PENGUIN BOOKS

NO ROOM IN NEVERLAND

Joyce Chua is the author of *Lambs for Dinner* (Straits Times Press, 2013), *Land of Sand and Song, Kingdom of Blood and Gold,* and *Until Morning* (Penguin Random House SEA). She graduated from the National University of Singapore with a degree in English, and is now a personal finance editor by day and author by night. When not writing, she can be found on Instagram and TikTok at @joycechuawrites sharing her random poetry or fangirling over Asian dramas.

T0288793

Also by Joyce Chua

Land of Sand and Song, Penguin Random House SEA, 2021
Kingdom of Blood and Gold, Penguin Random House SEA, 2023
Until Morning, Penguin Random House SEA, 2023

No Room in Neverland

Joyce Chua

PENGUIN BOOKS
An imprint of Penguin Random House

PENGUIN BOOKS

USA | Canada | UK | Ireland | Australia
New Zealand | India | South Africa | China | Southeast Asia

Penguin Books is part of the Penguin Random House group of companies
whose addresses can be found at global.penguinrandomhouse.com

Published by Penguin Random House SEA Pvt. Ltd
9, Changi South Street 3, Level 08-01,
Singapore 486361

First published in Penguin Books by Penguin Random House SEA 2023

Copyright © Joyce Chua 2023

ISBN 9789815127782

Typeset in Garamond by MAP Systems, Bangalore, India

www.penguin.sg

To all the Lost Children who have had to grow up

Contents

Chapter One: Gemma   1

Chapter Two: Cole   11

Chapter Three: Gemma   20

Chapter Four: Cole   29

Chapter Five: Gemma   35

Chapter Six: Cole   48

Chapter Seven: Gemma   59

Chapter Eight: Cole   67

Chapter Nine: Gemma   73

Chapter Ten: Cole   76

Chapter Eleven: Gemma   86

Chapter Twelve: Cole   89

Chapter Thirteen: Gemma   98

Chapter Fourteen: Cole   107

Chapter Fifteen: Gemma   115

Chapter Sixteen: Cole   130

Chapter Seventeen: Cole   133

Chapter Eighteen: Gemma   140

Chapter Nineteen: Cole   145

Chapter Twenty: Gemma   156

Chapter Twenty-One: Gemma   166

Chapter Twenty-Two: Cole   169

Chapter Twenty-Three: Gemma   174

Chapter Twenty-Four: Gemma   183

Chapter Twenty-Five: Cole   188

Chapter Twenty-Six: Gemma   197

Chapter Twenty-Seven: Gemma   208

Chapter Twenty-Eight: Cole   213

Chapter Twenty-Nine: Gemma   217

Chapter Thirty: Gemma   223

Chapter Thirty-One: Cole   225

Chapter Thirty-Two: Gemma   229

Chapter Thirty-Three: Cole   235

Chapter Thirty-Four: Gemma   242

Chapter Thirty-Five: Cole   245

Chapter Thirty-Six: Gemma   247

Chapter Thirty-Seven: Cole   251

Acknowledgements   257

Back then she was only three, barely old enough to remember much.

But she remembered the feel of her silky new pyjamas, the bed sheets pooled around her, her mother's cool dry hands as she tucked her into bed.

'It's time, Gemma,' her mother said, 'for me to let you in on a secret.'

Her little heart sped up, fluttering in her chest like butterfly wings. There was a glimmer in her mother's eyes and a shiver in her voice. 'What, Mama?'

'You have to promise not to tell anyone.'

Gemma nodded, leaning forward from her pillow.

'There's a special place all the children go to when they don't want to grow up. Now, we can't all go there, otherwise it gets too crowded. And then it becomes no different from where we are now. That's why only the best children know about the place.' She gave Gemma a smile that made the little girl straighten with pride.

'Would you like to go to Neverland with me, Gem?'

'Yes!' Gemma chirped, because anywhere with her mother was an adventure.

Her mother pulled the covers tighter around her daughter and smoothed the hair off her face. 'Then I'll start with the story of Peter Pan.'

Her father appeared at the doorway, smiling as he left his wife to take their daughter on her maiden journey to the magical land.

One

Gemma

No one knows the real story of Peter Pan. Maybe they've read the story countless times, watched every play and movie; maybe they even wrote a paper on it. But no one knows it like my mother did. They don't know Neverland like the back of their hand, much less how to navigate their way around it. They don't know the Lost Boys, the mermaids, the Indians, or the pirates.

But my mother knew. She knew Neverland because it was her home. It was where her mind drifted to even though she was right here with us. She could be talking about how the mailbox looked a little crooked from where she sat on the front porch, and off to Neverland she would go.

My mother was a denizen of that magical land as much as she was of this physical one, maybe even more so. Sometimes, she would pop in for a quick visit—five minutes and she was back. But sometimes it took longer—hours, days. Sometimes, she took me with her. But most of the time, she traversed it alone and I could only hope to meet her there.

Then one day, she went and never came back.

* * *

There were days when Neverland called out, clear as a voice next to my ear, and days when I found my way there on a wisp of memory.

1

Today, the promise of magic and miracles hung heavy in the air. This was a day that favoured even the cynics, a day when wishes uttered in low breaths could be heard and lost things could be found years later. I would lay my trust in that.

My footsteps rang in the near-empty park grounds as I made for the gates. Time slowed for no sentimental child in search of her mother, and today I was a girl on a mission.

The afternoon sun bore down on the amusement park grounds. Overhead, clouds rippled across a clear blue canvas. It was much easier to sneak out these days. No more milling crowds to wend through or giant, clumsy mascots to dodge or puddles of melted popsicles to skirt past. The soundtrack of carnival music continued to wear itself out as I strode unobstructed across the park grounds. These days, even on a weekend during the school holidays, this place saw more staff than visitors.

But that didn't necessarily mean this was the end of the Wild Ride. No, we were just experiencing a temporary lull while people flocked over to the new playground. What the Wild Ride lacked in novelty, it made up for in familiarity—unlike Wonder City 2.0. The name itself was stupid. Who called their amusement park that?

Yet, here I was, on my way to catching its opening ceremony. Right at the start of my shift, no less.

After two years of revamping—or, as Wonder Entertainment called it, 'reconfiguration'—Wonder City was now 'a better version of itself, with state-of-the-art entertainment capsules and rides that promised to take you to the infinite reaches of the universe and the future', according to a local news report.

I could see how kids could be bought over by that: it was practically their version of Neverland. But employee pride made me abhor Wonder City by default.

Still, it was hard to fight that swell in my chest or slow my quickening footsteps. Pretty soon, I was running. I hurtled past the Peter Pan ride that doubled as a clock tower, the games booths with their sun-bleached bunting, the souvenir shop that stocked more mascot-printed fans and coasters than anyone would ever need.

As I passed by the ticketing booth, Laura stuck her head out through the glass window and called, 'Where's the fire, Gem?'

In me, inside my heart. It burned away the nights I had spent wondering if I would ever find my parents, if they would ever come back for me.

But I told Laura none of that. Instead, I yelled over my shoulder, 'I'll be back in an hour!'

Laura sighed. 'We are all fools for hope.'

* * *

Wonder City 2.0 had spaceships. You do not underestimate the allure of spaceships when it comes to twelve-year-old boys or twelve-year-old boys stuck in thirty-five-year-old men's bodies.

As I neared Wonder City, the first thing I saw poking out through the canopy of trees was the giant silver disc that rotated and spun like a spaceship on crack.

I wasn't going to linger, I told myself. Of course, I could stay here on the pretext of scoping out the competition, but already the crowd was giving me a headache. Cars and bicycles spilt out from the parking lot, and people streamed by in droves. I should be used to crowds. I grew up in an amusement park, after all. But the Wild Ride had never experienced this sort of mob, even when it installed the new water features and brought in buskers.

Peter would love this.

The thought came unbidden, and I knew it was true. Peter Pan loved a party, even if I had never actually seen him in one. The stories I had heard about him came from my mother, and they were the ones that gave shape to the boy who never grew up. Still, I could easily picture him bouncing off the gleaming new rides like he cavorted around Neverland.

Wonder City looked nothing like Neverland. Yet, that was where I slipped dangerously into. Already, the scent of Neverland's wild fruits was drifting in on a warm breeze.

Focus, Gemma. Remember what you're here for.

I only had one clue to go on, a memory so faint I wasn't sure if it was just a figment of my imagination: my father's voice uttering the name Wonder City as though he was staking claim to it. But it was something, at least. A clue, much like the soggy ticket stub for the Wild Ride I'd had in my pocket when I was eight, when Jo and Boon found me. Clues to the mystery of my past I had spent the last ten years trying to solve.

I would take whatever I got.

The last time I stepped foot into Wonder City, it had seemed like an entirely new and different world on its own, far removed from the pathways littered with pamphlets outside, or the smoky food street just down the lane. Inside Wonder City, everything was aglow with a strange, otherworldly light. The Wild Ride amusement park was a faded vintage photograph compared to the technicolour Wonder City. Boon could loathe theme parks and the blockbuster rides all he wanted because of how high maintenance they were, but he couldn't deny that the commercial rides were what drew in the crowds.

Against a hyped-up theme park like that, we were just an old carnival past its prime. We had never had as many people gather around our go-kart ring the way Wonder City did (although they weren't called go-karts here, but 'speed mobiles', which roved around the ring like squat flashy insects under the sun).

The 'voyage schedule' stated that the 'secret mission' was starting here in five minutes. Right on schedule, the pint-sized emcee stepped forward from the ring and tapped his microphone.

More people gradually joined the crowd, jostling from behind and pushing me closer to the car ring. Skin brushed against mine, sweaty and slick; music soared, strings lilting. Every colour and touch and smell here was a thousand times more potent, heady, like a fever dream or half-forgotten memory struggling to resurface. Fighting all that, I tried to focus on the image of my father's face and craned my neck for a glimpse of him in the crowd. But in this writhing mob, it was a near impossible task.

'I know you've all been waiting for this,' the emcee declared. 'The highlight of today, the Secret Mission. Chasing Cars!'

The crowd cheered and applauded, but somewhere on my left came a snort. 'They're not actually *chasing* cars,' said a boy to two others flanking him. 'More like standing there and waiting for a car to run them over.' He was unapologetically loud. People around him turned to stare, but the emcee barrelled on like this was all part of the script.

'Indeed, today's challenge will be a nail-biting one, because mind you, these aren't your regular go-karts,' he intoned. 'These are speed mobiles with special engines that make them comparable to an actual car.' To punctuate this, the cars revved their engines and whizzed helter-skelter around the ring, sliding inches past one another.

'We'll need one valiant volunteer from the crowd to stand amid a choreographed performance by our speed mobiles with this flag.' He waved a red flag for emphasis. 'One of our riders will get *just* close enough to grab this flag from our volunteer. Rest assured our drivers are well-trained so no one will be losing any limbs.' His sharp laughter made up for the silence from the crowd.

'So, anyone?' The emcee waved an encouraging hand. The audience shifted uncomfortably, avoiding eye contact with him. 'Come on, our drivers are raring to go! Plus, proceeds will go to charity!'

The boy's voice rose above the crowd again. 'How many people actually buy that?'

I craned my neck to seek out the source of all that cynicism.

The boy seemed about my age, with well-defined features, brows quirked in disdain, and a stare that seemed determined to cut through all the bullshit.

The emcee's smile faltered, his eyes flicking towards the boy, but he said, 'Ah, who better to demonstrate the power and beauty of our speed mobiles than the heir to Wonder Entertainment? Cole, would you or your friends like to take on this challenge?'

The heir to Wonder Entertainment seemed to bear no love for the place he was set to inherit. 'The old man's not going to make me a part of this,' Cole said, turning to leave.

Just then, one of the cars zipped by me, too close for comfort despite the barrier that separated us. I stumbled backwards, treading on someone's foot.

'Sorry,' I muttered.

When I looked back up, Cole was staring at me. It was not the passing glance of a stranger, but of someone who recognized an old acquaintance.

And for some reason, it was there in his gaze that I found myself falling right back into Neverland.

Entering Neverland used to be easier when I was little. Peter taught us to think happy thoughts and let them take us away. My mother taught me to look for the crack in the sky, a trick of the light, a ripple in the air, anything that might indicate the spot where Neverland bled into the edges of the real world. Once you'd found it, you stepped right through—into a moment of weightlessness, where even your heart seemed to hold its breath.

But with Cole, there was none of that. No shift in the light or struggle to dredge up a happy thought. No word, no warning. His eyes brought me straight to the heart-drop moment itself, luring me in with a story. In his eyes, I slipped through the cracks easily, plummeting through the sky and crashing through the emerald foliage, finally landing on the soft-padded earth. The free fall never got old.

The din of the amusement park died away, leaving only the sound of lagoon water gurgling in the distance, punctuated by the hoots of the Lost Boys as they dove in. The air hummed and made its own melody; the scent of wild blooms and wood smoke threaded through trails of fairy dust and cloud wisps. There were parts of my childhood that grew murky over the years, but my memories of Neverland remained vivid, surreal as a waking dream.

I looked around for Peter. He wasn't any specific person in mind, but more like a few sensations combined into an experience of a boy. A voice close to my ear whispering about the wonders of Neverland, a warm hand wrapped around mine, a figure silhouetted by sunlight. And, always, that impish smile. The one that I remembered Neverland by, the one that I returned to every time I started thinking about my parents.

A muffled shout came from my right, but I ignored it. The grass was dewy and cool beneath my feet as I left the commotion behind. Heat lapped at my skin and the air shimmered like lagoon water, making me giddy and hopeful, ready to throw reason out of the window.

Neverland was not a place where you could stay long. It took a bit of you away each time you visited. But I didn't want to leave until I had found the people I'd lost. They *had* to be here. My mother had to have been hiding here all this while, having a laugh with Peter Pan.

Someone screamed, and then everything else dissolved into a roar of noise. A screech pierced through the din. Arms caught me, yanked me off the soft cool grass, and we went spinning out of control.

My eyelids flew open. Reality took a sharp bite out of me as my eyes adjusted to the glare of the late afternoon sun. I might be aware that Neverland was imaginary, but that didn't make it any easier to extricate myself from that place in my head.

Cole's face was inches away from mine; his breath fanned my hair. We were caught in an awkward stance that involved his foot being hooked around one of mine, his arms around me, and our bodies pressed against each other. Other sensations hit me all at once—the acrid stench of burning rubber, the crush of people around us, and voices woven into a discordant melody.

Next to me, a couple of drivers from the bumper cars got out. The emcee had stopped talking, and everyone pressed closer for a better look.

Cole straightened, hoisting me up. A frown worked its way between his brows. 'Are you ...'

I didn't break the silence or interrupt his thoughts. The ghost of a memory, so dappled and faded it was almost a mirage, was shimmering into existence. I didn't know if it was in a dream or in real life that I had seen him somewhere before. If not in Neverland, then someplace forgotten along with the rest of my childhood.

'Are you okay?' he asked at last.

I blinked. I'd expected him to say *crazy* instead of *okay*. That was what the kids at school called me. Maybe I was, but I didn't know or particularly cared. People pinned all sorts of labels on the things they didn't understand. They didn't know about Peter Pan or Neverland, much less go on adventures there. They could call me crazy all they wanted, but I knew the truth.

'I'm fine,' I said.

'Are you made of steel?'

'No,' I said again. Where was this going?

'Then why did you walk into a ring full of speed mobiles waiting to run you down?'

I should be used to it by now. But embarrassment still unfurled in my gut whenever I was caught red-handed between waking and dreaming, Neverland and the real world. The problem with being one of the few people who knew about Neverland was that you always had to explain yourself to those who didn't.

Cole was still waiting for an answer, and people around us were still staring. 'Is she okay?' the emcee asked, to which Cole gave a noncommittal thumbs-up. Real life was calling, expectant as ever, and I was not ready to respond to it yet.

'Cole?' a girl called, cutting through the crowd to join us. She wore a white shift dress and shiny black brogues that seemed as pristine and untouchable as her. Her attention shifted from Cole to me, then back to him again. 'Cole, what are you doing?'

'Hard to say, Chels,' Cole replied, still not letting go of me, his unsettling stare still fixed on me. 'What does it look like I'm doing?'

I wasn't sure if that was a rhetorical question or if the girl was accustomed to his snark—either way, she ignored his remark.

A boy in sunglasses appeared next to us. Cole's friend. 'Chelsea, did you see? Our guy here totally swooped into the middle of that ring!' He slapped Cole on the back.

Chelsea responded with a look carved from ice. 'Yes, Kas. I saw.'

'Although you might be getting a little too comfortable there,' another boy in a plaid shirt added with a smirk.

Cole let go of me and shoved his hands into his pockets, but his eyes never left me. 'Shut up, Josh,' he said.

Chelsea cut him off before he could say anything. 'Cole, your dad's been looking everywhere for you.'

Cole tore his gaze away from me at last. 'Well, here I am. In his territory, no less. That should please him.'

'He wants you to be at the press room in an hour.'

'To be clear, I'm not here because of him. So, no, I won't be at the press room later.'

Chelsea let out a sigh. 'Cole. Are you really going to do this? I'm tired of being your messenger.'

'You don't have to, Chels. You're not obliged to take his message or get on my case on his behalf.'

Chelsea went still. 'You think I'm doing this for him?'

My phone shuddered in my pocket then, saving me from third-party awkwardness. This venture into Wonder City had soured more quickly than I had expected.

'Gem, where are you?' Thomas said as soon as I picked up.

Given my track record for wandering around by myself (getting a little carried away on a trip to Neverland was not, I learned, a valid reason—it was cute when you were eight, but less so as you grew older), my absence from the Wild Ride was sometimes a cause for concern. Okay, *alarm*. (Thomas, in particular, was prone to freaking out.)

Cole's attention had returned to me. I could tell there were words sitting on the edge of his tongue, but they were melting away in the heat before he could get them out. I turned away.

'Did you see my message?' Thomas went on.

'What message?'

'Boon and Jo called for a meeting. Doesn't sound like good news.'

Around me, the crowd let out a cheer. The emcee had finally managed to rope in a hapless spectator for the stunt.

'Where are you?' Thomas asked again.

'On my way back,' I said, hanging up in case he caught any more background noise. Under Chelsea's hawkish gaze, I muttered a word of thanks to Cole for saving my life and scurried away before he could say another word.

Wonder City 2.0 was nothing like Neverland: it left you behind in time, it changed, it moved on. The world suddenly felt much bigger than before. It kept growing and moving and changing, while I remained where I was, unsure of which way to go. It hadn't stopped growing since the day my father left me at the Wild Ride for good.

Two

Cole

It was her. I knew that with more conviction than I ought to. It was her, right down to the tiny scar sitting atop her left eyebrow.

I wanted more than anything to tear through the crowd right then. It had been nearly ten years since I last saw her at Wonder City, and five years of misdirected text messages as the only connection to her. And now, at last, she was standing before me in the flesh.

To date, she had sent almost a thousand text messages, starting from the day she turned thirteen, when she received a cell phone as a birthday gift. Almost a thousand messages worth of raw hope, folded up and sent out to the wrong person almost every day.

I would have missed them all if I hadn't found the old cell phone lying in my father's desk drawer when I was thirteen and ready to shelve away the memories of Neverland and the girl who brought me there.

From her first day in secondary school to her first crush on a guy called T to her guardians to her dreams and nightmares about being lost in Neverland, I knew all about them. I knew that she was adopted by Jo and Boon a couple of months after her eighth birthday, when her father abandoned her with a bag of her belongings. That she recalled little of anything that happened before she turned eight. I knew how much she longed to see her mother again, how she sometimes felt guilty for loving her guardians more than her father, whom she barely remembered anymore. *But I still love you most*, she would hurry to assure her mother.

I also knew that she had been sending letters ever since she was ten, letters that had obviously found a recipient too, and were replied with postcards containing storybook quotes or quotes by dead people that revealed nothing. Gemma would crack her head trying to figure out what those quotes meant and how they pertained to her, and I would be tempted to text back, *Stop wasting your time and effort. They don't mean anything at all.*

But I didn't. I never told her who I was, which was probably cruel, except that I never replied to any of her messages either. I neither encouraged nor discouraged her, mostly because I didn't want to be the one who completely obliterated her hope of finding her parents. It got harder and harder to tell her the truth with each message she sent, and it sat in my gut like a stone I carried everywhere.

Now, I watched as the crowd ate her up, the girl I knew better than I should. There were a million things I wanted to say to her, but none of it came out in words, much less coherent sentences. *Where have you been all this time?* was probably the first thing I wanted to ask. It was ridiculous how I had received close to a thousand messages from her and still had no clue about her whereabouts, because she only revealed that she was living in Neverland now. All I had aside from her text messages were just the patchy memories from a time when I was still happy to wander around Wonder City, playing make-believe games so I could forget about my parents' divorce, if only for a while.

The largest distance between people lay in all the things they longed to know about each other.

But we were in the wrong place for nostalgia today.

The emcee had invited the volunteer, a guy in his twenties cajoled by his friends, into the ring and positioned him right in the middle. The guy's friends hooted in support, and Kas and Josh were making bets on whether he was going to make it. But all I could think about was Gemma and the way she drifted out into the ring. Like she was lost in a dream or a place that didn't exist.

I had come this close to asking her if she was still living in Neverland and how I could get there. Because I knew she wouldn't laugh or call me sentimental. Neverland might be just a ghost of a memory now, mostly because I never told anyone about it, but Gemma still believed in it. She was the one who had first brought me there, and there was no forgetting someone who changed your life like that.

But she didn't seem to remember me at all. Not once had she mentioned me in her text messages, the boy she spent countless hours exploring Neverland with. Even if I ran after her now, what would I even say to her?

Chelsea was watching me in her usual way, the one that unnerved all the guys in school but me—probably because they were afraid that she might read their thoughts and kick them in the balls.

'Who was that?' she said, nodding in the direction Gemma had left.

'What?'

'You seem pretty concerned. Was she someone you know?'

Did it count as knowing someone if I knew her mostly through misdirected messages? I had never told anyone about Gemma's messages, not Chelsea, not Kas or Josh, and certainly not my father.

Chelsea's eyebrows slid up. Having known me since I was eight, there was no one in my life that she wasn't acquainted with. 'Cole?' she prompted.

'No one,' I heard myself say, even as I continued watching the spot where Gemma last stood, as though she might suddenly materialize again.

'As I was saying,' Chelsea said, 'your dad's looking everywhere for you.'

I turned back to her. 'And I heard you.'

'So?'

'So what?'

'So, will you go talk to him or am I going to have to take a message again?'

'Neither. I didn't come here for him.'

I started walking. Away from the roar of the crowd as the cars did their choreographed figure eights around the idiot pretending like he wasn't this close to wetting his pants. Away from all these strangers who knew nothing about what went into creating this place of manufactured happiness. They left after having had their fun here, but the ones who remained saw this place for what it really was.

'Cole, come on,' Chelsea called. 'Don't you think this ridiculous feud with your dad should end already?'

'Nope.'

The crowd took a collective intake of breath as a pair of mobiles skimmed past the guy in the ring and one of the drivers reached for the flag. He failed. I continued walking.

'Where are you even going?' Chelsea went on.

'Nowhere near him.'

'What am I supposed to tell him?'

'That he should find another messenger. Better yet, deliver the message personally. It's only good manners.'

'Cole!'

Something in her voice—as if she was standing across a chasm far away from me and was about to fall over trying to reach for me—made me stop.

I turned back, watching her catch up with me. Chelsea once told me that people only got as close to you as you allowed them to, and when you turned your back on someone too many times, they would eventually get the hint and leave. But she was the only one who never did. Even when I shut the door on her many times before. Even when I told her I only saw her as a friend after she tried to kiss me when we were fifteen.

I took her hand, and she squeezed mine in response like she always did. Around us, the crowd erupted in cheers and whistles as one of the drivers managed to snatch the flag at last.

We cut through the triumphant mob silently as Wonder City clamoured around us. I kept my eyes peeled for Gemma, but there was no sign of her. As always, she had one foot in and another on the way out while I remained right where I had always been, not knowing which way to go.

From the night Gemma's mother introduced her to Peter Pan, the story of the boy who wouldn't grow up trailed through the house like a vine reaching for the sun.

It was everywhere Gemma went—twisted in the threads of the sofa, caught between the lines of laundry in the backyard, creeping under the doors into the rooms—and every shadowy nook of the house was dusted with the magic of Neverland. Gemma and her mother, who spent her days caring for her daughter and giving art classes, would sit on the swing in the backyard, chasing clouds, and her mother would describe a figure cutting through the dappled sky and holding out a hand to whisk them away.

'Someday, Gemma,' her mother said one day. 'We'll go to Neverland with Peter. Would you like that?' Gemma nodded eagerly as her mother scooped her up and buried her face in Gemma's hair, squeezing her a little too tightly for comfort.

In the afternoons, her mother would go to the nursery to draw. From her playpen, Gemma would watch her mother's frenzied hand move across the canvas to create portraits of a bright-eyed boy with a smile that let you in on a secret, or smudged drawings of a lush dreamscape populated by sunbathing mermaids and wild boys with painted faces.

Peter arrived on one of those lazy afternoons, after they had had their fill of playing with the Lost Boys in the backyard and retired to the nursery. Inside, the air churned hot and sticky in the prelude to a storm.

Her mother's movements were feverish, almost hypnotizing to Gemma. There was only the sound of pencil scratching against paper as clouds gathered outside, closing in with increasing urgency. Inside her playpen, Gemma launched into a jiggly dance along with the chime of the dreamcatcher hung by the window. Something was brewing—the air had transformed from static to electric.

When the first crack of thunder shattered the taut silence, her mother dropped her pencil. It clattered to the ground and rolled under the cupboard where she kept the brushes and rolls of canvas. Her head whipped towards the window. In a flash, she was perched on the windowsill, her eyes peeled as she scanned the sky.

'There you are,' she breathed.

Gemma saw no one, but she knew it was Peter who had come to visit at last. She craned her neck and leaned out of her playpen, but all she saw was the tower of dark grey clouds advancing towards them.

A surge of panic took hold of Gemma when another clap of thunder rattled the windowpanes. They were in the belly of the beast, and Peter was nowhere to be seen. She watched her mother raise a shaky leg to climb up the windowsill and let out a plaintive wail that was equal parts desperation and fear.

Her mother stopped. 'Oh, of course, baby,' she murmured, doubling back for her. 'How could I forget you?'

Gemma held out her eager arms, ready to be taken away.

But no, something was wrong. Something was very wrong. Her mother's grip around her was too keen. And they were going right into the eye of the storm, towards the sky that belched steel-grey clouds occasionally split by brilliant flashes of light.

'Mummy,' Gemma squeaked. 'Inside. Inside.'

Her mother's eyes were glazed, and a faint smile played at the corners of her lips. Gemma could tell that her mother was far, far away despite her firm grip. 'But Peter's here. Don't you want to meet him?'

'Inside,' was Gemma's only reply as she reached for the safety of her playpen.

'Peter's waiting for us, Gemma. Let's go!' She mounted the windowsill again. The first drop of rain hit Gemma's cheek, and she could barely open her eyes from the wind gusting in. 'We'll fly to Neverland. You like flying, don't you, baby?'

Gemma liked flying, but only when her father spun her around in the room or pushed her on the playground swing. Falling seemed awfully possible with this sort of flying. The ground was lying in wait for them. Worse, what if they were sucked into the grey belly of clouds and never found ground again?

Over the roar of thunder, the sound of the front door almost went unheard. 'Katie, I'm home! Katie? Gemma?'

'Daddy!' Gemma cried, straining towards the nursery door.

Maybe he heard something in her voice, or he had expected something like this to happen. His footsteps pounded up the stairs as he yelled, 'Katie! Gemma!' By the time her father appeared at the door, Gemma had started to squirm and wail. 'Katie. Come down, sweetheart. What will the neighbours think?'

Indeed, they must have been a sight for the neighbours, a woman with a distressed baby in her arms perched on the narrow windowsill.

'I don't care about the neighbours,' her mother snapped, unrelenting in her grip around Gemma. 'What do they matter now that I'm leaving for Neverland?'

'Katie.' It seemed to cost her father everything in him to keep his voice steady and low and as gentle as possible. 'Come back down. Come to me.' When that didn't work, he said, 'You're upsetting Gemma.'

Her mother turned to the sky, one hand braced against the window frame and the other holding a writhing Gemma. In that split moment of hesitation, her father dashed across the room and reached for her. He wrapped an arm around her whittled waist and another around Gemma, pressing the little one close to him.

As the three of them went crashing back to safe ground, her mother wrenched Gemma back, and the girl's forehead scraped against the edge of the wooden cupboard by the window. Gemma's cry rose in a sharp crescendo. The room spun, and Gemma saw colours burst around the corners of her eyes.

It would take eight stitches to seal the gash over the outer corner of her left eyebrow.

From then on, her mother would sometimes stare at the tiny, white crescent-shaped scar on Gemma's eyebrow with her lips pursed and her eyes red and wet. They would not speak of that incident again, although Gemma would catch her father on the phone with Doctor York more often, intent as he paced the length of his study. Her mother would stay in her studio more to paint, and Gemma would learn to colour and doodle. But really, she preferred to think of it as keeping watch over her mother.

Gemma's resolve hardened from that day on. She would make it into Neverland, if only to really be with her mother, so she would never again be left behind like she had that day in the nursery.

Meanwhile, Peter's shadow remained in the house, a silent companion lying in wait for the day Gemma found her way to Neverland.

Three

Gemma

I came to a stop in the middle of the crowd, trying to catch my breath and calm my racing heart in the aftermath of the memory.

The memory faded away under the glare of sunlight, but I couldn't tell if it was an actual memory or if my mind was fabricating its own stories now. Sometimes, what felt like a memory ended up as just another Neverland chronicle, while a snippet of my second life in that fabled place could contain a fragment of truth that led me closer to my parents.

But it had felt real enough. I could still feel the weight of the storm on my skin, the electricity in the air. And my mother's voice—its cadence I had almost forgotten, along with the gentle lilt whenever she spoke about Peter Pan—was as comforting a story told many times before.

My finger went up to the scar above my brow. I was too young to have remembered that accident, but could that have been how I got my scar? If so, why was that memory resurfacing *now*?

Cries echoed in my head, out of place on a day this open and bright. I scanned the skies, watching the towering mounds of clouds for a sign of the boy my mother and I had both believed in.

But someone bumped into my shoulder, jolting me out of my thoughts. Around me, people skipped along to their next destination, laughing and jostling, undisturbed by memories.

This trip to Wonder City was a bust. Not only did I not find the people I was looking for, but I had also slipped again. Slipped into Neverland, despite promising everyone—including myself—that I wouldn't.

But no one needed to know, right? Besides, nothing happened. I didn't *actually* get run down by a car, thanks to—

His face flashed to mind. With it came fragmented images of a clearing shadowed by a canopy of leaves, the sound of running water (a stream?) nearby, and a barbed wire fence hidden behind a wall of creeping vines and thick undergrowth.

Trying to recall my childhood sometimes brought on massive headaches, so Jo and Boon told me to let it come to me in good time. But how was it that Cole, a complete stranger, could trigger a reaction and memory like that? Everything was fine until he appeared.

Dusk was settling by the time I returned to the Wild Ride, fighting the pounding in my head. The amusement park was already slipping into a sleepy pall, far quieter than the last place I had been.

'Gemma!'

Thomas appeared before me, wearing that ghastly red Wild Ride employee polo tee that Jo and Boon (mistakenly) thought would help brighten up the place. Not only did it not live up to its intended purpose, but it had also scared a child to tears once (even though his mother explained that he had an unusual fear of the colour red, I still blamed us for setting him off).

'There you are.' He smiled, and my heart did a little backflip. 'We were just getting worried. Where did you go?'

'No cause for alarm, Thomas. I just . . . popped out to buy something.' I pulled a box of mint out of my pocket and offered him one.

He eyed the box of mint, then fixed me with a look. 'Gemma.'

'Okay, okay. Promise you won't tell Boon.'

'That doesn't sound good already.' I waited for the answer I was looking for. 'Okay, I promise.'

'I popped by Wonder City.'

It was better to not tell him about my trip to Neverland too, or the little accident that Cole rescued me from. Thomas might be a lot more tolerant of my obsession with Neverland, but that didn't mean he understood it more than anyone else did. And what people didn't understand, they deemed wrong.

'I assume you weren't there to check out the competition.' Thomas peered at my face. 'And you didn't find who you were looking for.'

I gave a half-hearted shrug. 'It was a long shot, anyway.'

If Thomas was considering the futility of my efforts, he didn't voice it, only throwing an arm around me as we made our way to the main office.

'Maybe she didn't know you were going to be there,' he said at last.

'But I texted her the day before. I *told* her I'd be there.' I'd had grand visions of reuniting with both my parents at Wonder City today, but of course, why would today be any different from all the days before this? I had waited long enough to know better than to act on false hope.

My feet slowed to a stop. 'Maybe she doesn't want to see me,' I said. 'That would explain why she never replied to any of my text messages.'

'She replied to your letters, though,' he pointed out.

She did, but sporadically, by way of postcards that featured abstract art and quotes that revealed nothing about her whereabouts. She was nothing like the person who had regaled me with stories of Neverland and taught me how to navigate my way through it— more like the person in the memory that surfaced at Wonder City.

In the office, Jo and Boon were conversing by Jo's desk. Even in her seat, Jo looked like she might collapse any minute. Her tiny frame, next to Boon's sturdy one, appeared even frailer. The past few months had taken a lot out of her, despite her repeated reassurances that she would be around longer than the amusement park. I didn't find that particularly funny.

'Where have you been all morning?' Boon asked. What if he knew I was at Wonder City running on nothing but a dim memory? With Boon, it was best not to bring up my parents unless I wanted to get into another argument with him.

'Market research,' Thomas said without missing a beat. 'Gem was at Wonder City to check out the competition.'

I sank into the couch in what I hoped was a nonchalant manner. 'So what's the urgent matter you said you needed to discuss?'

'It's about the Wild Ride.' Boon glanced at Thomas. 'Thomas, maybe you should—'

'He's part of the Wild Ride, too,' I said, grabbing Thomas's wrist before he could leave.

Jo and Boon shared a glance. Boon took a deep breath and announced, 'We're thinking of closing this place. For good.'

That got me leaping up from my seat. '*What?* You can't close the Wild Ride!'

Jo reached for my hand. 'Gemma . . .'

'We've been considering this for a while, and this is really for the best,' Boon said.

'But you can't. I mean, it's . . .' I was floundering. '*Why?*'

'We don't want to have to do this either,' Boon said. 'But how many people did we have last week? Not even a hundred each day. That's barely enough to cover the cost of maintaining the rides, much less all your pay cheques.'

'You can't close this place,' I said again. It sounded more like a plea this time.

'Oh, Gemma,' Jo sighed, exchanging a look with Boon.

I saw the look in their eyes and knew that they understood right away my real reason for protesting the Wild Ride's closure. I hated how blatant my intentions were, how easily anyone could read me. I was starting to regret making Thomas stay to witness this.

Jo and Boon had promised they would keep the amusement park open at least until my parents came back for me. When I was younger, Jo told me that my parents had taken an extended trip around the world, that it was better to stay put so they could find me. If the Wild Ride was closed, then there was no way my parents would ever be able to find me.

'We've already received a few offers for this place,' Jo said. 'Wonder Entertainment is particularly keen.'

Wonder Entertainment. The property development organization that created Wonder City, along other attractions like the Midnight Aquarium and the umbrella street market, two other tourist traps.

Resentment growled and snapped in my chest. They already had a newly revamped amusement park. What did they want with this old place?

'You made this decision without telling me.' It was hard not to sound accusatory, but at least it masked the hurt underneath.

'We're sorry, Gemma. We really are,' Boon said.

'You promised you wouldn't close this place until I found them.'

'Holding on to this amusement park isn't going to bring them back.'

'There are other ways to look for your parents,' Jo added. 'Just be patient.'

'She's not a child anymore, Jo,' Boon said. 'You don't have to keep protecting her from the truth.'

'She needs to remember everything on her own,' Jo insisted, like always. And like always, it drove Boon nuts.

'What *is* the truth?' I demanded.

'I've told you before, Gem,' Boon said, ignoring Jo's disapproving glance. 'Your mother is not coming back. She—'

'She sends postcards now and then, and her phone number is still in use!' I protested. 'And my father . . . Well, he just needs time to find me.'

'If they wanted to find you, don't you think they would have already?' Boon said quietly. 'It's been almost ten years, and goodness knows *you've* tried.'

I could only send him a mutinous glare, even as the silence that followed reached a deafening pitch. So much for avoiding the topic of my parents around Boon.

We had worn out this argument a long time ago, ever since Boon learned of the extent that I had gone to search for my parents. But neither of us was willing to budge. While Jo had never stopped me from finding my parents—even though my efforts had yielded nothing so far—Boon had always been far less accommodating, shy of just outright ranting against my father for leaving me in their hands with nothing but a note. In fact, he once even let slip the word *obsession*. Like this plan to find them had become a quest gone out of hand.

But my parents *would* return. Of course they would, despite what Boon kept telling me. If not, I would find them—as soon as I could recall everything that had happened before I turned eight.

'Maybe,' Thomas piped up, breaking the brittle silence, 'what we need is just some good marketing. Or a change in strategy.'

'Exactly!' I cried, latching on to this chain of hope. Never mind the logistics for now.

'Boon, you said the maintenance fees are killing us, right?' Thomas said. 'We could sell the rides and swap them for lower-cost attractions.'

'I don't know . . .' Boon said, glancing at Jo.

Jo leaned back in her seat, considering. 'It could work.'

Boon sent her a coded look. 'But we've dragged this on long enough. We can last for one more month—two at the most—before we sell this place.'

'Leave this to us then,' I said. 'We'll try Thomas's way for these couple of months—you won't have to fork out a single cent. If it doesn't work, then . . . then Wonder Entertainment can have it. Please?'

I was grovelling. But it didn't matter, as long as I could delay the inevitable. Jo and Boon were used to my stubborn streak anyway, which was why they never stopped me from texting and writing letters to my mother although my efforts seemed futile and even ludicrous.

I appealed to Jo now; my chances were higher there. Jo would always listen to my fragmented, patchy accounts of Neverland even though she barely understood a thing about it. Jo had always tried to keep my hope alive, and she would likely keep doing so now.

She reached for Boon's hand and gave a squeeze. I couldn't help but notice how papery her skin looked over her knuckles.

Boon let out a sigh big enough to fill the entire room. 'Two months,' he said at last.

Relief washed over me. 'Thank you. You won't regret it, I promise.' Then I grabbed Thomas and dashed out of the office before they could change their minds.

Now that we had averted an immediate crisis, the dusk air suddenly felt lighter as Thomas and I made our way to the bench in front of the Peter Pan ride.

The ride didn't feature Peter Pan per se (copyright issues and all that), but a mini clock tower with freewheeling carriages, spray-painted with glitter and silhouettes of flying children. The carriages spun in leisurely circles around the clock tower when the ride was in operation. Now they just hung limply, illuminated by the light from the clock face.

Thomas and I sat in silence, watching the sky turn from pink to indigo. At length, I said, 'Thanks for what you did earlier.'

'I know what this place means to you. We're still not out of the woods, you know. Revamping an amusement park is a big project, and we have no experience. We might fail.'

'We'll get through this. We have to.' A beat lapsed. 'Everyone thinks I'm foolish for believing my parents will come back. Sometimes, even I do.' I was glad for the cover of darkness; it was easier to make that confession when he couldn't see it written all over my face.

'I don't think you're foolish,' said Thomas. 'No one can leave their child behind just like that.'

'That's because *your* parents would never do that.'

'Jo and Boon won't either, you know.'

It was true. Jo and Boon would never dump me at an amusement park without warning the way my father had. Ever since they took me in, they had never been absent for one minute of my life, much less left me behind anywhere.

Some days, I felt like I could explode from all the longing inside me. Other days, it took tiny, fervent bites out of me. When would I finally be left with nothing to go on? When would I finally listen to Boon and give up searching for my parents?

Still, I said, 'My father wasn't—*isn't*—a bad person.'

'I know. He'll come back for you. Your mum, too.' He stared up at the Peter Pan ride. 'Someday, Gem, you'll finally get on that ride. With the person you're meant to.'

He knew how my father had left me in front of the Peter Pan ride, promising to return after getting me a cup of sweet corn. He knew how I had waited there for hours before starting to cry. He knew how I always imagined my father would find me where he left me, like no time had passed between that day and now.

I stared at Thomas, lingering on each feature of his I had come to know so well, from his kind smiling eyes to the gentle slope of his nose. If he asked me to go on that ride right then, I would have agreed to.

But then he reached over to ruffle my hair and I was reminded of the way he chuckled at me whenever I said or did something that made the two-year gap between us seem unbridgeable.

'I'll see you tomorrow, Wendy,' he said, getting up. 'Tomorrow we'll talk shop.'

I watched as he rounded the gift shop and headed out the gates.

The threat of the Wild Ride's closure loomed like a shadow, and I felt like I was losing grip on something that I had always counted on being there. Jo and Boon had been planning their retirement for years, but this decision still caught me off guard.

I couldn't bear to be in the amusement park tonight, not with the threat of closure pressing so close. It was almost time for my appointment, anyway. So, I made sure Thomas was well out of sight before rushing out to the park across the street.

Four

Cole

By the time I got home that evening, I was kicking myself for letting Gemma go without confirming her identity. What kind of idiot spent years quietly pining after a childhood friend and then did absolutely nothing when he finally met her again? Wasn't that the whole point of going to Wonder City today, to find Gemma again after all these years?

I didn't know what I expected from her. Perhaps a sign that Neverland had not only changed me but her as well. That we were both survivors after visiting it and would forever bear its marks, despite my father and Chelsea's attempts to make me forget about her and our Neverland adventures.

There was only a week to go before I turned eighteen and could finally move out. Until then, I planned to keep my presence in the house to the barest minimum. But when a house only had two people living in it, it was impossible to fly under the radar. I had barely made it halfway past the study to my room before I was waylaid.

'Where do you think you're going?'

My feet slowed to a stop.

'I barely see you for an entire week and now you're just waltzing past me without even a greeting?'

I made sure to look him dead in the eye. 'Hello, Father.'

'I didn't see you at the opening today, even though I distinctly recall telling you I expected you there.'

Oh, I was there. Just not for the same purpose as his. If Gemma hadn't sent that text to her mother the night before saying she'd be there, I would have continued avoiding amusement parks of any sort, especially Wonder City.

But even when I was at Wonder City, I steered well clear of the route my father took. When he was cutting the ribbon at the entrance and giving his spiel about 'moving forward and embarking on the next phase in entertainment', I was in the planetarium with Josh and Kas, fiddling with the lights. The guys got over the novelty after ten minutes, so we went to the sky-train and spray-painted our mark on it. The plain silver carriages looked a little dull, anyway.

'I was there,' was all I said.

In the pause that followed, his stare conveyed all the things he wasn't saying, but it was nothing I hadn't heard a million times before. I leaned against the door frame, holding his gaze.

'Have you packed?' he said at last.

'What?'

'For London. Don't tell me you forgot—'

'I already told you I'm not going.'

'But since you didn't provide a reason, I assumed you were just disagreeing for my sake.'

I pushed off the door frame and crossed the room. The door closed behind me with a *snick*, sealing us in. Behind my father, the window revealed the starless sky pressing close, trapping us in a place with too much carpeting, too much stillness, coldness, too much everything.

'In case I haven't made myself clear,' I said, 'I'm not going.'

'Why? What do you have here that's worth staying for? School? Please. Friends? How many do you have? Family?'

I tried to maintain my poker face, but he saw something in it anyway.

'Oh, you poor hopeful boy.'

Hate coiled around my chest like a barbed whip.

'How many years has it been? Eight?' he went on. 'If she wanted to have anything to do with us, don't you think she would have at least bothered to call?'

'Nine.'

'What?'

'It's been nine years.' Nine years, three months and eleven days, to be exact.

My father's look of pity deepened, as though he had heard my thoughts.

'I've already told Chelsea you're going,' he said. 'Everything has been settled. I will not let you upset everyone's plans. Not everything is about you, Cole.'

In here, there was no room for breathing, much less dissent.

'Of course it isn't. The Plan is the most important.' My father wouldn't know how to do anything without a plan; anything that strayed from it had to be reeled back. It was the only way his universe could function.

'You are going with Chelsea and that's final,' he said.

'It is, huh? Was that what you said when you drove Mum away?'

The silence that followed was ugly and cold. My father's stare was frosty and relentless, but I had long ago learned the art of mirroring his gaze.

When he spoke at last, his voice sounded wearier than I expected. 'I did not drive her away. She left on her own accord. I don't understand why I have to keep explaining this to you.'

Whatever. 'Look, I'm turning eighteen in a week,' I said. 'I'll be out of your hair soon. Why bother going to all this trouble of sending me away when I can easily move out?'

That brought the condescension back to his voice. 'Move out? And where can you go?'

'I have options.' Which wasn't really a lie, since there was the apartment that my father meant to give me as my eighteenth birthday present.

'Without my backing? You know I can always take away your privileges unless you hold up your end of the bargain.'

'You're cutting me off?'

'It's an *option*. Where have you been these past few days?'

'Why bother asking when you already know?'

'I will not bail you out again if you get caught spray-painting public property. And you will not get the apartment if you're not going to London,' he snapped.

If he thought threatening me was going to work, then he didn't know me at all. 'Fine, I'll find somewhere else then. Cut me off, whatever.'

He shook his head. 'I've been excusing everything you've done because of the divorce, but this has gone on long enough. Grow up, Cole.'

I prepared to walk out the door.

He rose from his chair. 'I'm not done talking.'

'I am.'

'Yes, run from a proper conversation again like a child. I forgot that's what you do best.'

'Well, at least that's one thing I'm good at.' I made my escape not a minute too soon, bursting out into the cool evening air.

When she was four, her parents told her she would have to start going to school.

You'll have friends there, *her father said.* Friends your age that you can actually see and talk to. *Gemma didn't quite see the need for that. She had her mother and she had Peter, and that was all she really wanted.*

On the first day, she clung to her mother's hand as they stood in front of the red double doors of the preschool. She had promised her father she wouldn't cry. 'You'll be a big girl about this, won't you, Gemma?' *he had said, and she had nodded and even pinkie-swore.*

But as she made her way down the winding path flanked by yellow daisies, she could feel her breaths getting shorter and a sob beginning to form in her throat. She clutched her mother's hand tighter and pursed her lips.

'Now, Gemma,' *her mother said, stooping to her height and taking her shoulders.* 'Remember, don't tell anyone about Neverland.'

Gemma nodded, solemn and silent.

'Most people would just say, "Play nice with the kids," you know,' *her father said, his smile tightening.*

Ever since that incident in the nursery, he became nervous whenever Neverland was brought up, but Gemma knew he held back only so he wouldn't get into another fight with her mother about this.

Her mother pretended not to have heard him.

Gemma took one last look at her parents, both beaming proudly at her, and made for the double doors.

* * *

She spoke about Neverland in the end.

She couldn't help it. When kind Mrs Tea told them to introduce themselves and talk about their family, she couldn't not *include Peter. He was as much a part of her family as her parents were.*

But then Jimmy Yu called out from the audience, 'Peter Pan isn't real,' like she was stupid for believing so.

Gemma stuck out her chin. 'He is. He lives in Neverland and he'll take me there one day.'

'Neverland isn't real too.'

'It is, too!' Gemma stomped her feet, making a hollow thud against the wooden podium.

'Then how come you've never been there?'

'Now, Jimmy,' Mrs Tea said.

'I will go there one day,' Gemma said. 'Just wait.'

'That means you are craaaaazy,' he sang, making a circular motion around his head with a finger.

'Shut up!' Gemma knew it was rude to tell someone to shut up, but this seemed forgivable given the circumstance. It was how she justified leaping off the stage and pushing him against the wooden book rack. Jimmy made her angry. Jimmy called her crazy. Jimmy was an idiot.

Mrs Tea made it just in time to stop Jimmy from retaliating. Later, she would report this incident to Gemma's mother when she came to pick Gemma up. It sounded a lot worse than Gemma expected, and she began to cry. The other children narrated the incident to their parents, casting her glances on their way out of the school grounds.

'What happened, Gemma? I thought we agreed not to tell,' her mother said on the way home. Her dismay made Gemma break into fresh sobs.

Gemma struggled to catch her breath. 'He said Neverland isn't real. He called it a place for mad people. I'm not mad, right?'

'Of course you're not, Gem. Birds in a cage think flying is a disease.' She wiped away Gemma's tears. 'I know it's hard to keep it a secret, but you have to pick the right person to share Neverland with. Only the special ones get to know about it, remember?'

They drove without another word all the way home as Gemma and her mother each sank into their own thoughts.

When she finally pulled up to their house, her mother broke the silence. 'We don't need to tell Daddy what happened today.'

Five

Gemma

The park loomed ahead, but my footsteps slowed as the last echoes of my mother's voice died away. Another memory. The pounding started again in my head, making it hard to gather my thoughts.

My mother's belief in Neverland had never made sense to anyone else but me, and for that we were called mad. In the early days of living with Jo and Boon, when Jo kept trying to coax a word out of me, a sentence, then finally a story, Neverland was the first thing I brought up. It was all I could remember, and while my foster parents tried to make sense of it for my sake at first, eventually they gave up. Neverland was too complex for the non-believers.

The park at this hour was deserted. It wasn't near any residential area and was a little too far away from the main road for anyone to visit in the middle of the night.

Which was why the voices from behind the pavilion wall sounded especially loud, even though the boys weren't yelling.

I made sure to keep out of sight as I walked past the pavilion to my meeting point.

Of all the pavilions in the park, I hated that one the most. Half of it was bordered with stark white walls that served no purpose other than to let people vandalize them and for the park council to put up notices telling people not to vandalize them.

If only someone would paint those walls.

There were three of them, two of them hanging in the shadowy part of the pavilion while the third stood closer to the wall illuminated by the beam of fluorescent light. It wasn't until I got a closer look that I recognized him.

He had a spray can in his hand. As he held out a hand for another can, he took a step back to survey his work.

The fluorescent light cast shadows on his face, making his cheekbones and jawline appear much harder. Yet, his eyes shone with a strange youthful wistfulness. He looked different somehow, as though daylight made a mockery of his features and night revealed his true face. He didn't seem like just a spoiled rich kid with socks for brains, especially when he had created something astoundingly beautiful on that sad little wall.

First, there was the blue, stormy indigo at the top of the wall that bled into a stunning turquoise and eventually a thin gold line where the horizon lay. Below it was a riot of hues, green like the emerald sea, red and pink and yellow like morning light scattered onto the sea. Off the coast in the left corner, three mermaids were sprawled across boulders, their tails fanned out before them . . .

He was painting Neverland—or at least, my version of it. I had never fully described it to anyone, not since I could remember.

I stood motionless, watching Cole bring Neverland to life. How could he know? It was a secret, my mother's and mine.

Could Cole be a potential clue to Neverland? I had gone for years unable to recall the slightest detail about my life before Jo and Boon took me in. It couldn't be a coincidence that my memory was dredging up two disturbing anecdotes in a day after meeting him.

Cole was not a quiet worker. He spent a good part ranting against his father, who had apparently threatened to cut him off, as the two other boys—the ones I saw at Wonder City today, Josh and Kas—watched on.

'Pass the blue,' Cole said.

'What are you painting?' Josh asked.

'Demonic mermaids,' Kas supplied.

'It's weird, man,' Josh said.

'I asked for the blue, not your opinion,' Cole said. Josh tossed him the canister.

The air was ripe with the smell of spray paint and slumbering trees. Fairy lights winked from the shadowy foliage of trees, and suddenly Peter was right there, a voice in my head telling me about the outsiders who tried to steal into Neverland and expose its existence to the world.

The drumbeats started up in my head, calling up images of a clearing bathed in deep purple twilight.

It was quiet, but the sounds of a river floated in the distance. Someone was next to me, his hand grasping mine as we emerged from the clearing and dove into a shaded nook . . .

A clatter made me jump. Cole had tossed the empty can aside, letting it roll against the foot of the wall. I was back in a park dimly lit by street lamps. What was it about Cole that triggered these random memory flashes?

'So, can I crash with either of you for a while?' he asked.

Josh, whose neon yellow sneakers squeaked when he walked, said immediately, 'My relatives are staying over tomorrow.' He gave a loose shrug. 'Sorry.'

Cole nodded at Kas, who started shaking the can and making the ball bearing inside rattle. 'What about you, Kas? Your distant cousins moving in?'

More rattling. 'No, but you know how my mum gets about guests.' He stopped. 'Why do you need to squeeze with us anyway? Just ask your dad for the apartment.'

'Long story. I'm not getting the apartment until I *grow up*.' That last bit was uttered in a tone that suggested inverted commas.

'He gave you the keys to your car when you were seventeen,' Josh said. 'Why not the keys to your apartment now?'

'Because that's how he gets me to do shit he wants me to do. By dangling my freedom on his fingers.' He snatched a canister from Josh's hand and aimed the nozzle at the wall. In jerky, haphazard strokes, he sprayed his frustration all over his work. The cloud of colours drifting atop the sea was now ensnared in a tangle of angry red lines, and the mermaids obliterated without hesitation.

All that beauty was ruined in seconds, leaving only a garish mess. The little regard he had for his art felt like a slap to the face. Now, it just looked like vandalism.

'No wonder Mum left him,' Cole went on. 'I would too, if I could. I could have gone with her.'

At the mention of his mother, Josh and Kas shared a look.

'Except, you know, she's not loaded like your dad,' Josh said, braving Cole's wrath.

Cole whirled around to glare at him. 'You think I give a crap about that?'

Kas raised a hand, detaching himself from the conversation, but Josh went on, 'You say you don't, but you've never actually lived without your dad's money. Who knows? You might hate it at your mum's.' He shrugged. 'Just pointing out a possibility.'

'At least she won't treat me like something she dragged off the street,' Cole said. A moment later, he kicked the wall, leaving a smear of dirt on it. 'I'm bored. Let's go for a ride.'

Kas perked up. 'Then supper?'

Cole rolled his eyes. 'Fine.'

'I don't have enough cash, though,' Kas said immediately.

Josh raised a hand 'Me neither.'

'It's on me, okay?' Cole said, rolling his eyes again. It sounded like an exchange they had had countless times before. 'Let's go.'

'We can't exactly leave this like that,' Kas said, gesturing at the vandalized wall.

'Nobody cares about a stupid wall, Kas,' Cole said.

I took a photo of the wall and sent it to my mum, wishing only that I had managed to capture it before its creator destroyed it. Cole pulled out his phone when it pinged suddenly.

'Silent mode, man,' Josh said. 'Amateur move.'

But Cole ignored him. He gripped his cell phone and scanned the surroundings like he was searching for someone. I pressed closer into the shadows.

'What are you looking for?' Josh said. 'Let's go already.'

'Let me finish this up first.'

'What's there to finish? You've already turned it into shit.'

My phone vibrated then, so I didn't witness Cole take affront at that.

I'm here—RL

When RL first contacted me about my father a month ago, I was ready to write him off as a fraud trying to exploit someone else's quest. He did ask for a five-hundred-dollar deposit up front, plus another five hundred after we met. But then he showed me that photo he had of my father. They were supposed to be doing business with each other, he said, but it fell through.

It might have been a slightly grainy, time-weathered photo, but I would recognize my father's face anywhere.

I headed over to the adjacent pavilion a few metres away from Cole and his friends. RL had on a cap and sunglasses—at night—because of course that wasn't shady at all.

'What have you got for me?' I asked as soon as I reached him.

'It's nice to meet you too, Gemma.' He cocked his head. 'You look just like your mother.'

'Just tell me where my dad is.'

'He's doing fine.'

'That's not what I asked.'

'That's all you need to know.'

'And I'm supposed to just buy whatever you say?'

'Look, you wanted me to bring news of him and I've brought it. My job here's done. It's up to you whether to believe me.'

'That's not what our agreement was. You're supposed to tell me where I can find him.'

'I said I'd bring you news of him. I was very careful with my wording.'

I folded my arms. 'I'm not leaving until you give me more answers.'

'Stay if you want. Just pay me and I'll be gone.'

I only stared at him.

'So you're *not* going to pay me.'

'How did you know him? What kind of business did you two do exactly? Where did you get that photo of him? Come on, give me something—*anything*—so I can trust you.'

His eyebrows flew up. '*Trust* me? You should've thought of that before you asked to meet with someone you found on the Internet.'

'But you had that photo . . . '

'That can mean anything. He should've made up his mind whether to sell his house. I had my deposit down and then he fled. I should at least try to recoup some of my losses with his daughter.'

'He tried to sell his house? Which house? Where is it?'

'You want to know? Pay up. This information doesn't come for free.'

'This wasn't part of the agreement.'

He took a step towards me and grabbed my wrist. 'It is now.'

I made sure my voice came out steady. 'Let go, or I'm calling the police.'

He let out a bark of laughter and reached for my bag, grappling with the strap when I wrenched it out of his hands and gave him a shove. But he yanked the purse strap and sent me tumbling down.

RL had all the advantage now. With one arm and his legs, he had me pinned to the ground. He rooted through my purse with his free hand. His knees bore against my ribs; it hurt when I struggled. The tightening in my chest spread to my neck, then my face. I clawed at him, but it was futile.

Just as RL had almost squashed the air out of me, his grip relented. Air rushed back into my lungs, and my breath returned in rasps and coughs. When I looked up again, Cole shifted into view. He had RL in a headlock, but after elbowing Cole in the gut, RL pulled free and threw him against the wall.

'Look, kid,' RL said. 'This is none of your—'

Cole swung a wild fist across RL's jaw and knocked him to the ground. RL lay there, motionless.

'What the hell, Cole?' I nudged RL's prone form with a foot. 'He's not dead, is he?' My voice echoed in the pavilion.

Footsteps squeaked as Josh and Kas stepped out of the shadows. 'Shit, Cole,' Kas said, staring at RL. 'What did you do?'

'Knocked him out. He'll live.'

'Should we . . . call an ambulance for him?' I asked.

RL stirred then, thank goodness. Before he could come to, Cole grabbed my hand and hauled me away. My hand was warm and slick in his, but his grasp was firm. We hurried out of the pavilion and down the pavement.

'Cole.' I could barely hear myself over the roaring in my ears. 'I really think we should get him some help.' RL probably hadn't bargained for this when he first decided to cheat me of my money.

'He'll be fine,' Cole said without breaking his stride. 'My fist probably hurts more than his jaw.'

But I couldn't let RL leave without at least getting some answers about my father. 'Wait, stop. You've got it all wrong.'

'Which part? The part where he was extorting money from you or strangling you?'

Behind us, RL was already picking himself up and stumbling down the lane away from us. 'Well, he's just a little impatient,' I said, trying to tug my arm out of Cole's grasp, 'but he's fairly harmless—'

'*Fairly harmless?*' Cole echoed, glancing at me in disbelief. 'Why did you even agree to meet him? In the middle of the night in a deserted park, no less.'

'He said he had news of my dad.'

He came to a stop at last. 'And you just took his word for it? Unbelievable.'

'When you've been searching for almost all your life, you take what you can get.'

His gaze softened a fraction. Before he could respond, a voice appeared next to my ear, making me jump.

'Hi, I'm Kas. We met earlier today at Wonder City.' Kas held out a hand. This entire situation couldn't be any weirder. But I shook his hand and gave him my name anyway.

Josh was about to introduce himself when a fresh set of footsteps clipped down the path, past the graffitied wall. The boys squinted into the distance behind us.

'Shit,' Josh muttered as flashlights arced through the night and revealed a uniformed pair of police officers led by the park-keeper. The abandoned canisters of spray paint and destroyed walls were all the evidence the police needed.

Cole shoved me behind a hedge. 'Hide!' he hissed, before putting as much distance between us as possible.

The boys scattered. They were fast, but the police had the element of surprise. Josh was the first to get caught, most likely due to his conspicuous footwear. Cole tried to escape but didn't resist once he was nabbed. Kas was the only one who managed to sneak off into the dark.

'Asshole!' Josh called, which earned him an arm wrench from the police officer, who thought he was being verbally assaulted.

I took a step out from my hiding place, but a look from Cole made me remain where I was. I watched as Cole and Josh were led away, my heart still racing. From the soured meeting with RL to the strange second encounter with Cole, this night could not get any more horrid. Yet again, I had acted on blind hope and yielded nothing but trouble.

I emerged from the hedge and went to examine the wall. The vivid colours leapt out at me, drawing me in.

And the memories came drifting back to the surface.

She was six years old when she finally made her first trip to Neverland.

'The first thing you need to know about Neverland, Gemma, is that it is a secret,' her mother said. 'Neverland loses its magic if too many people know about it. Never ever tell anyone unless you know he or she is a believer.'

With her mother's warning in mind, Gemma began to explore Neverland alone. Other children had their little cliques and playdates at each other's houses, but Gemma never needed them. Neverland was her playground; it was her home, as well as her mother's. Even when her teachers remarked that she always seemed to have her head up in the clouds, her mother only smiled, attributing it to a lively imagination, then gave her a conspiratorial wink.

After the tedium of school in real life, Gemma began her actual lessons with her mother. She learned about the seventy-four types of corals found in the shallows of the Bronze Sea, the direction and speed of the Moontide winds at different times of the year, the various uses of skeleton leaves; she learned about mermaid lore, the border wars between the islanders and mainlanders, Neverlanders and Otherworlders, and the petty politics between the air sprites and fairies; she learned about Captain Hook and his various nemeses, including Peter Pan, and the trade holdings and pirate businesses.

She barely needed any help getting to Neverland when the time came. Second to the right and straight on till morning. It was easy enough if you knew where to look.

Neverland was a vast kingdom, as lovely as it was lonely. Sapphire seas and emerald islands, pink beaches underneath a bejewelled sky. Gemma drifted across the choppy waters, taking to flight as easily as breathing.

When she arrived at Halcyon Coast, her first instinct was to look for the mermaids. Sneaky harlots, her mother had called them. They stole up on you and toyed with you for laughs—and then they robbed you clean.

But the coast was clear, the beach unmarked by foot- or tail-prints. Gemma dovetailed through the sky, dodging a flock of robber kites as she headed for land.

Flying might have been easy, but landing proved to be tricky. Gemma tried to manoeuvre her way down to the strip of sand, flapping her arms for extra support. But the winds of Neverland had a mind of their own. A gust eddied around her and disrupted her landing, transporting her instead to a huddle of trees. Gemma let out a squeal and struggled towards safe ground, but the second she doubted she could fly was all it took for her to fall.

She plummeted through the air and plunged straight into the trees. Her scream, which sent the cocktail birds squawking as they fled, died when she finally landed on compact earth. The ground punched the air out of her, and her vision grew dim around the edges.

As she gave in to the darkness, the gold-green forest and its hushed melody faded away.

* * *

Speckled darkness greeted her when she came to. The sounds of bird calls and voices sharpened as she drifted back to consciousness.

Around her was a circle of children her age, some older, a couple younger. She counted them. Ten, but she couldn't trust her blurry vision just yet. They were dressed in torn, mud-stained shorts, and those who weren't shirtless sported loose tunic tops that were equally soiled. There was no mistaking them. The Lost Boys were a motley bunch, but they directed the same hostile look at her.

As she struggled to sit up, the oldest-looking Boy bent to peer at her face. Gemma shied away.

'An Otherworlder,' the Boy reported.

A collective groan rose from the group. 'Not another one.'

'I'm not an Otherworlder,' Gemma said.

'Yes, you are,' replied a pudgy Boy with a ruddy face. 'You have no business here and will only give our secret away.'

'You were an Otherworlder once too,' Gemma pointed out.

'Yeah, but I stayed on.'

'What makes you think I won't?'

Another Boy piped up. 'They always leave. They always stop believing.'

'Not me,' Gemma said, thrusting out her chin. 'Neverland is my home too. How do you stop believing in somewhere you belong to?'

'There's only one way to test if she has what it takes to be one of us,' the oldest Boy announced.

Gemma leaned forward with her request. 'Will you take me to see Peter?'

The Boys shared a look, and if Gemma recalled how the story went, she would not be so eager to believe them when they chimed, 'Sure!'

But in her excitement to meet the legendary Peter Pan, she followed the Lost Boys out of the woods towards the beach. She was still feeling a little woozy from her fall, but one of the Boys held out a hand to help her along.

At last, someone let out a sharp cry and the gang came to a stop at the edge of the beach. Soft dewy grass gave way to warm sand, but it was the sight before her that made Gemma rub her eyes and stare.

Right before her was a group of three life-sized mermaids, their scales glittering in a myriad of colours under the sunlight as they lounged atop a broad slab of rock half-submerged in the water. When they spotted the Lost Boys, they paused in combing their silken sun-bleached hair long enough to wave.

Gemma needed no prompting to go up to them. The throb of her injuries had dulled in the face of these mythical beauties before her. 'You're real,' she said to the mermaid with the amethyst tail closest to her.

Her gaze sharpened. 'My name is Marelina, actually. Marelina of the Halcyon Sea.'

'I'm Gemma. Gemma from . . . Otherworld.'

'Well, Gemma from Otherworld,' Marelina said, her gaze slicing to the other mermaids, who now flanked her. The Lost Boys stayed safely on the shore, watching. 'We always welcome newcomers.'

'You do?'

'Of course. You made it all the way here. That counts for something.' She took Gemma's hand in her cool, slim one. Her smile was dazzling. Gemma had never seen anything quite as lovely as her.

In one swift jerk, Marelina seized Gemma by the waist and yanked her into the water. The second mermaid pushed her head down.

Gemma thrashed and kicked, drinking a mouthful of briny seawater laced with something bitter. Her chest tightened as seconds passed.

Finally, the mermaids let go of her. Gemma burst through the skin of the water, spluttering and gasping for air, and reached for the rock. Her sodden clothes made it difficult to crawl up, but she succeeded after several tries. The mermaids laughed at her effort, their tails catching the light as they flashed whip-fast in the water.

From the shore, the Lost Boys hooted and laughed along. 'Welcome to Neverland,' the oldest one said.

The mermaids flipped their merry tails one last time, spraying water at Gemma before diving back into the sea.

Six

Cole

Josh was wearing a hole in the ground in the fluorescent-lit holding room. While I wasn't a stranger to the police station, this was a first for him.

'Quit pacing, will you? It's just a damn wall,' I said.

But it was hard to stop him once he had given in to his nerves.

He whirled around to glare at me. 'It's not just a damn wall, Cole. My parents had specifically told me to stay away from you.' He continued his antsy march before me, his stupid neon yellow sneakers squeaking every time he turned. The noise filled the dingy little room we were holed up in.

'Why?' I asked, even though I already had an idea.

'Because of the crap you pull on a regular basis.'

I could understand why he felt a little wronged at being locked up here with me. Josh and Kas might be friends with me because of my credit card, but they didn't have to be in for my crime too. All they did was pass me the spray paint—they didn't even have anything to do with the altercation.

Good thing Kas was slick in escaping, even if Josh now hated his guts.

'Appreciate the skill, not the intent,' I said when he let out a few choice descriptions about Kas.

'Intent on this,' he said, making a rude gesture with his hand.

'Profound.'

'It was your stupid phone, Cole,' Josh said. 'It totally gave us away.'

'Sure. It wasn't your ugly shoes.'

But I stared at my cell phone sitting in my hand. The screen was still frozen on the photo Gemma sent me—no, sent her *mother*.

I hadn't given much thought to what I was spray-painting. Halcyon Coast, the mermaids, and everything else I could remember of Gemma's description of her first visit to Neverland had spilt out onto the wall.

It was only then that I realized how much I still wanted to believe in Neverland and everything it stood for. But only fools held on to the past. How pathetic was it to keep holding on to some make-believe place from my childhood? So I destroyed the whole thing.

Some guy painted Neverland on a wall, Gemma had said in her message. *It was the most beautiful thing I had ever seen, before he destroyed it. I wish you could have seen the original artwork. You would have loved it.*

As I read the message over and over, rolling each word over my tongue and imagining her saying them out loud, regret started to set in. A part of me was still going, *She said my piece was the most beautiful thing she had ever seen!*

But another part was telling it to shut up. Some guy, *she said. She doesn't remember you. What are you so excited about?*

Granted, we hadn't seen each other in almost ten years, after she failed to show up at Wonder City like we had planned. But still.

Josh's pacing squeaked to a stop, signalling the big kids' arrival. My father led the little pack, shoving the door open. Josh's parents, who looked as tired as two people who had worked an entire day in their bakery could look, stepped in after him. A police officer brought up the rear.

Josh launched into his explanation before his parents could say anything. 'Look, I—'

'I will settle the bail,' my father said, his voice a metal wire that could draw blood.

Without a glance at me, he left the holding room. Josh's parents followed him out. I thought about apologising to them but couldn't find the right words. At least Gemma was safely out of this mess.

Josh and I slumped in our seats, staring at our shoes.

'Who was that girl, anyway?' he said at length.

'Gemma,' I reminded him.

'I mean,' he said, 'who is she to you? Seems a bit one-sided, if you know what I mean.'

Our parents returned before I could come up with an explanation that made sense. My father was nothing if not efficient, especially when it came to settling bail. That was something you got better at with practice.

Everyone left after it was agreed that we would, aside from paying for the damages, wash the walls and restore them to their original ugliness within the next twenty-four hours.

My father gave a measured apology and thanked everyone for their time before throwing me a frosty glance. That was my cue to get up and follow him. We walked in silence to the car. Street lights drifted by as we cruised down the streets, a blur of orange orbs caught in the windows.

'I thought you said you wouldn't cover my ass this time,' I said at last.

My father didn't respond, just stared resolutely ahead, and told Praj, our driver, to pick up speed.

I tried again. 'How long is the grounding going to be this time? Remember I only have one week to go before I turn eighteen.'

Still no response. I gave up, turning my back against him and counted the number of street lamps that passed until the house came into view.

Once we got in, I kicked off my shoes in a hurry, eager to hit the shower and knock out. This night had dragged on for too long. It was supposed to be just a quick paint job, an explosion of colours on a wall. But seeing Gemma there tonight had somehow made everything worse, like my dirty deeds had been laid bare, even though I had spray-painted far uglier, pointless things before without caring what anyone thought.

My father's voice broke through my thoughts. 'I want you to move out.'

I stopped midway up the stairs. 'Excuse me?'

'Leave,' he said. 'I will give you one day to find somewhere to stay. By tomorrow evening, I want you out of this house.'

'Does this mean you're giving me the apartment?'

His words cracked like a whip. 'No, you are *not* getting the apartment. Don't you get it? I am sick of—how did you put it—*covering your ass* every single time you pull stupid stunts like that. I'm not here to clean up your mess. You're almost eighteen, Cole. I've excused your behaviour over and over because of your mother, but all you're doing is wasting your life on meaningless pursuits.'

'It's just a wall,' I said.

He only stared at me in exasperation. 'Don't you care about anything at all?'

Caring was a tricky business. You had to ration it, give it out in measured amounts, or you ended up giving away parts of yourself as well. It was just easier not to care.

Besides, if it was anyone who made me stop caring, it was him.

'Pack your bags and find a place to stay,' my father went on. 'You can take the car, but you're on your own until you grow the hell up and do something about yourself.'

'You're not seriously cutting me off,' I said.

'Pack your bags.'

* * *

'This is Seamus. Leave a message.' I hung up the call and dialled another number. Maybe it was too early in the morning. Seamus was a late riser, after all.

'Al here. Sorry, can't come to the phone now. Call back later or state your cause after the beep.' Al was an early riser. I hung up and tried someone else.

'I'm busy. Call back lat—' I hung up.

'*Beeeep.*'

I would fling my cell phone onto the ground if it weren't for the fact that I had just been driven out of the house and had nowhere to go. This phone was my last lifeline.

Chelsea was the first person that came to mind. But she was also the first person my father would expect me to turn to, and he would ask her to keep tabs on me. Besides, how lame was it to run to a family friend after my melodramatic departure last night?

I scrolled through my list of contacts, mentally striking out those who ran in the same circles as my family and would have heard of my estrangement.

Estrangement. That was quite a word. Like someone had been forced to become a stranger. And maybe that was exactly what I was now, to my father, and had been for a while.

Finally, my thumb landed on a name. I stopped. How many times had I thought about calling her at this number? I could call her, text her, and end this lie. But what good would that do? It would only upset her, and I still wouldn't have a place to stay.

I scrolled some more, coming to a stop at Thomas's number.

In the days after my mum left and Gemma disappeared, Thomas had come over every other day, providing some form of distraction as my parents dragged out the custody battle. When I was twelve and failed my first exam, he lent me all his notes and helped me study until I managed to get my grades up to scratch again. Even after we'd drifted off to different schools, he had always taken my calls without trying to score a meal or a favour from me.

Thomas was one of those friends you could always count on. I wish he could say the same of me, but the truth was, I was the shitty friend he didn't need, who called him only when I required help. Maybe my father was onto something when he said I only cared about myself.

Still, now that word had got out that I had zero financial backing from my father (the grapevine was much smaller than you'd imagine), Thomas was probably the only one of my friends who hadn't got the memo, since he worked part-time at an amusement park, and his parents ran a cafe in the quiet little neighbourhood he grew up in.

Thomas was my only hope now.

As before, the Wild Ride amusement park looked as inspiring as a pile of wet socks. It wasn't just the rusted gates or the peeling paintwork that protested the park's slogan, 'Be prepared for the ride of your life!' It was the music that really did it, the canned amusement park music that whinnied through the grounds like the sad peal of a violin. I wondered why the hell Thomas would continue working here until I remembered his sentimental streak.

I approached the ticketing booth, where a middle-aged woman sat filing her nails behind the glass panel. She was clearly into the whole retro look, if her cat-eye glasses, red lipstick and copper-coloured curls were any indication. Some garden seemed to have just vomited all over her dress, it was so flowery.

'Excuse me,' I said.

'Half the place is closed for renovation,' she said, still focused on her nails. 'You sure you want to pay the full price for half the ride?'

'I'm here to look for someone.'

At that, she looked up.

'Well.' She curled the word over on her tongue and quirked a brow. The once-over she gave me was so quick I almost didn't catch her eyes flit down and up. 'When my horoscope said I'm about to meet a special someone today, I wasn't expecting someone so young.' She cocked her head and flashed me a smile.

I wasn't sure if she was joking, but I didn't care either way. 'I'm looking for Thomas, actually. Where can I find him?'

'The Ferris wheel. He should be on his lunch break. Go left after the turnstiles.' She returned to her nails.

I didn't go left after the turnstiles. Instead, I wandered through the grounds for a bit before following the signs that pointed to the Ferris wheel. Half the rides, like the ticketing woman said, were closed, and there was only a handful of staff manning the games booths.

It was a dismal ending to the place it had been ten years ago. The amusement park had been a hotbed of activity then, filled with music and people and lights and sounds. It was a world you could lose yourself in as a child.

Until you found yourself one parent short at the end of the day. No explanation, no apology.

I'd waited for a long time at the souvenir store that day, hoping someone would come and collect me. Bringing me to the Wild Ride had been my mother's idea. It had also been her final attempt to hold us all together, but I wouldn't know that until an hour later, when my father found me standing before the shop, trying to hold back my tears and panic as the day wore on.

He had grabbed my hand and led me out towards the main gates of the Wild Ride. 'Let's go, Cole.'

'But what about Mum?'

'Your mother is not coming.' He tugged at my hand, but I pulled away.

'What do you mean?'

'I mean,' he said, reaching for my hand again and tugging with more force, 'that it's just us now.'

Everything around me slowed to a painful stillness then. All that chaos from the amusement park was now inside me, spinning erratically. I was convinced it wouldn't stop until I could return to that day and do everything all over again. I wouldn't get lost this time; I wouldn't let her out of my sight.

Thomas was scribbling in a notebook while checking his cell phone when I found him. He got up from his chair when he saw me. 'Cole! What are you doing here?'

'Just here to see my old friend.'

He stared at me. 'Okay, what have you done?'

'Can't I just pop by for a nice chat?'

'You? Not likely. What's wrong?'

I considered how best to broach this. I had thought about it all morning, how I was going to beg for a place to crash. It felt more difficult with Thomas than with anyone else on my list of contacts.

'How about I show you?' I said.

Thomas kept up a steady stream of fretful muttering as I led him out of the amusement park. At the entrance, the ticketing woman, now accompanied by a girl slightly younger than me, watched us, bug-eyed, through the glass panel.

'Laura, I'm heading out for a bit,' Thomas called. 'Be right back!'

The painting looked a lot angrier than I remembered. I had spent a disproportionate amount of time getting the colours just right, but now all that stood out were the red streaks. Night was too forgiving; daylight showed me just how my anger and boredom and frustration were nothing more than a little tantrum. Like a balled-up piece of scrap paper.

I gestured at the pavilion wall. 'My masterpiece went unappreciated by the park-keeper last night. Josh and I got caught.'

Thomas took in every inch of the painting. '*You* did this?' His brows pulled together. 'Didn't you get caught last time too?'

'Obviously, that wasn't the last.'

I reached over to the foot of the wall to retrieve the rag draped on the bucket of water. Josh was supposed to help me, but he wasn't here yet. I doubted he would come—this wasn't really his mess to clean up, anyway. The water was slick and gave off a sickly lemony smell when I dunked the rag in and wrung it. I started wiping, but the colours refused to budge.

'Oh, and my dad finally threw me out,' I went on. '*And* cut me off. That was after he settled bail for me and decided I have to do *this*.' When it became apparent the paint wasn't letting up, I gave up and tossed the rag back onto the edge of the bucket. It missed and landed on the ground next to the bucket with a splat.

Thomas shook his head. 'Wow.' His eyes were still on the ruined painting. 'Wow,' he said again. 'You finally pissed off your dad badly enough. What are you going to do now?'

'I was hoping you'd have a clue.'

He tore his gaze away from the wall and considered me. To our left, music blared from the speakers a group of obnoxious idiots doing aerobics had brought. A woman walking her dog passed us by. Her eyebrows rose at the sight of the wall.

'Well, you can borrow Joel's room,' Thomas said. 'He'd be glad to stay on campus anyway. And we need a replacement here for someone who's gone on maternity leave. It's just for two months, though.'

I perched on the back of a park bench, propping one foot on the seat. 'Where?'

'Here at the Wild Ride.'

'Isn't it on its last legs or something?'

'It's just going through a . . . conceptual change.' He laid a hand on my shoulder. 'And you, my friend, are the best person to help us. Besides, beggars can't be choosers. You need income now that your dad's cut you off.'

I probably owed him way more favours than this anyway. 'Fine. So what's the plan?'

The plan, it turned out, was to turn the entire amusement park into an even more watered-down version of itself.

'Tell me again how a carnival is supposed to fare better than an amusement park?' I said.

'I told you,' Thomas said, sounding as maddeningly patient as usual. 'It's a long shot, but it might work. We have to try.'

'You know, there's an easier solution to this. Find another part-time job.'

Thomas sighed. 'I've been working there for four years. I can't just abandon it now when it needs help.'

'This is way too sentimental, even for you.' I considered taking another stab at the wall, but the slimy water turned me off.

'Besides, I promised Gemma I'd help,' Thomas added.

My hand froze halfway through reaching for the rag. 'Gemma?'

I tried to quell the hope sprouting in me. *Don't get too excited, Cole. There are many other Gemma's in the world.*

But didn't she mention her friend, the 'kind and sweet T', in her text messages?

'So it's for a girl,' I said, struggling to keep my tone light.

'It's not like that. Gemma's just a friend. And you'd know her too if you weren't so busy trying to be the biggest inconvenience to your dad.'

'Okay, point taken. I'm a lousy unconcerned friend. Now, how about taking me to your crib?'

'If I give you a place to stay, will you come work at the Wild Ride?'

A grin split across my face before I could pull it back. 'Fine.'

'And will you help us with the revamp?'

'Why do I get the sense that I'm being manipulated into this?'

He gave me his best puppy stare, the one I had seen grown women and little girls alike melt over. Gemma probably did.

'Fine,' I said, even though he couldn't throw me off this idea even if he tried now. I would be a park mascot and put on a suffocating suit if that was what it took to see Gemma again. 'You have my word. Happy?'

He shot me a wry smile. 'Unfortunately, your word often doesn't mean much.'

'Now I'm flaky too. My list of attractive qualities just keeps growing.'

Thomas only shrugged.

I didn't blame him. I would doubt my words too if I were him, given how many times I had bailed on him despite promising to help cover his shift at the amusement park. He didn't know how much I had grown to hate amusement parks and went out of my way to avoid them. Partly because of the tacky cheeriness it tried to sell that eventually fell apart like cheap paintbrushes, but mostly because this was where so many promises were left unfulfilled.

We'll come back again another day. We can come here every weekend if you want. Next time, we'll go on that ride. Next week, we'll meet in Neverland again.

It gave you something to look forward to but eventually left you hanging, wishing, waiting like a fool.

Seven

Gemma

Despite myself, I spent the better part of the night wondering if Cole and his friend were okay. Rude as he might be, he had come to my aid a couple of times now.

RL avoided all my calls and messages demanding the information I was owed. Maybe that altercation with Cole had made him decide it wasn't worth pursuing this venture, but I couldn't just let go of this link. What if the house RL had tried to buy from my father held all the answers I was looking for?

The next day at lunch, Jo and Boon and I settled into our regular window booth at the Wild Ride Bistro. They were both blissfully oblivious to what happened last night, and I planned to keep it that way.

Shelving aside thoughts of RL and Cole, I waited until after Harris had yelled our usual orders to the kitchen before launching into my proposal.

'So,' I said. 'I've put some thought into this place.'

Jo and Boon shared a look.

'We'll start with the rides. Since we only have two months to work our magic, we have to pull something dramatic.'

'Gemma, you only have two months,' Boon said. 'Are you sure—'

'Exactly. We don't have time to hesitate anymore.'

Boon observed me through his bifocals. Even when I was younger, his studied gaze always made me nervous, as if he could read me as easily as a book.

'Gem, you don't have to go to this extent,' Boon said. 'We have enterprises fighting to take this out of our hands. It's not just Wonder Entertainment—J&K Enterprises also has plans for it.'

'No. The Wild Ride is not going to end up with those people.' I needed to do this. Without this project, without a solid plan in my hands, I didn't know what else I could do. This—finding my parents, one memory at a time, starting from the Wild Ride—was all I knew.

'There are other ways of finding your parents,' Jo said quietly.

I hated how she thought right away that this was less about them than it was about my biological parents. I hated how she wasn't entirely wrong. Jo and Boon deserved better than me, some abandoned child they found all cried out at the foot of the Peter Pan ride who couldn't move on from the past.

'Don't worry,' I said. 'Just leave this to me and go on a holiday, or something. By the time you two get back, this place will be a boom town!'

Jo gave me that indulgent smile she used to give me in the early days when I had finally stopped crying and started getting used to having Jo and Boon around instead of my parents. Then she and Boon did that silent exchange again, where they conferred with their eyes. I swear, they communicated through telepathy half the time.

Finally, Boon gave a grudging shrug. 'I guess we still have the cafe for our retirement in case this—'

'Don't say fail,' I said. 'It won't fail—I won't let it.'

Harris arrived with our food and set it down with his usual flourish. 'Here you go, boss.'

'Thanks, Harris,' Boon said. 'It'd be a shame if we stopped making these fantastic pancakes.'

'I'm sure Liza will make them for you anytime. We both owe you that at least, for giving us a job here.'

'You both owe me nothing.'

Thomas found us after Harris left us with our food. But he wasn't alone.

'So this is the replacement I was talking about,' he said, stepping aside to reveal a boy in a dark chambray shirt and jeans. His face was all too familiar, from his dark, proud gaze to the defiant line of his jaw.

The memories came fast and furious, but only revealed themselves in flashes too fleeting to mean anything—a break in a song, the call of birds, the sleepy, exotic scent of wildflowers in bloom.

'Cole?' I said, blinking through the fog in my head.

He seemed far too happy to see me given how our last encounter went. 'Nice to see you again, Gemma.'

Everyone turned to stare at me.

'You two know each other?' Thomas asked.

I shot Cole my best baleful stare, daring him to reveal any more about last night. 'We've met.'

'Understatement,' Cole quipped.

Boon nodded. 'Maybe we should start over. Take a seat, boys.'

Thomas slid into the booth next to me, while Cole grabbed a chair from the next table. He sat straddling the chair in the middle of the aisle, watching me avoid his gaze.

Boon tucked into his pancakes. 'Now, Thomas, you were saying?'

'Right,' Thomas said, glancing at me. 'This is my friend, Cole. I thought he could replace Anika *and* help out with the revamp project.'

That got me raising my brows. 'Help out? Does he even have any experience working in an amusement park?'

'No,' Cole said simply. 'But how hard can it be?'

A snort escaped me. 'Very confident.'

He frowned. 'Is that how you talk to someone who saved your life twice?'

'Wait, what?' Thomas said. Jo and Boon stared at me and Cole.

'It's nothing,' I said, shooting Cole a glare.

'Yeah, it's nothing to you since you didn't have to get involved with the police—'

Jo's eyes widened. 'The police?'

'Just a little misunderstanding,' I hurried to assure her.

'Gemma.' Boon's face looked like a gathering of storm clouds. 'Please explain yourself.'

I could try to lie, but we all knew it was futile anyway. Jo, Boon, and Thomas were all too aware of the trouble I could get myself into in my attempts to find my parents. 'I was just going to get some information from this guy.' A hard edge crept into my voice. 'Who knew he would get so ornery?'

Cole snorted. 'Yeah, who knew?'

I glared at him, daring him to say more.

Boon frowned in confusion. 'You mentioned you saved her life twice,' he said slowly, like he wasn't sure he was going to like the answer. 'The other time was . . .?'

'When she walked right into a ring of speed mobiles and almost caused an eight-car pile-up. Quite the showstopper.'

Thomas buried his face in his palms as Jo let out a sigh. They knew what was coming.

Boon dropped his fork with a clatter and rounded in on me. 'Gemma. How many times are you going to risk your life to find them?'

'But I'm okay! That's all that matters,' I said.

'No, that is *not* all that matters. What matters is your inability to move on.'

'Move on,' I echoed. Boon's gaze faltered, but I charged on before he could take back his words. 'You want me to move on from being abandoned by my parents? Why, because I have you guys now and that's enough to erase everything that happened before? You think I should go about my life pretending like I'm okay with not remembering anything about my past, or that I still get inexplicable nightmares about drowning and being chased around in Neverland? Everyone thinks I'm stupid for being so hung up on Neverland, but don't you see? There's no moving on for me if I haven't figured out what I've forgotten or where my parents are.'

I was aware of my voice growing shakier with every word, of Thomas and Cole witnessing all this, and the unbearable cruelty of what I had just said to my foster parents. But there was no taking back the things that had already been thrown out in the open.

An ugly silence settled at our table like an unwelcome visitor.

'Gemma . . .' Jo reached for my hand but thought better of it and retracted hers.

Boon let out a sigh. 'If you want to waste your time and effort chasing people who clearly don't care, go ahead. We're just trying to make sure you stay alive and in one piece.'

'I *know* what I'm doing,' I said.

'Oh, really? Is that why you keep hitting dead ends searching for your parents? Look, we've held on to this place longer than we intended to, all because we promised you that we wouldn't close it before you found your father. I know you want answers, but I'm not going to let the three of us suffer just because your absent father can't be bothered to turn around for you. If you think he's worth all the effort, then keep looking. But don't expect me and Jo to let you risk your life doing stupid things to find him.'

'You're just afraid that I'll leave if he ever comes back for me.' It was presumptuous of me to declare that, but Boon's gaze fell.

'You're right,' he said, the fight gone out of him. 'I am.'

This was worse than having him yell at me. I wanted him to berate me and tell me I was in over my head, not agree with my accusation. There was nothing more I could say that wouldn't hurt them.

I edged between Thomas and Cole and tore out of the bistro before anyone could say anything more. Harris tried to stop me, but Boon told him to let me go.

I had had fights with Boon before, but never like this. Neither of us were ever willing to back down from an argument, and it usually took some mollifying on Jo's part before we both grudgingly agreed to disagree. Boon had never retreated with a subdued response before. But then again, I had never mentioned the possibility of me leaving them.

Cole found me by the back of the souvenir shop, stooped at the foot of the wall, mangling a weed growing out of a crack in the ground.

'And here I thought my dad and I couldn't get along,' he said, leaning against the wall with his arms crossed.

'Boon and I get along fine,' I snapped.

'Sure, that's why you said those things to him back there,' he said. 'Hey, I get it, sometimes our folks just don't get us. But—'

'Go away, Cole,' I said, getting to my feet. I still wasn't sure what his motives were, why he wanted to help us, and I certainly wasn't going to talk about my domestic affairs with a stranger.

I was about to go around the corner when he called after me. 'You want to remember?'

Despite myself, I stopped and turned around. His gaze, dark and resolute, rested on me. In my moment of hesitation, he caught up with me in two large strides, closing the space between us.

'I can help you remember,' he said.

He was as good as a stranger. But no matter how I kept telling myself that, I couldn't bring myself to believe it. I might have placed my trust in the wrong people before, but Cole didn't seem like he was having me on. His eyes spoke a half-forgotten tale, one that went much further back than yesterday.

It scared me how easily I fell back in.

Ever since that Otherworld girl appeared, Neverland had been abuzz. It wasn't every day that an Otherworlder showed up here, especially not alone. Peter picked them carefully, the ones who believed, the ones who didn't want to grow up.

And since Peter Pan, leader of the Lost Children of Neverland, had been missing for three moons now, it meant someone else had divulged the secret to entering Neverland.

The fairies thought it was one of the Neverlanders given to treason; the mermaids thought it was the work of an intruder, like that Wendy girl they all disliked; the natives fretted about security and burned more pyres to pray for the safety of their world; the Lost Children hoped it was Peter sending them an envoy; the pirates wanted to know if the girl came with any treasures from Otherworld.

But Gemma did not care for the mean pranks the mermaids played on her or the fairies' distrustful glances and whispers behind her back. She had bigger things to worry about—a more important mission to accomplish—for Neverland was under siege.

Every day, there were people trying to break into the fabled kingdom to claim a piece of it. Some of them wanted to stay. Some wanted to own it. And some just needed a place to hide.

Gemma wasn't sure she belonged to any of those, but she knew she was going to fight to protect Neverland with her mother by her side. It was their duty to do so. So what if she was only seven and had only been here once? She was as much a part of this place as Tinkerbell was.

Speaking of whom, Gemma wondered if the ball of light now flitting around her was the fairy in question.

'Excuse me,' she called out. If the fairy wasn't going to be discreet about her hovering, then she wasn't going to pretend that she was alone too.

The ball of light stilled above her head, and the fairy revealed her lithe form. She wore an emerald-green dress that bloomed like a flower when she twirled in the air.

'Are you . . . Tinkerbell?' Gemma asked.

'Certainly not!' the fairy said. She drew herself up to her full six inches and raised her chin. 'My name is Anisel, but you may call me Nix.' She took a little bow.

'Pleasure to meet you, Nix. My name is Gemma.' Her mother had told her to always be polite with fairies—they had terrible tempers if you got on their wrong side. 'I'm looking for one Peter Pan,' she said, mimicking the way her father spoke on the phone. 'Have you seen him around?'

'That depends,' the fairy said. 'If you're asking if I have ever witnessed his brash, hedonistic, cocky self, then yes. But it's been three moons since anyone saw him, so if you're referring to a recent sighting, then no I haven't.'

Gemma didn't know what brash or hedonistic meant, but judging from the look on Nix's face, she wasn't a fan of Peter as much as Tinkerbell was.

'Only that lovesick Tinkerbell thinks the world of that . . . child. The rest of us know better.'

Nix's aura soured with her mood and turned into a bruised purple shade, throwing the clearing into a darker gloom. It was then that the nape of Gemma's neck started to prickle. The air was sick with the smell of sweet rot, and even in the clearing sunlight filtered in with an anaemic will. It was day, but she stood in a gloom too thick and heavy to be lifted with fairy light. The breathing of the hostile forest made Gemma's skin crawl.

This was wrong. Neverland wasn't supposed to make you feel this way, not according to the stories her mother had told her.

This was not Neverland anymore. A world under siege was an ailing world. Already the skylight was dying along with the song of the trees.

Gemma realized then that Nix was shaking in unbridled fury. She never thought fairies could possibly look this hateful. In the chilly hush of the clearing, Gemma found her voice, but it came out only as a whisper.

'Nix, what happened to this place?'

'Peter Pan abandoned us, is what happened.'

Eight

Cole

It seemed even more cruel now to keep her in the dark about the messages, especially after hearing her frustration first-hand. Was this how she had been living all these years, tormented by memories and trapped in the past?

'I can help you remember,' I blurted now.

She shot me a look that wasn't completely hostile. There was something like bewilderment in it, like I was something too far beyond her grasp.

'Why?' she said at last. 'Why do you want to help me? Twice yesterday, and now with the Wild Ride. We barely know each other.'

I shouldn't be this disappointed; I shouldn't expect her to remember me or our shared experiences that felt like a lifetime ago. But how could she forget? She was the one who had taken me on those adventures and made me believe in Neverland.

'We don't? I'd say we are very well acquainted,' I said.

Never mind that I had spent the last ten years looking for her, waiting for her to return to Wonder City. Never mind that I had dreamt about her more times than I cared to count, each time waking with an ache in my chest. Never mind even that I still believed in Neverland and the girl who took me there, even though I would never in a million years admit it to anyone else. I couldn't let her forget everything we'd been through, make-believe or not.

She shook her head. 'I don't see how you can help, given that you lost me my lead last night.'

'Your *lead*? He would have robbed you blind last night. What even made you think he was legit?'

She stuck her chin out. 'He had a photo of my dad. I'm not completely stupid.'

I shook my head. 'No. You're just insane.'

Her gaze sharpened. 'Just because you saved my life before doesn't mean you get to judge it. You don't know how hard I've been trying to find my parents.'

Oh, believe me. I know a thing or two about your efforts.

My cell phone rang before I could voice that thought. I pulled it out of my pocket and checked the screen. Chelsea always had a knack for calling at the most inconvenient moment.

I turned my attention back to Gemma. 'You don't remember at all, what happened to them?'

'Aren't you going to answer it?' she said, nodding at my phone.

'No need.'

'Seems urgent.'

'It's not. How can you not remember anything about Neverland. Or this.' I drew a circle around my face with a finger. She frowned. 'What about the Council, the Lost Boys, the mermaids, Nix—anyone?'

Her eyes widened. 'How do *you* know all that?'

My phone rang again. I considered turning it off—we couldn't afford any distractions now.

'Look, I've been trying,' Gemma said, squeezing her eyes shut. 'If I could just remember what happened that day, I might finally find my parents.'

'What day?'

'My eighth birthday.'

We were supposed to meet in Wonder City as usual on her eighth birthday, but she never showed up. I had waited at our regular spot in the clearing with her birthday present, but the light had turned from gold to violet and finally died before I made my way back out alone. I never saw her again after that.

I wanted to know what happened that day too. The day she disappeared from my life and left me in pieces.

'Follow me,' I said, taking her hand and leading her out of the amusement park.

* * *

Chelsea continued calling a couple more times as we made our way across the park grounds—once while Gemma changed out of her Wild Ride uniform, and again as we headed out of the amusement park.

On the second call, Gemma snuck a glance at the screen before I moved my phone out of her sight. 'It's not very nice to keep a girl waiting like that,' she said.

'None of your business.'

'It is if my sanity is involved. If you're not getting that, I will.'

She reached for my phone, but I held it up above me. A moment passed between us before she lunged at me. I couldn't help but laugh at the sight of her determination. The sound took me by surprise as much as it did her.

She tried again, this time tripping over my foot. I threw out an arm around her waist and grabbed her hand before she went tumbling down. When she looked up, our faces were close enough for me to feel her breath on my skin. Neither of us moved an inch.

'Cole!'

We both jumped. Gemma hurried to put some distance back between us, her cheeks decidedly pinker.

Chelsea's eyes were fixed on Gemma as she strode down the lane.

'Chelsea. How did you . . .' I gave up on the dumb question halfway. Like my father, she had her ways.

Under Chelsea's gaze, Gemma rubbed her neck, glancing between me and Chelsea like she was already planning her escape.

'I heard you're working here now. The amusement park, I mean,' Chelsea added with an *everything's fine* smile.

'If this is about London, I'm not going,' I said.

Her eyes gave nothing away, but her smile wavered.

'Sorry,' I added as an afterthought.

Up went the smile again. 'Why not? You liked London.'

'Sure. For about a week.'

Her composure came crumbling down with a sigh. 'I don't get it. Is it such a torture to go overseas with me? We're supposed to be a team!'

'This isn't about you, Chels.'

'I know,' she said. 'I know it's about your mum. But don't you think you should let that go already? She doesn't want to see you.'

I was aware of Gemma standing next to me, pretending like she wasn't listening in on our conversation, and evened out my voice for her sake. 'That's not true.'

'It *is* true. If not, why hasn't she called you once? Why are you always the one reaching out to her?'

'Thanks, Chels,' I snapped. 'I'll keep that in mind if I ever need an unnecessary opinion.'

Gemma rubbed her neck again, suddenly very taken by the overgrown hedge next to the Wild Ride gates.

I considered apologizing, but I was tired of apologizing for every single thing I did.

'Your dad is not the enemy, you know,' Chelsea said quietly. 'He just wants the best for you. This trip to England is supposed to be a good start for all of us.'

'My father's intentions are not as good as he'd have you think, Chels. He just wants me out of his life, and I just showed him a less inconvenient way to do it. I've moved out.'

'You *what?*'

I had expected her to have received the memo by now. But apparently, things were slow-going in the grapevine today. 'Don't look so surprised. It was only a matter of time.'

'But where are you staying? Your dad gave you the apartment?'

'Funny you should mention that. He cut me off, actually. Told me no London, no deal. And since Thomas's brother is staying on campus, he offered me a room.'

'Thomas? You mean the amusement park guy?'

Gemma shot a fiery glance at her.

'Yes,' I said. 'But he prefers Thomas.'

'Why didn't you call me? I would've prepared a room for you right away.'

'It's better this way. Different. Better.'

Thomas's flat might be the size of my room, but I found it easier to breathe there.

'How?' Chelsea demanded. 'How is this any better? Because you have your pride intact? Because I'm part of the life you wish to run away from? How long are you going to live in the past, Cole?'

'I'm not living in the past, can't you see? I'm starting a new life here. One without him.'

'One without me?' She glanced at Gemma, and I saw then how ugly her territorial streak could be. For some reason, that made me want to reach for Gemma's hand, but I willed mine to stay where it was before it did anything stupid.

'You can't stay there forever,' Chelsea went on. 'Eventually, you're going to have to come home.'

I shrugged. 'Until then, I'm not.'

'You're being stubborn, Cole. What makes you think your mum's going to take pity on you and come back to you when she doesn't even bother calling?'

Silence stretched taut between us. A lone car cruised by and kicked up a flurry of leaves. Gemma looked like she would give up her lung to be anywhere else right now.

'I am not,' I said, 'looking for her pity.'

Chelsea's eyes darted away from me. 'I-I know you're not. I just mean—'

'You think I'm moving out so she'll take me in? You think everything I'm doing is just so she can pay some attention to me?'

'No, I just mean—'

'What, Chelsea? What *do* you mean? That I should just give up trying to bring my mum back and, in the meantime, go along with everything my dad says? Pretend I—*we*—don't need her?'

'You don't have to put your life on hold for her. Your dad has a plan for you, for *us*.'

'I don't give a shit about his plans for us,' I spat.

'Or maybe you just don't care about *us*. And that would be just typical of you, not caring about anyone or anything other than yourself.'

Her breaths came shallow and fast, and her eyes were reddening. I didn't understand the growing panic in my chest until I realized this was the first time Chelsea had ever cried because of me.

'I cancelled my plans just for you. *I* put my life on hold for you. But you don't even want me in yours anymore.' With a final filthy look at Gemma, she stormed off.

Gemma nudged me to give chase, but my legs remained rooted to the ground. There were a number of things I thought to say, but by the time I decided to apologize after all, Chelsea was already gone.

Nine

Gemma

After Chelsea stormed off, Cole and I made our way to Wonder City in silence. He didn't say a word and I didn't pry.

When we arrived at Wonder City, every other thought faded away. Standing before Wonder City with Cole now felt momentous, like I was perched at the edge of a cliff about to dive into the rapids of my memories. Images—snippets of a tale whether lived or told, I was no longer sure—flashed through my mind as my heart clamoured to return to Neverland.

Sometimes, I couldn't tell where the dreaming ended and the waking began. Had I told Cole about Neverland all those years ago and invited him on the rescue mission? Was that when we first met?

More importantly, would I be able to make it out of the dream if I stepped back into it now? Or would I end up like my mother, lost in my fantasies of a fabled place?

I wanted nothing more than to succumb to them now, to ask Cole if he would like to join me in Neverland again.

As though he had heard me, Cole glanced at me. 'Ready?'

I steeled myself, trying to tame my wild, thumping heart. Neverland was calling, and I didn't have the strength to keep away anymore.

We stepped through the gates.

Shortly after her last visit to Neverland, Gemma found someone who would help in her quest to save the besieged kingdom.

She met him on one of her regular visits to Wonder City, where her father would take her while her mother visited Doctor York at the cream-coloured building on the other side of the hill.

Cole was perfect for Neverland. He wasn't in a hurry to grow up; he was simply content to explore the world one nook and cranny at a time. And while he might have started out sceptical, he soon warmed to the idea of another kingdom ruled by children who didn't have to worry about grown-up things. It took Gemma just three more visits to Wonder City to convince him that Neverland needed their help.

He was, like her, eight years old then, and eager to set off on a quest of his own. Gemma taught him how to fly (although he had some initial trouble thinking of something truly happy), how to get to Neverland ('You have to believe in it wholeheartedly. Only believers can find Neverland') and warned him about the natives ('Mermaids are the worst').

'And how do we rescue Neverland?' Cole asked, interrupting Gemma in the middle of her lecture on mermaids.

Gemma kicked a stray twig out of the way. In Wonder City, everything was gleaming and tidy, so she was more than surprised when Cole showed her this little chaotic corner behind the theme park.

'My dad says behind this hill is where all the disturbed people go, so we should keep away,' Cole said.

'Hopewood?' Gemma thought about the sprawling brick building surrounded by neat squares of manicured green lawns. 'It's not that bad. My mummy goes there quite often.'

'I never said it was bad. I'm here, aren't I?'

Here was the forgotten backyard of Hopewood Sanatorium. It was a densely forested area at the foot of Hopewood Hill, where the undergrowth was as tall as them and snagged at their clothes. But it made the perfect place for planning a secret rescue mission and for taking off on secret trips to Neverland.

'We need a plan,' Cole suddenly declared.

'A plan?' Gemma echoed.

'Well, we can't just charge in and expect to change things.'

'We do have a plan. Find Peter Pan.'

'My dad always told me not to pin my hopes on one thing. What if we can't find him? We need a backup plan.' It sounded important when he said it.

'We'll find him. Mummy has met him before.'

'Then we ask her.'

'She's in Hopewood right now.'

So there was nothing left to do now but set off on their own. Her parents weren't due for another hour or so. Ever since her father saw how well Gemma clicked with Cole, another lonely boy wandering around the park grounds, making up stories in his head, he had trusted her to be safe in Cole's company. At this point, he was probably just glad that she had a friend.

Gemma nodded at Cole. 'Let's do it.'

Ten

Cole

As usual, Wonder City was packed with clusters of tourists and families with one too many screaming babies. I had almost forgotten what it was like to be in a normal, crowded amusement park.

Wonder City was everything the Wild Ride wasn't. While the Wild Ride had ticketing booths where you got your all-day pass at twenty dollars for adults and fifteen dollars for kids, Wonder City had 'admission platforms' where you stepped into some kind of sci-fi looking silver box and get registered as an all-day or half-day visitor. While the Wild Ride had a bistro for diners to have regular food like roast beef sandwiches, Wonder City had a dining gallery that served food named Sky High Platter and Rocket Monster without explaining what any of that entailed. (According to my father, it was supposed to add to the experience.)

When I was younger, and the idea for Wonder City first came into conception, I thought it was the most complicated plan I had ever heard. Then, when Wonder City was built in a matter of months and I got to get on the kiddie rides before anyone else, I thought it was the most terrifying and marvellous kingdom I had ever been allowed to roam about.

'This,' my father had intoned in a *Lion King*-esque manner, 'will be yours one day.'

That was before, when amusement parks still meant make-believe games and gratifying three-minute rides, not unexplained departures and an interminable wait for someone who was already gone.

Now, there was no going back on my revulsion for Wonder City and its contrived thematic rides and booths, its unapologetic over-the-top-ness like a smarmy smile from a stranger about to grab you and go.

As we queued in line to get on the registration platform, Gemma took deep breaths with her eyes closed like she was bracing herself for, well, a wild ride. She seemed no different from that little girl way back then, determined to save Neverland and find her mother there.

When she opened her eyes, my gaze darted to the hotspot TV monitors (which showed where the visitors were scattered in the City) and I studied them like they were the most fascinating things I had ever seen.

'You never answered my question,' she said. 'Why did you agree to help us with the Wild Ride project? This place belongs to your dad—to *you*. We're essentially your competitors.'

'Let's not kid ourselves here. In terms of competition, the Wild Ride doesn't even register as a worthy competitor.'

'Still, you're helping us to become a worthy competitor. Why?'

Maybe I did this in the hopes that my mum would come back to us. Maybe I just didn't want my dad to succeed in taking over this place. Or maybe I was just hoping to create my own version of Neverland, one where people could forget the rest of the world just for a while. Whatever the reason, I wanted this to work.

'Because I root for the underdog,' I said with a shrug. 'By the way, just so we're clear, I am not getting on any of the rides. It's bad enough we're paying to enter a theme park.'

'Can't we get free tickets? You own this place—or will, someday.'

'That would defeat the purpose of leaving home, wouldn't it?'

'So I'm paying forty dollars to preserve your pride?'

'That's one way of looking at it.'

She raised her brows. 'I'd have thought your pride would be worth a lot more than that.'

'You'd be a lot nicer if Thomas were here.'

'Actually, no. I have an attitude reserved for you that will never change.'

I felt a grin split across my face. 'I'm flattered.'

'Chelsea's right, you know,' Gemma said as we inched towards the platform. 'You'll have to go back to your own life eventually. Regardless of why you're helping us, you can't keep hiding out at the Wild Ride.'

'You're one to talk about hiding out.'

She frowned. 'What's that supposed to mean?'

'You've been hiding at the Wild Ride all this while, waiting for your parents to come find you, because then you don't have to deal with the possibility that they didn't bother looking for you.'

She started to protest, but I knew she had no argument coming. She had mentioned that fear in a text message to her mum once, then proceeded to apologize for that message, as if her anxiety might further deter her mum from returning. It was one of those moments I could have ended the lie but didn't.

'Admit it,' I said. 'You've considered that possibility.'

She shot me a mutinous glare.

After we bought our tickets, we climbed into the capsule that would take us into Wonder City on a conveyor belt, which moved along to an annoying series of beeps. It was funny how a place that used to hold so much allure could be so off-putting now.

Our destination was seven stops away from the entrance. People got on and off the capsule, and at each stop Gemma glanced at me, expecting to get off. But where we were headed, it was so remote that we were the only passengers left in the capsule. Everyone else had opted to explore by foot.

'Where exactly are you taking me?' she asked at last.

Separated by a densely forested area, Hopewood Sanatorium was a place my father used to warn me to stay away from. And until I met Gemma, Hopewood was a place for 'disturbed people', as my father put it.

But Gemma was *normal*—or as normal as someone who sincerely believed in Neverland could be. But if she was 'disturbed', then so was I for believing in Neverland too.

I kept my gaze trained on the cream-coloured building in the distance. The private sanatorium was in pristine condition even after all these years. The capsule hissed to a stop as we reached the final station. I got up and headed out.

'Cole,' Gemma called, and I turned to find her rooted in the same spot. There was worry in her eyes, but also something else peeking through. Something like hope. 'Where are we going?'

'Back to where we left off,' I said.

Once they reached Neverland, they dove straight for the clearing, Gemma taking the lead. The air was ripe with the smell of rot and ruin—the sign of a sick forest—and they stood in a hush that sent Cole's hairs standing on end.

'Those cocktail birds usually make a racket up in the trees, but even they are quiet,' Gemma whispered.

Cole couldn't tell if this silence was normal here in Neverland, but this place didn't look as magical as he had expected.

'So about this key,' he began.

Gemma shushed him, her gaze roaming around the empty clearing. 'I told you,' she whispered. 'It will lock the gateway to Neverland and keep the outsiders away.'

What they needed to do, she said, was find Peter. Without him to lead the search, they had almost zero hope of finding the key.

'Outsiders. You mean us?' Cole said.

'We're here, aren't we?' Gemma shot back. 'We're not the outsiders.'

'But you still talk like one,' said a voice between them. Cole yelped and jumped away from Gemma, but Gemma broke into a grin.

'This is Nix, my fairy friend,' she told Cole.

Cole barely had time to register the little ball of light flitting around him before it dove straight into the bushes and wove an intricate pattern through it. Her movement was so rapid that her aura trailed in a pink streak behind her.

'Show-off,' Gemma said.

'Who's your friend?' Nix said, coming to a stop before Cole's nose.

Cole's eyes slid towards each other. He almost swatted the little thing away and was glad he hadn't. She was pretty, though he couldn't tell how old she was. He drew himself to full height, the way he had seen his father do. 'My name is Cole. It's nice to meet—'

'You said we need a key to lock people out of Neverland the other time,' Gemma said.

Nix straightened mid-curtsey. 'Gemma, it's rude to interrupt.'

'We're running out of time. Look at this place!' Gemma threw an arm around.

'I am well aware of the dire state of things here,' Nix replied. The edge in her voice made Cole, who didn't quite know what to expect from fairies, slightly nervous. 'But there is always time for manners.'

Gemma pursed her lips, looking suitably chagrined.

'Now, before you go running off to find some magic key, there's somewhere we need to go.' Her gossamer wings began buzzing again. 'Follow me. And for goodness' sake, stay close. Those cocktail birds aren't as nice as they look.'

Gemma and Cole broke into a run to keep up. 'But where are we going?' Cole asked.

'To see the King and Queen,' Nix said, without a backward glance. 'At the Private Council of Neverlanders.'

* * *

The Private Council of Neverlanders was a fancy name for a motley assortment of creatures and beings—magical and non-magical—although Cole thought you had to be somewhat magical to even be here. It was all incredibly bizarre and becoming even more so.

When Gemma first told him about this place, he had assumed it was just a very elaborate game, but now he wasn't so sure. This felt too real, surreal, like a story come to life.

And now, with Gemma by his side, he stood before a long rectangular table, where twenty representatives sat peering at them. Cole was used to being paraded about. He had experience wearing uncomfortably scratchy suits, having his hair combed and parted neatly, and smiling at the people his father regularly invited over for his work parties.

But this. This was completely out of his league. Cole had no idea what he was supposed to say or do when facing a bunch of supernatural creatures, winged and scaled and beaked, all of whom were watching him as though expecting him to break into song any minute.

There were the fairy sovereigns, Queen Arabelle and King Titus, who sat at the head of the table in gilded, high-backed chairs; the mermaids, who folded their tails awkwardly beneath them; the pixies, goblins, gnomes, a pair of harpies with red and blue plumages respectively, dwarves, elves, adults (humans!); and finally, two Lost Children, who looked as they were named, quailed by the solemnity and grownup-ness of the Council.

Peter Pan should have been here, even Cole knew that. He wondered if he should sing, just to break this stalemate.

But then Nix broke the silence. 'Your Majesties, I present to you the Otherworlders.' She flitted aside and gestured to Cole and Gemma.

'The rumours are true, then!' shrieked the blue harpy as everyone leaned out of their seats to stare some more.

'Question is, how did she learn of Neverland?' said a goblin with a lumpy nose. 'And how did she break in? We know it can't be Peter Pan. That idiot boy has been missing since before the girl arrived.'

'Indeed,' the fairy king said. 'And it seems she has brought a companion this time, too.'

'See, this is how it spreads. This epidemic of Otherworlders,' snarled a gnome with a full snow-white beard. 'Thanks to snitches like her. And that Wendy girl.'

Gemma looked up sharply. 'I am not Wendy Darling.' She wasn't some common Otherworlder who came here and disrupted the peace. She belonged here.

'Razzledorf, please,' Queen Arabella chided. She turned back to Gemma. 'So how did you learn about us?'

Gemma wasn't sure whether to bring up her mother. What if she got her into trouble as well? She was beginning to tell she wasn't entirely welcome here.

'Don't be afraid, child,' Queen Arabella said gently. 'Just speak the truth.'

Gemma's voice emerged as a squeak before she cleared her throat and tried again. 'Peter Pan brought my mother here. And she taught me how to come here.'

'Ah yes, when he is not bossing a bunch of kids around, he's off gallivanting with Otherworld girls,' Razzledorf remarked.

The pair of Lost Children bristled. 'Peter has a job to do,' said the girl. 'Those Lost Children need a guide.'

Gemma cut in before Razzledorf could retort. 'Peter will come back.' Cole tugged on her hand to shut her up, but Gemma paid him no heed. 'Peter Pan will return for Neverland.'

'We should hope so,' King Titus said. 'But until he does, we have to shore up our defences without him.'

'But he's the only one who can get the key,' one of the mermaids pointed out while braiding her turquoise hair.

'Nonsense,' the goblin snarled. 'He's not the only one who has crossed the Silver Sea.'

'No, but he's the only one who has spoken to Old Limestone.'

'Who's Old Limestone?' Cole whispered to Gemma. His hand was still around Gemma's, and neither of them had let go.

'A mountain,' Gemma muttered back. 'The key is hidden deep in his belly.'

'Peter Pan spoke to a mountain?'

'Storm!' the bearded man in a stained oversized coat bellowed, jolting Cole and Gemma back to attention. 'He's crossed the Silver Sea before. He can help find that key.'

Razzledorf raised a finger. 'Correction: he didn't cross it; he merely ventured into it. Besides, he doesn't know the key from his own pie-hole.'

'Razzledorf,' one of the elves chided. 'Not in front of the children!'

The gnome's female counterpart stepped in. 'What he means is, Storm never stays on land for longer than a day. He will leave us stranded there.'

'What about Captain Hook?' Gemma piped up. 'Has he crossed the Silver Sea before? Can he find the key?'

At that, the entire Council broke into peals of laughter.

'Hook's not going to help us, silly,' the scarlet harpy crowed. 'He's too busy hiding from that alligator in his head. Goodness knows his time is up.'

'Then we'll look for the key on our own,' Gemma said, quelling the urge to stamp her foot. 'We will find Storm and get him to take us to it—'

'Wait a minute,' the mermaid said, pausing in her hair-braiding. 'You know where the key is?'

Every pair of eyes fell upon her. Gemma shrank back in her seat. 'Peter might have mentioned it to my mother,' she squeaked.

Razzledorf and half the Council started up again, listing treason as one of Peter's offences. This time, the two Lost Children leapt up from their seats and joined in the argument.

'Peter Pan aside, are we to place our hope on two human children? Have we learnt nothing from Peter Pan?' the bearded man roared.

'You're human,' Cole pointed out. 'I think,' he added meekly when the man turned to glare at him.

'Exactly why I don't have faith in you two,' the man growled.

Queen Arabella called for order, and everyone sank back into their seats. 'Seeing as no magical being is able to cross the Silver Sea, and none of us here have any leads on the location of the key, these two children are our only hope. Neverland cannot wait for Peter Pan to come to the rescue, nor can the Lost Children wait for their leader to unite them.'

Not even Razzledorf or the bearded man could refute that statement.

'So,' the fairy queen said. 'All in favour of Gemma and Cole crossing the Silver Sea with Captain Storm, please raise your hand.'

At first, no one moved an inch.

And then, like the lantern shoots of Neverland that sprouted on the beach each night to welcome sailors to shore, hands rose. A pair. Then another. And another. The harpies perched on the table and raised a wing each. Soon, fourteen hands (or their equivalent) were in the air. The gnomes, goblins, and humans remained unyielding.

'It's settled then,' Queen Arabella pronounced. 'Gemma and Cole of Otherworld, you will be tasked with finding the key to Neverland, with the aid of Captain Storm and his crew.'

The harpies let out a loud squawk and the pixies clapped politely. Razzledorf gave a grunt and got up from his seat.

Cole leaned over to whisper in Gemma's ear, 'I sure hope you know what you're doing.'

Eleven

Gemma

We ended up in front of a nondescript wrought-iron gate tucked amongst uncultivated bushes. In this forgotten part of the theme park, memories grew heavier with each step I took.

My heart drummed to a rising beat as I finally came to a stop next to Cole.

The more I looked at him now, the more it became clear to me that he was the boy I had brought to Neverland, the one who had stood by me as I spoke before the Council of Neverlanders, and shared those adventures with me.

How had it taken me this long to remember him? How could I have forgotten those stories we had told each other?

The first whiff of Neverland hit me, and I yearned to give in to its heady scent. Cole was waiting, watching my face for any indication that I recalled something. But what if Neverland was nothing like what I remembered?

As though he had heard my thoughts, Cole said, 'I know you still believe in Neverland. Which means you can't have forgotten this place.'

I tore my gaze away from the gate to look at him. 'So you believe it's real?'

'Only believers can find Neverland,' he said, echoing my words then. 'That place is no realer than you are. Sometimes, I wonder if

I had imagined everything: Neverland, the Lost Boys, the Captain, the Council, you. But even if I stopped believing in Neverland, I never stopped believing in you. So don't tell me you've clean forgotten everything. I know you haven't. You can't have.'

He pushed the gate open, which let out a groan at its own weight. He waved me through, holding it open as I stepped through the weed-choked undergrowth.

The place seemed to have frozen in time, wild and rampant and teeming with secrets and stories. The smell of ripe fruits and soft earth lured me back into the world we had created, the one in which I had so badly wanted to stay but didn't quite dare to.

A tangle of voices rose in my head: shouts of the Lost Boys, of Captain Storm to his crew, of the Council in conflict, and Cole's nervous whisper. I was caught between here and there, almost washed away by the tide of memories—until a lone voice cut through the noise.

I'll wait for you there, Gemma. I'll wait for you in Neverland.

I remembered my mother's voice as the low, melodious one that recounted endless tales and schooled me in the ways of Neverlanders, not the shrill, raspy one that accompanied the fright-wide eyes of a hunted animal.

Everything else dissolved into a riot of noise and colour. For some reason, I could taste the salty tang of the sea, feel the weight of water on my chest. I was scrabbling to reach the surface, gasping for air. Cole's voice drifted close to me, but I couldn't make out his words.

Darkness closed in, hot and heavy. My throat tightened and my head felt weightless, like it had been snipped at the neck. Every noise was muffled, as though I was underwater.

Warm hands cupped my face. 'Gemma, look at me.'

I cracked open my eyelids and tried to focus. Despite his murky outline, his face was clear as day. He *was* that boy. Cole.

The one who had tried to save Neverland with me, who had stayed with me until the end. And I had deserted him.

Cole's gaze was fixed on me. The darkness receded and then all I could see was him. 'Gemma. Say something.'

'You *were* that boy.' My words trailed away with the breeze, but Cole heard me loud and clear.

A smile took over his entire face. 'Took you long enough.'

Twelve

Cole

When she opened her eyes again, recognition glowed in them. Her brows pulled apart and her clenched fists loosened. My hand slid off her face.

'You *were* that boy,' she breathed.

A grin slid across my face. My mother could distance herself from me all she wanted, and my father could pretend like I didn't exist, but there was someone who remembered me at least. At last.

'Took you long enough. I knew you couldn't have forgotten,' I said.

'I don't remember much either.' She dragged a shaky hand through her hair.

'Why don't you remember? What happened that day we were supposed to meet?'

Her lips curved into a wistful bow. 'I've been asking myself that since that day. But I don't remember much of anything that happened before I was eight.'

'You never showed up. I figured you were sick of Neverland, sick of me.'

She shook her head. There was a softness in her face now that hadn't been there before, as if her memories had brought her closer to herself.

'Better late than never?' she said.

'Better late than never.'

* * *

The gate was locked now. It was a measure my father took to prevent me from revisiting Neverland, not knowing that Neverland wasn't a place you returned to but a place you carried everywhere with you.

As we made our way back to Wonder City, Gemma sank into a pensive silence that only had room for one. My questions sat at the tip of my tongue, but I didn't want to bombard her with them yet. I fell into step with her, feeling more and more stranded with my doubts with each passing moment. Why hadn't she remembered? What exactly had happened that day she failed to show up at Wonder City? Why had Jo and Boon adopted her? What happened to her father?

Despite all the text messages I had intercepted, I still couldn't glean enough information to piece together the full picture. Gemma's messages mostly revolved around Neverland and the everyday details of her interim life. It was like she had never quite settled down since she lost her parents.

When the din of the amusement park finally hit her, she came to a stop, pressing a finger to her temple.

'It'll come to you,' I said, like I knew any better. 'Have some faith.'

'Faith?' Her smile was wry. 'Now there's something I never thought I'd hear from you.'

Watching her consult her Wonder City 'navigation chart', I wondered if she was right. If I *wanted* her to be right. It didn't seem possible that someone as achingly hopeful and trusting as her could possibly exist, that she could still believe so wholeheartedly in the people who had left her behind.

A part of me wanted to prove her wrong—show her that her optimism was sorely misplaced, especially when it came to me— but then I'd only be proving my father right. Proving that I was so dead set in my ways I was beyond saving, that I had been lost ever since Mum walked out on us and Gemma disappeared from my life. That I was really the wildest Lost Boy that ever existed. But if someone—even just someone who operated on blind faith like Gemma—believed in me, did that mean I might actually be worth the effort?

Thomas's phone call saved me from figuring that one out. This was too much navel-gazing for one day.

'I thought you'd like to know,' Thomas began. 'Your dad just came by the Wild Ride.'

'What did he want?' Chelsea was such a tattletale sometimes.

'He wanted to know what your current living arrangements are.'

'That can't be it.'

'He also wanted to remind you of the party this Wednesday evening on the boat. It's at seven sharp, and you're to wear a suit.'

Now that made more sense. Only when an event required my public appearance would he need me around. 'Didn't your mum teach you not to talk to strangers, Thomas?'

'Your dad's not exactly a stranger. Besides, what was I supposed to do, ignore him? He said he really wants you to be there. So just call him back, okay?'

'Whatever you say, Thomas.' I hung up.

'Rude,' was the first thing Gemma said to me after that.

I shrugged. 'I've been called worse.'

The days leading up to the divorce were the worst. Mum would purse her lips at every little thing Dad said or did, and he would blow his top, unleashing the ugliest words that Mum would counter with a frosty silence that coated the house and nipped at us. It was in those long, chilly days that I missed Gemma the most.

She peered at my face now, shifting entirely into my line of vision. 'It still hurts, doesn't it? You never really get over someone leaving.'

'What is this, pity?' I said irritably.

'You don't have to act like you don't care. It doesn't hurt any less.'

'And it will if you keep hanging on to the hope that they will care? I'm not like you, Gemma. I know a lost cause when I see one.'

'You say that, but I think you wouldn't be so afraid of the truth if you could look it in the eye.'

'And what,' I asked, 'might the truth be?'

'That you haven't given up hope that she will return.'

'Says the girl who has waited ten years for her parents. Maybe you're just tired of waiting alone.'

She flinched. I considered apologizing, but my apology sounded hollow in my head, so I kept it there.

Now that we had what we came for, we made our way wordlessly out of Wonder City. By the time we reached the gates, my guilt had caught up with me. It was strangely easier to apologize to her—I didn't have to plan my words and tread on eggshells like I did with Chelsea.

Gemma shook her head, dismissing my apology. 'It kind of becomes part of you after a while, the waiting. Sometimes, I dream up all the ways we'd meet again.'

I thought about all the text messages she had sent over the years ever since she got her first cell phone, and all the letters to which I hoped she received more satisfying responses. Because there was no way her mother was ever going to reply to her.

'Don't look at me like that,' she said. 'When I find my parents, it will be worth all the wait.'

I gave no reply.

She threw me a sidelong glance, ready to change the topic. 'So what else do you remember about our Neverland chronicles?'

We had written the story together, crafted each character's journey—including our own—passing it back and forth between us like a polished stone. Even if I could convince myself that I was well past make-believe stories, to Gemma those stories were part of her fractured memory. Each chronicle was crucial to her quest for the truth.

So I would visit Neverland again. For her.

Captain Storm was someone who guarded his ship so zealously he barely ever made port. He believed that the sea was his one true home, and to be on land was as unnatural as the hook on his nemesis's hand.

When he first caught sight of the two children, it was on the southern island of Almeta, where he had just gathered enough supplies for another voyage to the Silver Cape. He never stayed overnight on land, even in terrible storms that tore ships apart. But as his men loaded the ship with bags of flour, potatoes and seasoned meat, Captain Storm stepped off his ship.

His crew stared. But the captain's attention was fixed on the pair of children. They shouldn't look so out of place in Neverland, where Lost Children made their home. But the two weren't inhabitants. No, they were just visitors. Port Almeta hosted vagrants and visitors alike, and these drifters were from the Otherworld.

They were hardy little things, the captain could tell right away even from afar, not a day older than eight years old. They approached Storm with a steely determination that was uncommon among the Lost Children.

'We would like to cross the Silver Sea with you,' were the girl's first words to him. Storm could tell she was a lot more nervous than she sounded—her picking at a loose thread on her jeans was an obvious tell. The boy nudged her, and she added, 'Sir.'

'Captain,' the boy corrected, and the girl nodded.

The captain was being very un-captain-like so far, so he cleared his throat and growled, 'You want to cross the Silver Sea?'

The pair nodded.

'Why?'

'We want to know what's on the opposite shore.'

Tourists, the captain thought irritably. There was no other way to the Hinterlands but sea passage—flight was impossible because of the air sprites out for flesh. Many stubborn visitors had plunged into the watery depths of the tumultuous Silver Sea because of those greedy little sprites.

These children had no idea what they were in for.

'Hitch a ferry. I don't take passengers,' Captain Storm said.

'You don't understand. We're on a mission,' the girl said with enough passion to make the captain's brows slide up. 'To save Neverland.'

Storm narrowed his eyes. 'Save it how?'

The children shared a brief look before the boy replied, 'We know our way around. We've studied the maps and everything.'

'We're not just visitors,' the girl added with an eye roll.

A crew of sailors traipsed by with more bags of rations, staring at their captain and the two children he was entertaining. In the time it took for his men to pass, Storm understood.

'You're looking for the key, aren't you? It's a myth, kids. There is no key. Just an old cave and a treacherous jungle.'

'We don't know that for sure,' the girl said.

Oh yes, they were Otherworld children all right. Only they could be this stubborn.

'Neverland is not yours to save,' said Storm. There had been others who tried, but they all gave up eventually after failing too many times, moved on and left Neverland for good. The others ended up as Lost Children, drifting by each day for eternity.

'We don't know that unless we try,' the girl insisted. She was determined and solemn, unlike most children her age. Not that Captain Storm would know, given the number of children he came into actual contact with.

How then was he going to have two of them on his ship?

Yet, he looked at the pair standing before him now and heard himself say, 'Get on board, then. And try not to fall over. I won't bother doubling back for either of you.'

* * *

When Captain Hook first heard about the children's plan to lock the gateway to Neverland, he burst out laughing. And when he heard that Storm was helping them cross the Silver Sea to find the key, he laughed even harder. To think the old sailor would get involved in some foolish, starry-eyed quest of two Otherworld children!

The key was a myth. Storm—and the rest of them—should have known better than to place their faith in some fabled object. Ancient Neverlanders made that up so they could believe that they were safe from invasion, that there was an easy, convenient way to protect Neverland.

Neverland was never going to be safe. Not if idiot children like that foolhardy pair were going to keep entering the realm in the wake of that Darling girl. If Neverland were to counter this invasion, it would be because they fought for it. Staked their claim.

But Neverlanders were a weak-willed bunch, content to while away their days chasing fairies through meadows and sunbathing with mermaids. No one did any real work here but him.

Fine, and Storm too. The sailor was responsible for almost half the trading done around here; he, too, was doing something to keep Neverland alive, unlike those fairies and that stupid Council to which he had not been invited, even though he technically ruled the seas.

The Silver Sea. Good luck trying to cross that with two children, *he thought. Not just children, but Otherworlders. They wouldn't know the bones of those who had died trying to find the key from their own teeth.*

Hook paced the length of his chamber. He had to stop them from crossing the Silver Sea. Not only because their passage would disturb the sea dragon, but it would also diminish his chances of acquiring the weapons he would need against the Otherworlders. Although the sea witch had been most useful in getting rid of that crocodile, even she couldn't fight against an enraged sea dragon.

He had to act now. Peter Pan might be missing in action, but the other Neverlanders weren't entirely incompetent. He had learnt never to underestimate his enemies, even small children.

Hook headed to the upper deck and watched as his crew shuffled to attention. One of them let go of the sails in his panic, making it billow lopsidedly. Hook took slow, deliberate strides towards Kiyeogh, the old sailor. He was becoming more of a liability these days—perhaps it was time to let him go.

Before he could decide on Kiyeogh's sentence, the soft but unmistakable tick tock, tick tock *echoed through his head.*

Hook cursed inwardly. That blasted crocodile. *The ravenous reptile might be dead, but it would never stop haunting him. Time was his true enemy—he realized that after even the crocodile's death couldn't assuage his fear or worry.*

Punishing Kiyeogh could wait. Hook stepped away from the edge and looked every crew member in the eye.

'Make for land. Come moonrise, we're paying the old crone a visit.'

The crew drew a collective gasp. For them to go through the putrid, swampy labyrinth to see the sea witch again meant things were dire. The last time they did that was because Hook had been driven half-mad by that crocodile.

'But, Captain,' braved a sailor. 'We are too far from land to reach the shore tonight.'

Hook threw out his hooked arm and snagged the sailor's shirt front, then drew him up close. The blade tore through the sailor's shirt and pressed against the base of his neck. Waves rustled around the ship, filling the silence. Hook slashed the blade across the sailor's neck, sparing him not even a glance as he crumpled to the ground.

When he spoke again, his voice rang loud over the waves. 'I said, make for land.'

This time, no one else questioned his order.

Thirteen

Gemma

Boon was nowhere to be found when Cole and I returned to the Wild Ride, but Jo was there in the office. Cole left us alone just before Jo spotted us.

With Jo and Boon, I never had to coat my words. They always gave me space, never pressuring me to speak before I was ready. Now, though, as I hovered in the doorway, I found myself returning to my mute eight-year-old state, struggling to find my voice even though I had rehearsed my apology on my way back here.

'Hi, Gem,' Jo said, looking up from her computer screen. She smiled, but it only made me feel worse.

'Hi.' I rubbed my foot against the other ankle. 'Boon's not here?'

'He's making his usual round.' Boon always walked around the entire amusement park, starting from the souvenir shop all the way to the boardwalk and back again. He said it helped him sort out his thoughts.

I went over to Jo. 'About what I said earlier, I . . . '

She shook her head. 'We know, Gem. We're not mad at you. Boon's just worried about you. You know how he gets.'

'Yeah, but—'

'Gemma. There's nothing you can say that will make us love you less. Now, get busy with the revamp project. Thomas is all on board, and so is Cole. I've had a chat with him, and I think he might just be the person to help with this. And you two already share some history!'

That was an understatement.

'That should make things easier.' Jo got up gingerly from her chair and gave my shoulder a feeble squeeze. 'Well, I'm going to go look for Boon.'

After she left, I pulled out my notepad from the desk drawer and began to write.

I had been writing a letter a week to my mother for as long as I could remember. Never mind that I had no concrete mailing address. Or that Boon told me not to waste my time because it was unlikely to change anything. Or the tell-tale sadness in Jo's eyes even as she smiled and told me not to listen to Boon.

My pen sat poised over the paper as I considered how best to explain it to my mother. Even though more pieces were falling into place the more time I spent with Cole, it was still impossible to put everything into words for her to understand.

Dear Mum,

Remember the boy I told you about who accompanied me to Neverland—
I'm starting to recall the story, thanks to the boy I went to Neverland with—
I still don't quite remember everything, but Cole—

This was futile. Would she even remember Cole? I had nothing to go on, nothing to help me figure out my mother's current state, save for those postcards that offered pretty much nothing—just quotes that served more as riddles. If I could just figure out what she was trying to tell me, maybe I would find her at last. At least that was more promising than the text messages that yielded no reply.

Cole was right. I was holding on so stubbornly because I still believed that the next moment would make the wait worth it. Because any other alternative was too unbearable.

Dear Mum,

I found him at last. It took me longer than it should, but I'm starting to remember. Very soon, I'll find my way back to Neverland, back to you. Will you wait for me?

Love always,
Gemma

Later, with my letter sealed and ready to be mailed tucked into my back pocket, I emerged from the office and found Thomas with Cole in the common room outside, poring over the Wild Ride's floor plan.

'Oh hey, Gem,' Thomas said, glancing up. 'Cole was just saying he can help us sell the rides. We can start on the first phase of the revamp as early as next week.'

I had no choice but to acknowledge Cole then. '*You* can?'

'I've got contacts. They'll quote us a good price.'

I nodded and reached for the envelope in my back pocket.

'Is that your letter to mail out this week?' Thomas asked.

Ever since he knew about my weekly letters I wrote to my mother, he had offered to mail them out for me, claiming that he needed to send his letters to a pen-pal in Japan. There was no pen-pal, I knew, just Thomas doing whatever he could to keep my hope alive. So I handed him my letters every week and prayed that each one would bring me the response I wanted, that someday I would receive something more than a quote, something in her own voice to assure me that I wasn't, like everyone had told me, a fool for hope.

Cole stared at the envelope in my hand before I could think to hide it. I handed it to Thomas, avoiding his gaze. In front of Cole, my endeavour felt laughable, pathetic.

I turned to glare at him. '*What?*'

He pointed at the letter. 'Who's that for?'

'My mum.'

'Uh huh. Have you received any reply from her?'

I stuck out my chin. 'Actually, I have.'

'Really?' His brows rose. 'What did she say?'

'That's confidential.'

Cole had that look on, the one where he seemed to be waiting to see how long you were going to persist in your bullshit before he decided to call you out on it.

'She replies. That's all that matters.' I left before he could say anything else, diving back into Neverland without a care.

Life on board the Thunderstorm—*the rules, the daily schedule they stuck to religiously, the strictly out-of-bounds areas—was nothing like what Gemma was used to, although Cole seemed to be fitting in quite well. All Gemma wanted was to see two people: her mother and Peter Pan. But on a ship out at sea, it was easy to feel like you were entirely alone in the world, even in the company of an entire crew.*

Cole's presence offered some comfort. At least she wasn't the only Otherworlder child on board. Or in Neverland, for that matter.

While the rest of the crew were busy assembling armaments and a questionable assortment of ingredients that Storm claimed would help smoothen the passage through the Silver Sea, Gemma and Cole huddled in the lower bunk of their cabin, a borrowed map of Neverland unfurled before them.

'Do you know how we're going to find the key?' Cole said. 'What if it's not even real?'

'Mummy says it's as real as Peter Pan.'

'That's not very comfort—'

The ship gave a lurch, as though it were rolling over a large wave. Gemma and Cole grabbed each other's hands. A thump came from the upper deck, followed by a shout. Gemma and Cole scrambled to their feet, tossing their map aside as they charged out of the cabin and up the stairs.

Out on the deck, a chilly gust of wind howled as it swept past them, almost knocking them off their feet. Hand in hand, Gemma and Cole fought their way through the gale towards Storm's hazy but imposing figure at the helm of the ship.

The wind was stirring the seawater into a rage, making the ship rock from wave to wave. Even walking in a straight line was a feat. Twice, Gemma slipped in her ballet flats and Cole had to throw his arm around her to stop her from sliding across the agitated ship. Men yelled over the roar of wind and water as they drew the sails. A couple of them almost toppled over the rails before their crewmates saved them.

As Gemma and Cole reached Storm's side, the clamour rose to an unbearable crescendo. A fresh gust of wind picked Gemma up and tossed her overboard.

'Gemma!' Cole cried, reaching out for her.

Storm sprang into action. He flung out a strange contraption made of tentacle-like wires. With its eight limbs, the net reached out for Gemma's tiny falling body and grasped it with surprising gentleness.

Storm reeled the wires back in measured figure-eight loops, making Gemma swing from side to side as she was deposited back on board, sodden and shivering. Cole helped Gemma to her feet, keeping an arm around her.

But as suddenly as it began, the storm was over. The wind died to a gentle breeze, and the waters slipped back to an eerie calm.

Cole's voice broke the stillness. 'What was that?'

'That,' said Storm as he righted himself, 'was just the entry to the Silver Canal. Better hold on tight. It's going to be an even bumpier ride from here.'

* * *

Her mother was too ill to make the voyage across the Silver Sea with them, so Gemma took to updating her on their rescue mission. She told her about Cole and Captain Storm and his crew and his magical ship that contracted and expanded to fit through impossibly narrow canals and buffer against strong winds.

Gemma knew her mother was hiding somewhere in Neverland, but she didn't want to prod her for her whereabouts. Her mother was easily upset these days—an offhand remark could set her off. Doctor York and her father said she needed peace and quiet, and told Gemma not to talk about Neverland with her. But Neverland was the only thing that her mother responded to these days. It was the only thing they shared.

When Gemma first told her mother about Cole, her mother had furrowed her brows. 'You're sure he's willing to help us?'

'He is just like us,' Gemma said. 'A believer.'

Her mother told her about Old Limestone, the ancient mountain that had swallowed the key to Neverland to stop the natives from fighting over it. She told her how the mountain trusted only Peter Pan with it, because he was the only one who wanted the key not to rule Neverland but to help it. She told her how Peter had delved into its cavernous belly for weeks before he found it, how he had promised Old Limestone he would never take it out unless Neverland was under dire threat.

Her mother told her all she needed to know about the key. But she didn't tell her about the monsters in the deep.

* * *

The Silver Sea had its fair share of creatures, magical and strange, living in its depths. But none of them were as terrifying as the sea serpent. The crocodile that Hook so feared was a mere lizard compared to it, said Captain Storm. Many had tried to hunt it down and capture it, but no one could put a leash on the guardian of the Silver Sea.

'Our plan,' said Storm, 'is to cross the Silver Sea undetected by the sea serpent.'

It was unfortunate then that their journey involved passing through the creature's lair. They would have to burrow through the underground cave where the serpent slumbered before emerging to shore, where Old Limestone sat.

Storm seemed confident about making it through, although the rest of the crew whispered their doubts in the close quarters of their cabins.

Nights on the Silver Sea were busy because it was impossible to travel during the day. The sea blinded voyagers with its brilliant silver light that only diminished in the small hours of the night. But travelling by night had its own risks. More than once, they came too close to a reef or citadel of an underwater city.

'With all due respect, Captain,' one of the crew members, Hermit, said, 'we are crashing through these waters like clumsy sea cows. We will never make it through alive.'

'Nonsense,' Storm boomed, clapping Hermit on the shoulder. 'We have done this before, haven't we?'

'Not without a guide.'

'We shall have to make do without Peter Pan this time,' Storm said.

It was just as he uttered this that the Thunderstorm ran afoul again. This time, the force was large enough to rock the entire ship, causing several members of the crew to lose their footing and grapple for the railings.

Gemma and Cole were scaling the rickety wooden stairs leading to the deck when they heard the deafening boom that resounded as the ship began to sway. Cole's foot slipped on a step, and he went tumbling down the stairs.

Gemma, who had already emerged on to the deck, was immediately seized by one of the sailors, Bruck. She clutched on to him, unable to hear Cole's scream over the panicked cries all around as the crew scrambled to gather the sails.

'Hermit, honestly,' Storm admonished, righting himself with as much dignity as he could muster after collapsing into the sailor's arms.

'It wasn't me, Cap,' Hermit protested. 'Someone ran into us from behind.'

Storm turned and squinted into the darkness behind. Gemma did the same, peeking out from behind Bruck's massive form. 'Nothing's there,' Storm said.

'I swear, there's nothing before us that we could have run into,' Hermit said. The realization settled upon the ship like a chilling fog and only Hermit dared to give voice to it. 'We're being followed.'

* * *

It was terribly bad timing to have an accident. The sun had just slipped below the horizon and the light had dimmed. Gemma was all alone in the wild heart of the forest with an injured Cole and no means to find their way back to Wonder City.

The scream was real, and so was the fall. Except that it was not a flight of wooden stairs he had tumbled down, but a trap of sorts about ten feet deep and five feet wide, well disguised by a pile of leaves and twigs. This was the furthest into the forest they had ever ventured, away from the hubbub of the theme park, and the trees huddled close around them, blotting out whatever light there was in the sky and swallowing their cries for help.

Gemma reached for Cole. 'Take my hand.'

'I can't.' His voice sounded hollow and very far away.

'Well, then try climbing.'

'I can't,' he said again. 'My foot hurts.'

Gemma felt the first trail of panicked tears skate down her face. She got to her feet. 'Wait here.'

'Don't leave me here alone.' His voice was thin with fear.

'I'll be back soon, I promise.'

Gemma stumbled through the darkness before Cole could beg her to stay. She groped for stray branches in her way and kept her eyes peeled for dubious-looking piles of leaves and twigs. There were blind turns that made her wander in circles at times, and the slightest noise made her jump. What a poor navigator she made! She couldn't even save her friend, what more Neverland.

It felt like years later when she finally spotted the lights, then the rides, and finally the narrow wrought-iron gate that they had snuck through hours ago. After slipping through that, Gemma made a mad dash for the office building. It was late enough that the crowd had dwindled to small pockets scattered across the grounds.

Cole's father was just emerging through the sliding glass doors when Gemma skidded to a stop, her breath catching in her throat. He narrowed his eyes at her. 'Mr. Wu. Cole—he's hurt. I don't know—'

'Bring me to him.' His voice was deadly quiet in the empty lobby.

Cole's father would be furious to know that they had disobeyed him and ventured into the forest. But she didn't have a choice.

They moved at a brisk clip, Gemma leading the way. She struggled to find the right words. The older man stared straight ahead, his face tight and cold.

'I'm sorry,' she squeaked at last.

He pressed on, not bothering to acknowledge her.

Fourteen

Cole

Gemma flounced from the room, her dignity trailing after her. I waited until she had slammed the door behind her before rounding in on Thomas.

'So what's the address?' I said, nodding at the letter.

'I leave them in the P.O. box,' Thomas said. 'Her mother comes to collect them.'

I reached out for it, but Thomas whipped it out of my grasp. 'You're a terrible liar, Thomas.' I lunged again, but he ducked. 'Seriously, what do you do with those letters?'

He stopped. 'How did you know?'

'That girl has been waiting for her mother for nearly ten years. She's sent her letters every week and text messages every day. If she's not getting any leads on where her mum is, she's obviously not getting the answers she's looking for.'

'How did you know she sends letters every week?'

I snatched the envelope out of his hands. 'So you're feeding her this lie, and she's happy to be strung along?'

'We don't know if her mother is—'

'Her mother's dead, Thomas.'

Thomas froze. 'That's not . . .'

'Possible? It sure is a lot more possible than having someone reply to your letters for ten years without revealing her whereabouts.'

His voice turned hollow. 'How did you know?'

'Not long after she failed to show up at Wonder City, her mother got into an accident. My father told me. He was very smug about it, about how I'd almost hung out with "bad company" if he hadn't stepped in.'

'Wait a minute.' His eyes widened. 'You mean you knew her way back then? Why didn't you—'

'Why didn't I tell you? I didn't even know where she was,' I said. 'Or what exactly happened. Things just got lost over the years. Forgotten.'

Thomas sank into a long silence. 'Are you going to tell Gemma?' he asked eventually.

I waved the envelope at him. 'Are *you*?'

'Maybe we should at least find out what happened to her mother before we tell her anything. No sense prematurely upsetting her,' he said.

'Protecting her from the truth isn't going to make it any easier for her to swallow when she does find out.' Although wasn't that what I had been doing all these years, when I couldn't bring myself to stamp out her hope that her mother was alive? I was being a hypocrite calling Thomas out on the letters.

'What else do you know about her mother?' he said.

'She went to Hopewood. But they don't release patient info. Trust me, if I could've found out anything more about her, I would have.' But I still didn't know any more about what happened that day than what my father told me. An episode, an accident, and one family left adrift.

'Gemma will find out sooner or later, and I'd rather we tell her before she learns that we've been lying to her,' I said. 'In the meantime, you need to cool it with the postcards. Quotes, seriously? Do you know how obsessed she gets trying to work out what each one means?'

He squinted at me. 'How would *you* know?'

I shrugged. 'She seems neurotic enough to obsess over something like this.'

Thomas sank into silence. I could see him mentally weighing the consequences of his actions—or *in*action. With Thomas, everything was intended to deliver the softest impact as possible. But even he had nothing this time. There was nothing we could do now but help Gemma recover her memories over time.

'Mum's cooking claypot rice tonight,' he said at last. 'Join us?'

Thomas's mum tried to cook for her family every opportunity she got, despite having to juggle two jobs.

'Thanks,' I said, 'but count me out.'

'Why? Got plans?'

He wouldn't understand the truth, that it was easier eating dinner alone than sitting at the same table with him and his family. That being around his complete family reminded me of everything I wanted but couldn't have.

'I'm meeting a friend for dinner,' I lied. Thomas was the only friend I had left who would willingly have dinner with me now that I wasn't the one footing the bill.

I couldn't tell if he bought it, but he nodded. 'Okay, if you're sure. We'll save some food for you, just in case.'

I made a noncommittal gesture that could be interpreted as a nod or a shrug, then waited until he was gone before pulling out Gemma's letter from the envelope. It was flimsy, like it was very much aware of its frailty against the odds. I stuffed the letter back in. Text messages were one thing; letters felt a lot more intimate to be prying into.

By eight o'clock, the Wild Ride was empty. At Wonder City, the staff always had to spend an hour or so hurrying the stragglers out before closing time. But here, there was no need for that.

I bought a roast chicken sandwich and a can of Coca-Cola before searching for a place to have an uneventful dinner. Night settled in, casting its pall over the grounds. The world had never seemed emptier.

I found my way to the bench in front of the Peter Pan ride, spotlighted by the pool of ghostly light from the clock tower. The carriages hovered in mid-air behind me, bearing witness to my solitude.

It felt like another lifetime ago that I was here. But now the Wild Ride was the safest place I could think of, the furthest I could run from my father. He had hated amusement parks to begin with, but he reserved a special hatred for this one. It was the reason he was so intent on razing this place to the ground.

I knew why my father wanted me and Chelsea to go to England. On one hand, it was a move to cement our 'relationship' so her father would invest in my father's upcoming project. On the other, it was so that Chelsea and I could learn to helm said development project together. The one that involved buying over the Wild Ride and turning it into something unrecognisable so that the memories would be buried, as good as gone.

I could tolerate my father's futile attempts to use Chelsea to make me forget Neverland and Gemma, but if he thought I was going to fit nicely into his plan to erase our old lives, the one with Mum in the picture, then he was mistaken.

What would my father think about me being here with the girl he had tried so hard to keep me away from? *Her stories are poison*, he had once told me. *You don't want to end up like her mother.*

As if on cue, my second phone vibrated in my backpack just as I sat down to eat. Gemma had been silent since that altercation in the park, but now her text messages to her mother came fast and furious.

Mum, how do you take back words you have thrown out in the open? Is it too late to apologize when they've already done their damage?

I hate fighting with Boon. Jo said we're okay, but what about Boon?

I'm an awful person. Jo and Boon don't deserve this.

Like always, I fought the overwhelming urge to reply. Instead, I chewed absently on my already cold sandwich and sipped on my insipid drink. The sooner she remembered what happened, the sooner I could stop lying to her at last.

'Can you please chew quietly?' said a voice on my left.

I blurted an expletive, scrambling to hold on to my can of Coke, but my sandwich ended up by my feet anyway with its contents exploding all over the floor.

An irate-looking Gemma stuck her head out of the ticket booth next to my bench. Warm yellow light spilt out, illuminating the book open in her lap and her baleful glare.

'What are you doing, creeping about in there?' I demanded.

She waved the book, *The Geometry of Stars,* in her hand. 'I trust this isn't a foreign object to you. Why are *you* here?'

I gestured at my ruined sandwich on the ground. 'I trust that isn't a foreign object to you.'

She emerged from the booth to survey the remains of my dinner, then joined me on the bench. 'I mean why are you eating here *alone?*'

'You're sitting here alone,' I pointed out.

'I'm reading. It's a solitary activity, which you just interrupted.'

'Who said dinner had to be a social activity?'

'Guess all that money can't buy you good company.'

I was working up a retort when I noticed her fingers brushing the edges of the book absently. 'By the way, I don't think I've said this,' she said, her gaze trained on the book cover. 'I'm sorry.'

The sharp change in topic—and her demeanour—caught me off guard. 'For what?'

'For not showing up that day. For making you wait. For almost forgetting you.'

This wasn't quite what I expected.

Over the past few days, my relationship with Gemma had changed. There was a strange space between us now that was filled with the things we had and hadn't said. Our words, once thrown out in the open, made the air between us harder to breathe, though not in a bad way. I wasn't sure how to describe it.

My cell phone rang before I could find the right response.

'You have Chelsea on speed dial?' Gemma said, glancing at the screen.

'She put herself on speed dial.' I let the ringing go on for a while before deciding to answer. Gemma returned to the booth, giving me some privacy to take the call.

'Cole? How . . . how are you?'

'Never been better.'

'So we haven't talked since . . . I just thought . . .'

This awkwardness was making me break out in a rash. 'It's only been a day, Chels. Are you missing my sparkling personality and dashing good looks already? I heard my father wants me at the party on Wednesday.'

'I was going to talk to you about that.' A beat. 'You're going, right?'

'Actually, I'm not. I don't have any reason or inclination to be there.' I started to hang up.

'Wait! He says he'll give you your allowance for three months if you come.'

'Allowance for my attendance? What does he take me for?' My eyes drifted back to Gemma. She had gone back to her book. Her bangs fell over her face, and I fought the urge to brush aside the tuft of hair. 'Actually, you know what?' I said, watching her eyes slide across the page after each line. 'I'll be there.'

* * *

Gemma was still buried in that book when I got off the phone with Chelsea, but I could tell she had overheard our conversation. She looked up when I joined her back in the ticket booth.

'Why do you have to make everyone's lives so difficult?' she said. 'It's just a party, not an execution.'

'I *am* going—with you as my plus one.'

Her eyes widened in panic. 'What? Why? I don't want to go.'

'It's just a party, not an execution.'

She scowled.

Why *did* I want my father to meet her? Was it just to prove to him that he was wrong about Gemma, that she was nothing like her mother?

'Your father used to work at Wonder Entertainment,' I blurted before I could think better of it.

Gemma set her book aside and held my gaze long enough for the words to sink in. Outside the booth, the Peter Pan ride creaked in the breeze.

When she spoke again, there was a timid hope in her voice. 'So you're saying there's a chance your dad might know where he is?'

The look on her face made me want to take back what I said. It seemed cruel to plant that kind of expectation in her. 'No promises.'

She would take it, just like I knew she would. 'Just so we're clear, I am not your date.'

And that was that.

I gave her a nudge and gestured at the ride before us. 'What do you say we get on this thing?'

'There's no one around to operate it,' she said flatly.

'I'm sure you know how to.'

She narrowed her eyes at me. 'I'm not doing it.'

'Buzzkill.'

'Delinquent.'

'It's just a ride, Gemma. Live a little.'

'It's after hours.'

'It's *your* amusement park,' I said.

'Technically, it's Jo and Boon's. I lay no claim to it.'

'Why are you so afraid of going up there?'

She rolled her eyes. 'I'm not afraid.'

'Right. You're just staunchly law-abiding.'

She shrugged.

'Buzzkill,' I repeated.

Gemma ignored me, turning back to the ride. 'This is where my dad left me.' A cool breeze swept past, making a tuft of her hair dance. Her gaze was fixed on the ride as she toyed with the pages of her book. The light from the clock face shone in her eyes. 'I had just turned eight. My dad took me here.'

'What about your mum?' I asked carefully.

'I don't remember—she just wasn't there. Anyway, my dad told me to wait right here, said he'd be back to get on this ride with me.' Her smile was a sad, feeble thing trying to hold itself up. 'Jo and Boon found me after that, and I've been living here ever since.'

'So you never got to go on the ride.' She nodded. 'You mean you've never gone on this ride? Ever?'

'I will,' she said. 'Once I find him.'

'Gemma. He's left you waiting for almost ten years. If you love someone, why would you keep them waiting?'

'Maybe because you don't know someone's waiting for you.'

I had no response for that. Because I knew all too well about waiting for someone who didn't even know a fool like me was waiting for her.

Fifteen

Gemma

The next morning rolled off to a weird start. First, Cole sauntered by the office to inform us that the rides were taken care of.

I lowered the floor plan. 'What do you mean by taken care of?'

'It means someone is willing to buy them,' was his cryptic answer.

Then there was Thomas, who was, for some reason, clearly avoiding me. He wouldn't even look me in the eye when I asked him if he had sent out my letter, or when I sought his opinion on naming the food street.

Later, as we discussed the next phase of the carnival plan sans Thomas, Cole and I fell into a strangely harmonious rhythm, as if we were just picking up where we left off in Neverland, plotting our route to the key, working out our plan to save Neverland.

In the evening, as Laura narrated her latest failed blind date to me, Cory and Beth, I stole out amid their debate about Laura's impossible standards to meet Cole at the park opposite the Wild Ride, where he was waiting in his chauffeured Audi.

'Still don't get why we have to be this sneaky,' Cole muttered as I got into the car.

'We don't need to give the others more gossip fodder,' I replied.

When we arrived at the yacht club, there was already a procession of cars at the drop-off point. Wonder Entertainment did not hold back with its twentieth anniversary celebration. From the gilded, perfumed invitation cards to the white marquee that led to the boat *Wondrous*, Lionel Wu went all out. There were no more than fifty people present, but the setting was grand enough for a much larger crowd.

'Guess now we know where you got your showiness from,' I remarked.

Cole's lips curled. 'Please. I do it with better taste.'

After registering on the guest list, Cole led me through the throng of people mingling around the reception, flutes of champagne in their hands as they flitted from group to group. I felt underdressed and out of place. My gait was too ungainly, my intentions shabby. I shouldn't have come.

But I had to. This was my only lead now, and I couldn't let a little social awkwardness get in the way of getting some answers at last.

People pointed and whispered as we passed, but Cole seemed completely indifferent to the murmurs—some discreet, others not so—as he led me through the marquee. Under the weight of everyone's attention, I felt like a criminal.

'So this is your natural habitat,' I whispered.

'It's not my natural habitat. Or any habitat that you should put me within a ten-metre radius,' Cole said in a normal decibel, reaching for two mango-and-shrimp lettuce wraps from a waiter drifting by. He offered one to me, which I declined. He shrugged and popped both into his mouth.

Chelsea emerged from a group of women with similar up-dos and Oxford-shirt-and-pencil-skirt outfits, looking immaculate in a snug burgundy dress and nude pumps.

She made a beeline for us. 'Cole!' Her gaze drifted over to me as she pulled Cole into a hug, as though they hadn't parted on a fight the last time. Chelsea offered me a hand and a stiff smile. 'We haven't been formally introduced. I'm Chelsea.'

I slipped my hand into hers and let her pump it once. 'Gemma.'

She turned her attention back to Cole. 'Your dad will be glad you showed up. Even if'—her glance flitted my way—'it's for the wrong reason.'

'There are no wrong reasons, just different ways of looking at things.'

'Very profound,' another voice said. A boy our age appeared from behind me, holding a glass of champagne. He was coiffed in a way that made his proud jaw appear even harder. 'Very uncharacteristic of you, Cole.'

He gave the boy a brusque nod. 'Andrew.'

With his free hand, Andrew clapped Cole on the shoulder. Cole glanced at the spot where he had touched, then back up at Andrew like he expected a valid explanation for the gesture.

Andrew chose to ignore the look. 'Didn't think you'd dare to show up tonight, given your latest . . . shenanigans.'

'I didn't realize you had subscribed to my channel, but I'm glad you're up to date,' Cole said.

Andrew nodded at me, a smile spreading across his face. 'Who's your date?'

'Friend of mine.'

'Didn't realize you had any left.'

'You're mistaking me for yourself. If you'll excuse us, we don't really want to be in your presence.' He towed me away before Andrew or Chelsea could protest.

At the dock, we were waved through with just a look from Cole. I stumbled a little in those heels as I clomped across the wooden deck of the ship and down a flight of stairs into a plush ballroom.

The cruise was mostly empty, with a handful of suited men and women milling about, speaking into their mouthpieces. My clomping stopped thanks to the carpeting.

It was tranquil in here like my memories of the *Thunderstorm* had never been. The seas in Neverland had always been rough and vengeful towards trespassers. But as serene as it was aboard *Wondrous*, my insides curled with unease.

Cole leaned towards me and muttered, 'Just a heads-up: his last impression of you isn't the best.'

On the stage at the front of the room was a tall, slim man whose gaze settled on us as soon as we entered. I was aware of my hand in Cole's and tried to retrieve it, but Cole didn't relent. We came to a stop before his father with every reason for him to misunderstand our relationship.

'Dad, this is Gemma. Gemma, my dad,' Cole said.

His father stood stock-still before us, his stare as flinty as I remembered, one full of contempt for the girl with the troubled mother. I was six years old when I met him for the first time. He had shaken my hand with a daunting formality that drove me to duck behind my mother, even though he and my father spoke with the lightness of close friends. My mother would send him a fleeting polite smile before making herself scarce in his presence at the earliest opportunity, taking me with her.

'I see you found her in the end,' he said now, as though I was something he had thrown out that had come wandering back.

'No thanks to you,' Cole said. The bite in his voice earned him a glare from his father.

Lionel turned to me. 'Your father has stayed well out of the spotlight ever since he left Wonder Entertainment.'

Why did my father resign? Was it because of my mother? I had a flash of being scooped up in her arms, gripped by fear as I struggled to break free because she was holding me too tightly.

Cole gave my hand a squeeze, as though he could sense my discomfort.

'I hear you have some questions for me,' Lionel went on.

'I do.'

'My son doesn't usually ask me for favours.' He cocked his head. 'Except when it comes to you. Should I thank you?'

'I don't . . .'

'It's a rhetorical question,' Cole told me. 'Don't crack your head.'

'Unfortunately,' Lionel said, 'I need to make sure my son holds up his end of the deal before granting you my attention tonight.' He glanced at Cole. 'Come, I want you to meet some people.'

Cole grabbed a glass of champagne from a line of waiters that had appeared and handed it to me. 'Load up on the appetizers and champagne. They're the only good thing in this entire charade. I'll be back soon.'

Shortly after Cole left with his father, the guests began streaming in, chatting and laughing. It wasn't difficult to blend into the background here, where everyone was gathered in their little cliques. I stood in a corner, picking up snatches of conversation everywhere, including the one from the group on my right, a small gathering of two middle-aged women and a man.

'Is that the director's son over by the stage?' said one of the women. She had emerald earrings dripping from her earlobes, which she flaunted with a hairdo that looked a little too tight for comfort.

I glanced at where she was pointing and, sure enough, found Cole—and Chelsea—by the corner of the stage while Lionel engaged a group of older men in conversation. Cole's eyes drifted across the room. A tiny smile flickered across his face when he spotted me. Before I could respond, Chelsea reached for Cole's hand and dragged him away.

'Huh,' said the man next to me, not bothering to hide the fact that he was staring. 'Wasn't expecting to see him here tonight. I heard Lionel's finally had it with him. Cut him off and all that.'

'I heard he kicked him out of the house,' Emerald Earrings said.

'Wow, really?' said the second woman, who sounded more gleeful than concerned. Her lipstick was smudged but no one bothered informing her.

Emerald Earrings went on. 'I would've done so much earlier if he were my son. I mean, I get that his mother left him when he was young, but now he's just using that as an excuse to behave like a brat.'

'I still think it's the director's fault,' said the man. 'It's a classic case of negligence.'

Smudged Lipstick took a sip of her champagne. 'Well, if he had paid more attention to his family, his wife wouldn't have shacked up with that guy.'

'Cassandra!' Emerald Earrings said.

'Oh, come on, Dara. Everyone was talking about it.'

The man snapped his fingers. 'What was the guy's name? Starts with a J, if memory serves me well.'

'Your memory is a moth-eaten dishcloth, Adam,' Cassandra said.

'Give me a break. It was a decade ago.'

'It's Joseph. Joseph Young,' said Dara. 'They were business partners until Joseph's wife fell sick.'

The champagne glass slipped in my hands. I scrambled to keep a firm grasp on it but holding myself upright was sapping every ounce of energy from me. I took a bracing gulp of champagne, and felt it sizzle down my throat.

I didn't doubt fate. I didn't dismiss serendipitous encounters as coincidences. I believed in chance, sought it, and kept my eyes peeled for it. But what were the odds that Cole and I were linked in such a bizarre way? That this was how I was going to find my father?

'That's right!' Adam said. 'Joseph Young. Isn't he dead though?'

My fingers tightened around my champagne glass. I downed the remaining contents and left the glass on a table nearby, quelling my shaking fingers by digging them into my palm.

'What? That's ridiculous,' Cassandra said. 'Where did you hear that?'

'I agree with Adam,' Dara declared. 'Why else did he suddenly stop showing up to work?'

'Maybe because he backed out of the partnership to take care of his wife?' You could hear the eye roll in Cassandra's voice. 'I still think they had a thing going on, Lionel's wife and Joseph.'

A waiter drifted by, and I reached for another glass of champagne that turned out to be wine. When at last I decided to approach the three gossipmongers, it was after a mouthful of wine and two deep, shaky breaths.

'Excuse me.' My voice came out hoarse and feeble. The party of three didn't notice me until I spoke again. '*Excuse me.*' They glanced around in confusion only to find me glaring at them. 'Did you know Joseph Young personally?'

'Excuse *me*?' Dara responded, placing a hand on her chest as if *she*—not the one who wasn't there to defend himself—had suffered a personal affront.

'Joseph Young,' I repeated. The three of them flinched, whether from the blatant mention of the name or my flinty tone I wasn't sure. 'You seem to know him personally, given the way you talk about his personal life.'

'And who are you?' Adam said.

'I'm his . . .' There the words skidded to a stop. Adam raised his brows. Dara cocked her head.

Thankfully, the emcee invited Lionel to take the stage at that moment. Dara and company edged closer to the front, and I slipped away before I ran my mouth again.

Lionel stepped up to the podium. As he launched into his speech about the history of Wonder Entertainment and the milestones it had achieved, Cole scanned the crowd. He seemed straightjacketed in this place, especially when I knew inside him was a boy who splashed colours on the wall, who clung to the hope of reviving a dying amusement park.

When our eyes met again, all I could think about was the earlier conversation about my father and his mother. I glanced away and downed my wine for want of something to do. It scraped and burned its way down my throat.

What happened ten years ago that left me and Cole struggling to bring back the people who had left us?

They're just rumours, Gemma. Don't believe what they say. They know nothing about your father. They knew nothing about the rare Sunday brunches he used to take me to that were always such a treat, the way he called me Gem like the jewel, or the way his eyes always lit up whenever my mother was around, and the tiny smile he had whenever he looked at her.

But what if *my* memories were wrong? What if all those were just part of my imagination, and I was the one who barely knew my father? He must have had another life I hadn't known about if he had decided to leave me behind with no warning. Plus, I remembered the fights too. My mother's tantrums. The way he stared at her with heartache and resignation whenever she shut him out.

Could it be that my father had tired of us eventually and abandoned us?

The room started closing in and the air grew thin. An unbearable heat spread through my body and settled like a second skin. My head was a steel ball about to pitch me off balance. The room began to spin.

I needed to get out of here.

My getaway was almost a success when Andrew sidled up close, a glass of wine in his hand and a sloppy smile on his face.

'So I didn't manage to talk to you earlier,' he said.

I tried to focus on him, gripping the edge of the table to steady myself.

'Me?' I said.

'Yes, you with the pretty eyes.' He cocked his head and regarded me. 'Gemma, right?' I didn't bother asking how he knew my name. Andrew nodded in the direction of the stage. 'What are you doing with that tool?'

'He's not a tool.'

Up went his eyebrows. 'Takes a really misguided person to say that.' He stopped a waiter and grabbed two salmon-wrapped asparagus off the tray, then offered one to me. 'Asparagus?' I shook my head, then instantly regretted it when the room swam. 'The food at these things is the main reason I agree to come. My dad's on the board,' he added by way of explanation.

'That's nice,' I murmured. His words registered a couple of seconds later. 'You said your dad's on the board?'

'Yup.'

'Then have you heard of Joseph Young?'

His brows shot up, and a lazy smile wormed its way across his face. 'No information is free, you know. I propose an exchange.'

'An exchange,' I echoed.

He nodded and took a step closer to me so that I was backed against the wall. I was considering how to break free of him and not draw attention to myself when Lionel gestured to the screen behind him. The image projected on it was unsettlingly familiar.

'Ladies and gentlemen,' Lionel said, 'I present to you Wonder Town, a far better development than what J&K Enterprises has proposed.' Polite laughter tittered through the room. 'I am also pleased to announce that my son Cole will be joining the team in executing this upcoming project. The amusement park now known as the Wild Ride will very soon become Wonder Town, an al fresco dining plaza complete with an outdoor amphitheatre and modern art gallery.'

'What?' I cried, loud enough for a few people to turn and glare at me. Andrew backed away slightly.

'We are currently still in talks,' Lionel continued, 'but the old amusement park is our top choice venue-wise. Cole has recently been involved in the demolition of the Wild Ride and will participate in the Wonder Town project as a committee member together with Ms Chelsea Low.'

This. This was how Cole could get the buyers to settle on the old rides so quickly. This was how it was so easy to take down the Wild Ride piece by piece in such a short span of time. Of course he wasn't here to help us—that spiel about having a vested interest in the Wild Ride, it was all just to get insider information and destroy us from within.

'Are you okay?' Andrew asked, taking away my wine glass before I could slosh its contents onto the carpet.

'I'm fine,' I murmured, even though I couldn't even work up the energy to push Andrew away when he rubbed my arm.

Onstage, Cole stepped forward. He held the attention of the room with as much ease as his father. Seeing him here, it was easy to envision his future as the heir to an empire. But the Cole I knew wasn't a liar.

'I'd like to thank everyone for coming, for your continued support of Wonder Entertainment.' He paused, his gaze settling on me. 'I'd also like to clarify that I am not involved in this *unconfirmed* project and did not join the Wild Ride crew for this purpose. But most importantly, I'd like Mr Andrew Fan to stop harassing my date.'

Heads turned. The weight of everyone's stare pinned me to my spot.

Andrew dropped his arm and backed away calmly, flashing a sheepish smile, one that he was obviously certain would absolve him. Once the attention lifted off him, he shot Cole a stormy stare. From the side of the stage, Lionel had the same look directed at Cole.

'Enjoy your evening, everyone,' Cole said before leaving the stage. While Lionel tried to smooth things over by talking about Wonder Entertainment's other projects, Cole edged his way through the crowd, ignoring the whispers in his wake.

'I leave you for two seconds and the wolves descend,' he said when he reached my side.

'Shouldn't have brought her here if you were so afraid,' Andrew quipped.

Cole shook his head. 'Always wanting what's mine,' he said. 'Don't you have anything else to aspire to?'

'You're one to talk about aspirations. Last I heard, you've been chased out of the house and are now working at some rundown amusement park.' His gaze slid pointedly to the projector screen on stage.

Cole glanced at me, but the buzzing in my head was crowding out everything else. The amusement park, my mother's past, Cole's betrayal . . . Everything spun in my head.

The lights dimmed and we were asked to take our seats. Cole led me to a private table in the corner. As soon as the guests had settled down, waiters emerged through the double doors with trays of food.

Cole leaned closer to me. 'I might have just blown your chances of talking to my dad.'

Did I really want to talk to Lionel now? What if I accidentally blurted what I had heard about his wife? Worse, what if he confirmed it? I wanted to turn back and run away from the truth now that I was getting closer to it, but I couldn't back out now, not after all the time and effort I had spent chasing it.

'Look,' Cole tried again when I didn't respond. 'I swear I didn't join the Wild Ride as some kind of spy. My dad promised me he'd help the Wild Ride if I attended this event, and then he ambushed me with this Wonder Town project—'

'I don't want to talk about that right now.'

He paused to peer at my face. 'Are you okay?' He glanced at the champagne tray on the table behind us. 'I told you to appreciate the free flow of drinks here, not go nuts with it.'

I wasn't sure if the spinning in my head and the roiling in my gut was due to the alcohol or stepping too close to the truth. 'I'm fine,' I said.

Cole's gaze didn't let up. 'You want to leave?'

'Don't you have to be here?'

'Trust me, no one will miss me.' He took my hand and led me out.

I stumbled in his wake. With my thoughts and senses in a jumble, it was hard to tell where reality ended and story began. In the distance, amidst the sound of cutlery clinking, was the roar of a swelling sea, the cry of night birds, and the smell of briny waters. I knew, then, that I was drifting back to Neverland.

'We're being followed, Captain,' Hermit said into the chill. Fog swirled around them, bringing their faces into view before obscuring them again.

'Or it could be the sea's dead,' Marrow quipped. 'All those people who died out here, they have tales of their own to tell and vengeance to seek.' He snuck a glance at Gemma. 'Best to have the girl off the ship.' Gemma clutched Cole's hand, and he gave her a reassuring squeeze.

'I will have none of that superstitious nonsense on board, Marrow,' Storm said. Marrow dipped his head, suitably chastised. 'Take cover in the cabins,' the captain ordered the children.

The sea gave another lurch. Cole, whose ankle had just healed thanks to the sailors' salve Gemma applied on it, almost went sprawling again.

This time, however, they were joined by a newcomer. She appeared at the nose of the ship as though she had been washed on board. Her iridescent turquoise tail shimmered through the fog. In the ship in the waters below, her sisters surrounded the ship, ready to attack. They seemed less like mermaids and more like warriors. Gemma stepped away from the edge of the ship and huddled closer to Cole.

'Ladies, what can I do for you?' Storm asked with a smile that compensated for his slightly worse-for-wear state. Cole raised his eyebrows at Gemma, but Storm's crew seemed perfectly used to the switch in their captain's demeanour.

'Currency for passage,' said the mermaid. 'Of course.'

'Of course,' Storm echoed. 'And what will you require? I'm afraid we're running rather low on gold and rations.'

The mermaid sneered. 'We have no use for your worldly currency.'

'It would greatly expedite our journey if you would simply tell us how we can make payment for our passage,' Storm said.

'Guardian of the Iron Sea,' said the mermaid. 'Surely you must know that the Silver Sea needs to feed.'

'Feed? With what?' Cole blurted.

Hermit clamped a hand over his mouth. The mermaid arrowed her ice-blue gaze at him, then turned back to Storm. 'You dare make passage across the Silver Sea when you have Otherworld children on board. This is treason.' Her last words came out as a hiss, and the waters around them started to bubble and boil. The first trails of steam snaked into the air.

'They need the bones of three men from each ship to build their underground cave for the sea serpent,' Gemma whispered for Cole's sake. 'I forgot to mention that.'

Cole balked. 'Neverland is wild.'

Storm raised his arms in a placatory gesture. 'We do not want trouble.'

'Too late,' the mermaid sneered. Steam transformed her winsome face into a ghostly mien. 'You've already created it.'

* * *

As they journeyed deeper and deeper into the Silver Sea, things at home took a turn for the worse. Gemma wasn't sure how one could influence the other, but the further her mother descended into her own rabbit-hole the more turbulent their voyage became.

When Gemma wasn't on board the Thunderstorm, she was visiting her mother at Hopewood, where the latter now stayed in a private ward five days a week. After school, she would go to Hopewood on her own, and her father was none the wiser. On weekends, her father would take them to the beach or the park—places that normal, happy people went—but her mother never seemed fully present there.

On one of her solitary visits to Hopewood, Gemma took her usual seat by the window next to her mother.

'When can I see you in Neverland, Mummy?' she asked. Neverland was supposed to be their shared secret, a place they explored together. But she was having her own separate adventures now.

Sometimes, her mother was too drugged to even respond. All she did was send Gemma that blank, heavy-lidded stare that terrified her. On a rare occasion that her mother was lucid enough to make conversation, she reached out to brush Gemma's hair away from her face.

'I want to be with you in Neverland too, darling,' she said. 'But I can't tell you where I am.'

'Why not?'

'Because I'm held captive. If I breathe a word about my whereabouts, he will kill me.'

Gemma's gasp caught in her throat. 'Who?'

Her mother's reply came as a raspy whisper. 'Hook, darling. Captain Hook. Shh!'

She grew more and more fearful of shadows, easily startled by light and noise. Gemma felt like she had to hold her breath around her mother and could only rely on talking about Peter Pan to keep her together.

When Gemma got home from her visits, she would feel strangely drained and moody, and more than once she got sassy with her father, who was just as brittle and full of sharp edges these days. Each time they passed by each other in the house, they would jab each other with their newly grown thorns.

Her father had spoken of a work project to Doctor York, one that required them to move out of their little yellow house with the backyard full of geraniums and hibiscus her mother used to grow. Gemma was certain this was what's worsening her mother's condition and refused to speak to her father unless he promised her that they weren't going to move.

She missed Cole terribly. She missed exploring Neverland with a friend. She missed Captain Storm and his ragtag crew. She even missed the long, arduous days and tempestuous nights aboard the Thunderstorm. What with schoolwork and her mother's rapidly deteriorating condition, she barely had time to look for Cole in Wonder City these days. The occasions where he managed to sneak out and meet her behind Wonder City were always fraught with the fear that they might get caught.

Sometimes, Gemma wasn't sure what exactly she was meant to do in this waking, dreamless world. All she could do now was count down the days until she could disappear into Neverland again—although she was starting to realize that the most dangerous stories could happen in your head.

Sixteen

Cole

The top deck was empty, as I'd hoped. Below us, the water rippled under the light from the boat and trailed off into the inky darkness in the distance.

It had been ages since I last came up here. I would hide out here when my parents fought, and in the days when I didn't see Gemma. But after Chelsea, my father, and a string of pointless parties succeeded in keeping me busy, I stopped coming here. This was the first time I had ever brought someone up here.

It was chilly enough for me to offer my jacket to Gemma. She murmured an absent *thank you* and pulled it around her, but the glazed look in her eyes suggested that she was someplace far away from here. Had she disappeared into Neverland again?

'Gemma,' I said, careful not to startle her.

She gave no response.

I tried again, touching her elbow and seeking out her gaze. 'Gemma. Talk to me.'

She watched the light play off the water beneath us, unaware of her fingers worrying at the jacket sleeve as her words tumbled out of her.

'My mother grew afraid of her own shadow,' she began.

She picked up where we left off with Captain Storm and the mermaid crisis, faltering when she described her mother's

130

paranoia. As she reached the end of her memory, I continued with mine. After all this time, our story had merely been buried, waiting to be told again. As imaginary as Neverland might be, it had always been a part of us that neither of us could or wanted to escape.

Ever since that accident that left him in a cast for two weeks and grounded for another week, Cole was starting to feel more and more like an animal trapped in an enclosure. His father monitored him closely through a home tutor and caretaker who always hovered within a five-metre radius of him.

At the start of the fourth week since the accident, Cole's father announced that he was no longer grounded and would like to introduce a new friend to him. Cole stabbed the broccoli on his plate and muttered a resentful 'sure' when his father asked if he would like to meet her the next day. In his chest, his heart rattled and shook in its tiny cage, desperate for escape.

The next day, his father brought him along to the office, where he introduced her to a girl in a stiff pale green dress who introduced herself as Chelsea. Cole stared down at his feet until his father gave him a harder-than-necessary squeeze on the shoulder and told him to introduce himself.

Chelsea was nothing like Gemma. She was faultlessly polite and gave him a closed-lipped smile that made Cole feel like cracking her open to see if she was truly as nice as she appeared. So he behaved as sullenly as possible, even when she offered him half of her lunch.

Later, out of longing for Gemma and her fantastical tales, he asked Chelsea, 'Do you know any stories?'

Chelsea, delighted that he had initiated conversation for the first time, responded, 'I do know a few. What do you want to hear?' And then she proceeded to bore him with stories about captive princesses who pined away for princes and sleeping princesses who were awoken by princes.

Cole hadn't realized how much he had come to count on Gemma's presence in his life or her stories that kept him alive. In the days he couldn't meet her, he found his thoughts drifting to her, to Neverland and its plight. Soon, he began to devise a plan, one that would help them save Neverland and even help Gemma find her mother. Gemma would be so pleased.

But first, he needed to see her again.

Seventeen

Cole

Gemma was silent when I was through. Something else was weighing on her mind, something bigger than Wonder Town.

'Your father seems to have an agenda for everything he does,' she murmured at last.

'Look, the whole Wonder Town thing . . .' I began to explain.

It was exactly like my father to pull something like that. No agreement with him came without a hidden clause or, in my case, being strong-armed into a project. J&K Enterprises had always been our strongest competitor, showing tit for tat in practically every project or acquisition, so my father was doing whatever he could to wrestle the Wild Ride from them.

'I had no idea he was planning that,' I said. Gemma raised her brows at me. 'Okay, I did, but that's why I want to help the Wild Ride. I didn't know my dad would make use of my being at the Wild Ride to implement this project. That wasn't part of our agreement.'

'The Cole I knew wasn't a liar,' she said quietly.

The Cole she knew. Which meant she didn't trust me now. I could already see the doubt clouding her eyes when she looked at me.

But I knew there was more to her current emotional state than this. She'd had this thunderstruck look on her face even before my father mentioned the project.

'Gemma, what's this really about?' I said.

She shook her head. 'Forget it, it's stupid.' But her fingers were tight around the bars of the railing. 'I should never have listened to those people,' she added, more to herself than to me.

'Who?' I pressed.

'I'm going home.'

I didn't budge an inch. 'I'm not moving until you tell me what happened.'

'Fine.' She sidestepped me and headed for the stairs.

'Gemma.' I reached for her arm and spun her around to face me. But she kept her eyes doggedly away from me. 'Seriously, you're starting to freak me out here. What happened?' Something occurred to me. 'Did Andrew do something to you? I swear, if he did, I will—'

'It's Joseph Young,' she blurted, meeting my gaze at last.

My grasp loosened. 'Who?'

'My dad. I heard stuff about him earlier . . . with your mum.' She turned away again, and I let my arms flop back to my side.

'My *mum*? What are you talking about?'

As she narrated what she had heard at the party, I paced in circles on the deck, trying to hold on to reason and, funnily enough, faith. Faith in my mother. When Gemma was done, I came to a stop and looked her straight in the eye.

'My mother would never do something like that,' I said.

'But—'

'My mother,' I repeated, 'would never do something like that.'

In the distance, a ship horn trumpeted. We broke our gaze. I turned my back to Gemma and gripped the railing.

'I'm just telling you what I heard.'

I whirled around. 'But you believe them, don't you? You believe a bunch of hearsay over your own dad?'

'I want to believe him like you believe your mum. But the truth is, I haven't known him since I was eight. Maybe I never did.'

'So you think he hooked up with my mum, and then what? Ran away?'

'Maybe your dad found out, I don't know!' She threw up an arm. 'It's not entirely impossible that he fired my dad after finding out, and my dad—'

'Do you realize what you're doing?'

'I'm just trying to understand why he left out of the blue.' Her voice cracked.

'No. You're trying to justify your dad leaving you behind. There's a difference.'

'That is *not* . . . I'm not . . .' she spluttered. 'That's not true.'

'Because now you have someone you can blame. You're throwing out all sorts of reasons why your dad had to leave, so now you can blame someone other than yourself. All this time, you've believed that you're the reason he left, that there was something wrong with you that made him decide to abandon you. Now that there's another reason why he might have left, you're clinging on to it for all it's worth—'

'That is *not* true. Just because your mum isn't interested in having you in her life doesn't mean my dad is the same.'

'Yes, I'm sure that's why he left you for almost ten years and shows no signs of wanting to be found by you, much less *be* with you.'

We were taking jabs at each other, vicious enough to draw blood. But it felt almost cathartic to bleed.

'Just because we both had someone leave us doesn't make you an expert on my feelings,' she snapped. 'You don't know my dad. You don't know my family.'

I knew more than she thought I did. But I didn't say as much.

'Fine. You want proof? I'll give you proof.' I didn't know what I was expecting when I pulled out my cell phone and pressed two for my mother. 'It's me,' I said by way of greeting when she picked up.

'Cole,' she said, clearly surprised. 'What's the matter?'

'Can we talk?'

'About what? I'm busy now.'

Gemma was watching my face for a hint of the way our conversation was going. I turned away from her. 'It'll only take a moment. Please.' I glanced back at her, and this time she was the one who turned away, pretending not to have heard.

'Cole,' Mum said. 'Really, I don't—'

'I know about Joseph Young.'

Her breaths came long and slow over the line. At last, she let out a sigh. 'When and where?'

I rattled off a time and date, then hung up before she could change her mind. This was the first in a long time I had spoken to her and one of the few times she had agreed to meet me. I wasn't about to push my luck by making small talk.

'And here I thought you'd grown past your separation anxiety, Cole.'

Gemma flinched at the newcomer's voice. Andrew, with his dumb slicked-back hair, smarmy smile and oily voice, strolled towards us with one hand in his pocket.

'Piss off, Andrew,' I growled.

Andrew only smiled at Gemma. 'He makes such pleasant company, doesn't he? It's probably a good thing that your mother's not around to hear the kind of things you say.'

He was baiting me—I knew that, of course. But I couldn't let him get away this smugly. 'Shut your mouth.'

'I suppose all that pent-up rage has to go somewhere. And after what I just heard, your hostility makes so much more sense now. After all, knowing that you are unwanted baggage is one thing. Knowing that your mum ditched you for a tumble in some other guy's bed—'

In my defence, I was fully justified in shoving him. It wasn't enough that he had to try and one-up me in front of my father ever since we were kids. No, he also had to be malicious enough to insult my mother.

I didn't mean to push him overboard, but Andrew lost his balance and toppled over the railing. His shriek was cut off midway when I lunged to grab him before he plunged into the water.

Gemma screamed and dashed forward, almost pitching herself overboard too. Her hand was slick with sweat when I grabbed it.

'Gemma, stay back,' I said. 'I got him.'

Andrew clung on to my arm, still relentless in his kicking and screaming. 'Don't let me die, please don't let me die!' he screeched, thrashing against the body of the ship.

'Be a little more dramatic, Andrew.'

'*Please!*'

I gritted my teeth. 'Dammit, Andrew. Save your energy for getting back on board.'

Gemma reached for his other hand—no mean feat, considering how wildly it was flailing around—and pulled. Her face was flushed and damp with tear tracks, but she was too preoccupied with rescuing Andrew to notice.

We were making some headway, inching him up past the railings, when the emergency brigade came pounding up the stairs. My dad, Andrew's dad, Chelsea, and a bunch of nosy people from the party came to a stop when they saw us in our ridiculous state.

'What,' my father demanded, 'is going on?'

Gemma, startled by the number of people who had suddenly appeared, loosened her grasp on Andrew, who launched into a fresh round of shrieking. I was almost tempted to let go just so he would shut up.

'It's okay, Gemma,' I said.

But she wasn't listening to me anymore. 'I won't let you go,' she cried. 'Hold on to me, Mummy, please!'

Andrew's father shoved me and Gemma aside, then sprung forward dramatically to grab Andrew by the collar. Chelsea's father steadied Mr Fan, while everyone else contributed by crowding around with their necks craned.

Gemma was curled up into a shaking ball. Her fists, white and tight, gripped the railings. I pried her fingers off slowly and wrapped an arm around her.

'Don't let her go,' she kept saying over and over.

'I got you, you're okay,' I told her, but she couldn't seem to hear me.

Everyone was watching, their curious, wary gazes fixed on us. 'What's wrong with her?' someone asked, not bothering to whisper.

When Andrew was finally hauled back on board, the older men collapsed on the ground from exertion. Andrew shot me his best martyred look, the one he had mastered to perfection after countless attempts to set me up when we were kids.

'Can't a friend show some concern?' he said. 'Sometimes you just don't appreciate the people around you, Cole.'

I ignored him and helped Gemma up. She seemed to have just registered the presence of an audience and hurried to wipe away her tears. I gave her shoulder a squeeze.

'With all due respect, Lionel,' Mr Fan said, getting to his feet, 'your son is out of control.'

The chilly stare my father gave me was like the one all those years ago, when he found me with a sprained ankle in the middle of the woods behind Wonder City. Like he was a stranger to that place that Gemma and I had escaped to and he hated that.

I had humiliated him tonight. It wasn't the first time, and it was one time too many. In a parallel world, I might apologize. I might be as responsible as Chelsea and clean up my act. In a parallel world, I might become the person my father wanted me to be.

But there was no repairing my relationship with him. A sea of ugly words—and things unsaid—lay between us now, and neither of us was willing to plough through them to get to the other side. It was just easier to stay on separate islands now.

Things would have been different if Mum were here.

'I do apologize, Peter,' he said now. 'Cole has been troubled by the recent turn of events at home, but that is no excuse for his behaviour.'

I couldn't even work up the indignation at everyone's certainty that it was me who had pushed Andrew around. For one thing, Andrew looked like the sort who badly needed a fist sandwich from time to time to keep that ego in check. For another, this wasn't the first time.

'I'd have better control over myself if Andrew had better control over his damn mouth,' I said.

'Enough, Cole,' my father snapped. He took a step closer, but not to me. 'I'd like a word with you in private,' he told Gemma quietly.

Eighteen

Gemma

Cole told me not to go.

'You don't have to if you don't want to,' he said.

I knew he was worried his father might upset me even more. After that mortifying display of hysterics (although Andrew was comparably hysterical), all I wanted was to leave this party and forget tonight ever happened.

My memories came in starts and stops, but I could still taste the cold, brackish water in my mouth, feel my heart on fire. The fear and panic were real, even if I didn't know the exact reason behind it. Everything connected to my mother remained fuzzy, as though I was listening in on a conversation underwater or watching a scene through a grimy window.

As much as I wanted to, I couldn't leave. Not without getting some answers first.

'I want to,' I said. 'I need to.'

Chelsea dragged Cole away before he could say anything else, and Lionel invited everyone back to the lower deck. Once the crowd had dispersed, Lionel headed down the length of the deck and down another flight of stairs without glancing back to check if I followed.

We ended up in a room at the farthest corner of the boat, a study padded with thick carpeting and lined with bookshelves.

In here, there was only the sound of my shaky breaths and thundering heart as Lionel appraised me with his arms folded and his lips pressed into a grim line.

'It's been a while, Gemma.' He didn't sound quite as pleased about that as Cole had. 'I didn't expect you back in my son's life.'

'It wasn't Cole's fault back there. Andrew antagonized him.'

'I know.'

'You do?'

He threw me a bored glance. 'I am aware of the petty rivalry between Andrew and my son. He likes to rile Cole up with the subject of his mother, and Cole never fails to take the bait.'

'You seem to be making light of it.'

He shrugged. 'If he can deal with his mother's departure, he can deal with a few mean-spirited taunts from his peers.'

'What makes you think he's dealing with his mother's departure?'

Lionel narrowed his eyes at me, and I levelled his stare.

'As I was saying,' he said sharply, 'I didn't expect you to reappear in Cole's life, and I would appreciate it if you remained out of it. We all know how he fared in your company the last time.' He shrugged. 'But if he's going to mix around with you, then I should at least get something out of it. Wonder Town is a huge project, one that Cole will help me see through.'

'Cole said he had nothing to do with it.' I tried to keep the doubt out of my voice, but he caught it anyway.

He sent me a pitying smile. 'Ever since you left the picture, Cole has been poised to take over Wonder Enterprises. He has everything to do with my company.'

'So poised that he left home and never really got over Neverland?'

His jaw tightened. 'Kate's ridiculous obsession was a burden to everyone. I won't let you destroy the plans I have for my son.'

Turning to leave, he added over his shoulder. 'My guests are waiting. Please find your way out.'

It was in the cold snap of his voice that a memory sprang forth in my mind. A figure in the doorway, a stiff handshake, a tight smile. My mother's contempt was palpable in his wake.

I managed to find my voice just before he left the room. 'You knew my parents. I remember you coming over to our house. You spoke to my father, and my parents got into a fight later that day. My mother cried, threatened to take me away.' Take me away to Neverland for good.

The memory flashed in and out of my mind, surging forward in starts and stops.

Lionel was watching me with his brows furrowed. 'What do you remember of that day? The day your mother . . . left?'

I wasn't about to admit to him that I barely remembered anything, even if I was recalling more each day thanks to Cole.

'I offered your father a new position, he turned it down for the sake of your mother, and that was it. Whatever happened after that had nothing to do with me.' His voice rang with the conviction of someone who had spent enough time convincing himself of that.

He stepped out of the study. 'Your father was held back by you and your mother. You'll have to understand my efforts in preventing that from happening to my son now.'

He let the door swing shut behind him, leaving me behind with my useless shreds of memory. For some reason, it was Captain Hook who took centre stage again.

Hook could tell that Storm had grown attached to the Otherworld children. The mariner had always let his sentiments distract him from his job. Ever since Storm inherited the Iron Sea from Old Pistol the scar-faced pirate, the Blood Coast had been losing its crimson hue thanks to the significantly diminished body count that fed the hungry Iron Sea.

And now he was even risking his life and his crew's by smuggling two Otherworld children across the Silver Sea? Placing his hope in the most unlikely people was what got him into the blood pact to guard the Iron Sea in the first place. It seemed like Storm still hadn't learned his lesson.

Hook had made sure to keep a safe distance from the Thunderstorm. But thanks to the traitorous wave that lurched his ship forward, not only did Storm and his crew now know they were being followed, but the mermaid guards were also circling dangerously close to his ship.

'Draw the sails,' he barked, though he knew he could only rely on the fog as his best cover and hope Storm could distract the mermaids.

Although, why should he hide from a few fish-women? They were nothing but sea guards. Storm could pander to them all he wanted, but sometimes force was the only way to get anything done.

When the first mermaid appeared on his ship deck, almost like an apparition in the fog, Hook was decidedly calmer than his men. Several of them inched back but, on Hook's orders, didn't lower their weapons.

The mermaid's voice rang out clear as a bell in the gloom. 'State your business on the Silver Sea, sailor, and make your tithing quick.'

'Sweetheart, I'm a pirate,' Hook drawled, gesturing at himself. 'When have I ever paid for anything fairly?'

The mermaids never saw his sails coming.

They made barely a rustle when they fell from their masts, swift and silent as phantoms in the night, emitting their fervent scents of blood-rose and snow-aster that he pilfered from the merchants of Thalesea.

The sails, weightless though they seemed, carried the strength and tenacity of a thousand steel wires. No matter how hard his enemies struggled and squirmed—if they even managed to fight off the effects of the wicked scent—they would not be able to free themselves. These sails were one of the reasons Hook slept more soundly at night.

The mermaid on board lay crippled, tangled in swaths of black fabric. Hook didn't even have to think twice before he drove his knife into her heart. Thrice, for good measure. The good thing about black sails was that you could hardly see the blood.

He tossed the body overboard and had the sails reframed. The sea could have its dead soldiers back.

Nineteen

Cole

Chelsea stormed down the hallway away from the party, her hand wrapped around my wrist. The chatter sounded louder after that little scene on the top deck, but I had no interest in hearing what those people had to say.

Chelsea seemed just as determined to stay as far away from the party as possible. I could double back to find Gemma, but she *had* come here tonight to speak with my dad, so the least I could do was let them talk in peace.

'Chelsea!' I pulled my hand out of hers before she could drag me any further.

She whirled around. 'I can't believe you went at Andrew again. Your dad—'

'Is used to it.'

'I just don't think you should be pissing him off now.'

'I've been pissing him off since before I can remember. What makes this a special occasion?'

Her gaze was solemn. 'Cole. He just kicked you out of the house. What if he decides to cut you off completely? No house, no allowance, no car, no credit cards, nothing. Hmm? And for what, to defend *her* honour from Andrew Fan?'

Andrew's taunts resounded in my head. 'It was more to give Andrew what he deserved.'

'Why did you bring her here? You never bring anyone to meet your dad.'

'Is this what this is about? Chelsea, I think we need to—'

'I heard her asking about Joseph Young,' she said. 'Why is she so interested in him?'

'She has her reasons. Just like you and my father had your reasons for keeping me in the dark about the Wonder Town project.'

Her voice diminished. 'Nothing's confirmed yet.'

'Given that my father just announced all his plans in front of everyone, I'd say a lot of things have already been confirmed.'

'Why are you so upset about the Wild Ride? Is it because of Gemma?'

'Chelsea.'

'I just think it's strange how you're doing so much to help someone you haven't seen in ages restore her amusement park. You, who could barely be bothered about Wonder City, are helping to get *another* amusement park back on its feet?'

I stopped myself before I could explain why I was more invested in the Wild Ride than Wonder City. Gemma and the Wild Ride were a part of my life separate from Chelsea and my dad, and I liked it that way.

'Revamping the Wild Ride is what I promised *Thomas* I'd do,' I said instead.

'The old you wouldn't even care about some little promise you made.'

'There is no new me.' There was just me that she never really knew.

'There is. Ever since you left home and started working at that amusement park—ever since you met her again—you've been different.'

'Maybe I was never the person you knew, Chels. You don't know everything about me, so quit acting like you do.'

Her stare turned pitying. 'What do you think is going to happen when she finds out the truth, Cole? Her mother's dead. She's not going to thank you when she learns about that. She's just using you to reconnect with a past she's better off forget—'

'You checked up on her?'

She faltered. 'I'm just trying to protect you.'

'Chelsea, there is nothing you can protect me from.'

'I can protect you from losing your head—and your heart—over her. Why do you think your dad was so intent on making us friends when we were kids? He wanted to make you forget her and that ridiculous Neverland you kept going on about.'

'Chelsea. This is my life. I don't need you to tell me who to trust or what to do. Plus, Gemma is . . . a friend. She's my friend.'

'Gemma is your friend? Like Kas and Josh are your friends?'

An ugly silence sprawled between us. 'That's nice.'

She reached for my hand, lacing her fingers with mine when I didn't respond in kind. 'Let's not fight over this, okay? Why are we fighting over an outsider? Gemma—'

'Gemma is not the problem here, Chels. Look, part of the reason why I didn't want to go to London with you is because I want you to stop babysitting me for my dad. You don't have to make everything about us.'

'Babysitting you for your dad,' she echoed. 'Is that what you think I'm doing?'

'Why else do you keep trying to get me on board with Wonder Entertainment? I'm not like you, Chels. I'm not interested in the business.'

'I'm only a part of it because you are.'

'I was never a part of this. Wonder Entertainment belongs to my father, not to me.'

'So what are you part of? *Them*?' Disgust twisted her face into something barely recognizable. 'That's your problem, Cole. You hurt the people who actually care about you and want to help you, and you put your faith in the wrong people. That's why you always end up getting hurt. What do you think Gemma wants from you? Are you seriously going to help our competitor?'

'You don't know a thing about Gemma—or me, for that matter—so do us all a favour and, for once, stop acting like you're right about everything.'

Her grip on my hand tightened. When you got to a point where everyone was always disappointed in you, you stopped feeling sorry towards them. The word *sorry* didn't mean a thing anymore, and soon the people wouldn't either.

Chelsea's gaze bore into mine, the way it always did whenever she wanted something done her way. But when she saw that I wasn't going to yield to her—not this time, not anymore—she let go of my hand and stepped back.

'You belong with us more than you think,' she said. 'You're just going to do whatever you want, get hurt, and your dad and I will have to fix you back up the way we always have.'

'Fixing is what you do to a park ride that's broken down, not someone you claim to care about.'

There was no reason for me to stay here any longer. All I wanted was to leave this place with Gemma, to a place where only dreamers lived, if only for a while.

I found her at the end of the hallway, looking close to being devoured by this place. I shouldn't have brought her here. It had done neither of us any good.

She stiffened when I reached for her hand but didn't pull away. She seemed as eager as I was to leave.

In the tight silence of the car, our breaths came out ragged and loud. I drove without a destination in mind, intent on putting as much distance as possible between us and the *Wondrous*. The night raced past us in a series of blurred street lights. Shadows flitted across Gemma's face as she stared out the window mutely.

'Don't worry, Gemma,' I said, like I even had a clue. 'What happened back there, those people will barely remember it after tonight. They'll just—'

'Did you know about my mum?'

I slammed my foot down on the brake. A horn blared at us as a taxi sped past us, the driver shooting me a dirty look. I pulled to the side before we could get mowed over by an oncoming truck.

When she spoke again, her voice was hoarse. 'She's dead, isn't she?'

I didn't reply, but my silence was enough. It seemed like that notion had always haunted her, and now her fear was taking shape.

This was everything I had tried to spare her from.

'And you knew?' she said.

I considered staying as still and silent as I could, but she had torn her attention away from the dashboard and fixed it on me. The weight of her gaze was unbearable.

I gave her the barest of nods. 'You weren't supposed to find out this way. The plan was for you to remember it all on your own so you could come to terms with it.'

'The *plan*?' she spat. Before I could explain myself, she got out of the car.

I didn't blame her for wanting to get away from me, but she was in no state to be alone. I got out after her, abandoning my car on the road shoulder to catch up with her.

When I reached for her again, she whirled around and wrenched her hand out of my grasp. Tears sat in her eyes, ready to spill out. 'How long?' Her words came out low and shaky, as though it was taking everything in her to hold herself together. 'How long has she . . .'

I shook my head. 'I don't know the details.'

'And how long have you known she's dead?'

My hand fell back to my side. 'Since before we met again.'

All the fight drained from her, she sank to the ground, folding in on herself. I wanted to reach for her again, but I wasn't sure if she would push me away for good this time.

Neverland was a place she used to go when there was no room left for her here. Now I wished it would take her away again.

'But she replied to me. She replied to my letters.' Her eyes shone with a fierce hope that refused to die. I hated to be the one to kill it, but she figured it out on her own anyway. 'Thomas.'

'And the text messages—that was me.'

She blinked, setting free a tear that skated down her face. 'What?'

I pulled out my phone and showed her all the messages she had ever sent, seen by the wrong person. She scrolled through them, her face as brittle as glass.

Finally, a long breath rattled out of her. She shoved the phone back into my hand and turned away. 'I need to go.'

I caught her hand. 'Gemma—'

'Either take me home or let me go.'

I took her home.

We rode in silence. Tears slid down her face as she stared out the window. A million thoughts raced through my mind and died on my lips. There were so many ways to say sorry, but none of the words measured up.

It wasn't until we reached the first stoplight that she spoke again. 'What's the story?'

'What?'

She turned to me. 'Tell me the story.'

I saw in her eyes the desperation to return to the place where everything began and ended for her.

So I took her back to Neverland.

'You Otherworlder children are more trouble than you look,' Captain Storm muttered to Gemma and Cole.

But while the captain wasn't about to admit it, Cole could tell he had grown rather fond of them and didn't relish the thought of them being taken captive by the mermaids. Storm refused to give them up even though the mermaids promised to waive payment if he did.

When the blue-haired mermaid advanced towards Gemma and Cole, Storm planted himself in her way. 'Come now,' he said. 'Let's not make a tempest out of a drizzle.'

'Move aside, sailor,' said the mermaid, her eyes flashing. 'I will not repeat myself.'

Hermit squeezed Gemma and Cole's hands. 'Hide,' he whispered.

The children barely had time to consider his suggestion before the ship erupted in clamour and chaos.

In seconds, the other two mermaids had slipped out of the water and appeared on board, perched atop their scarlet and coral tails.

Meanwhile, half the crew had formed a barricade between the children and the mermaids, while the other half, including Storm, drew their weapons. A cold wind rocked the ship, tipping it into a precarious balance.

'Steady, boys,' Storm called. 'No blood on this ship, remember.'

'You cannot deny the sea its tithe,' the mermaid snarled, 'much less smuggle Otherworlders across it. Brazen fool.'

'Now, that's not a nice thing to call someone,' Storm said.

The mermaid lunged at him just as Storm whipped out a gleaming knife. She deflected his strike with a wave of her hand. Cole watched, entranced, as they engaged in a series of lunges and parries before the tight barrier formed by the crew blocked his view.

Gemma and Cole pressed close against each other, their hands laced. Cole could hardly breathe, only just realizing how huge a risk Storm had taken by letting them on board and sneaking them across the Silver Sea. Quite possibly, they might die if they broke free of the ring now.

A renewed gust of wind, this time accompanied by a crack of thunder, sent the crew sprawling and flung every which way. Gemma and Cole rolled down the length of the ship, and ended up right before the mermaid trio. Their bejewelled tails flashed under the streak of lightning that split the bruised sky.

Storm barked an order, but the wind drowned out his voice. Weaponless and with his crew scattered, Storm could only watch as the mermaids slipped back into the sea with the children.

Gemma and Cole tore through the skin of the Silver Sea, swallowing their screams in gulps of brackish water. The mermaids moved at a relentless speed even as they wound through tight sea tunnels and passageways lit by rows of luminous corals.

Cole soon felt his chest begin to constrict. He wondered how long it would take before his lungs exploded, but when they finally reached a cave-like chamber that glowed a deep, eerie blue from within, he found that he could breathe as easily as he had on land.

'We're sorry,' Gemma called, and Cole shot her a withering look. 'Being nice always helps,' she hissed in defence.

'Not when you're Otherworlders trespassing the Silver Sea,' the mermaid called over her shoulder. She came to a stop before the darkened mouth of a cage set against a rock wall. With a flick of her tail, she jostled the children in. The walls were slick with algae and littered with what appeared to be human bones.

The mermaid hovered at the entrance, watching them with a stoic gaze that suggested no room for negotiation or mercy.

'The serpent will have you for dinner now,' she informed them.

Then she ducked out of the cave, her tail flashing as brilliantly as the last sunset.

* * *

This was bad. Cole didn't need to be a Neverlander to understand that. His own father had caught a trespasser once and put him in jail. Trespassing got you behind bars in the real world. Trespassing in Neverland landed you in an underwater cage, waiting to be fed to an ancient monster.

'Whose idea was it to cross the Silver Sea again?' he said.

'It's the only way to get to the key,' Gemma replied.

'Well, that mission has failed. Obviously.'

'Will you shut up and help me find a way out?'

'They used their mermaid-y magic to seal us in, Gemma. I don't think there's any way we're getting out.' But he joined her all the same.

They couldn't even go near the entrance without being flung back against the wall.

Cole struggled to catch his breath and shared a look with Gemma as they picked themselves up. 'Told you so,' he said.

'There has to be a way,' Gemma insisted. 'As long as we're in Neverland, there will always be a way.'

Cole was about to challenge that statement when Gemma shushed him, her ears pricked. 'Do you hear that?' she whispered.

Cole stopped to listen. Sure enough, there was a low rumble in the distance. Soon, trails of bubbles parted the blue gloom as a shadow—no, two—broke through the water.

Shells, Cole realized. Conches, to be exact. Huge moving conches with equally huge clamshells tied around their spiral middles. They speared through the magically sealed entrance, coming straight at them. Cole gave a shout and pushed Gemma out of the way as the bars twisted apart under the force of the conches.

The rocket conches (as Cole mentally named them) and clamshells were much clumsier in landing, tumbling and skidding across the rocky ground before coming to a stop in front of them. The clamshells opened their generous mouths, revealing plush white middles with enough room for them to recline in.

Cole held Gemma back before she could take a closer look, just as a head stuck out from one of the conches. It was a tanned, sandy-haired boy not much older than them. 'Get in!' he hissed.

Gemma prepared to climb in, but Cole grabbed her hand. 'How do we know if we can trust you?' he demanded of the boy.

'By all means, stay,' said the boy. 'But the mermaids might be coming back any moment and I, for one, would like to disappear before they lock me in here too.'

That got both Gemma and Cole scrambling to crawl into a shell each. Cole's driver was an ebony-skinned girl who gave him a silent nod when he climbed in.

The interior of the clamshell, upon closer look, wasn't as magnificent as Cole first thought. Once you got over the size of it, you started to notice the hairline cracks in its walls.

'Hold on tight!' the boy called and let out a whoop as the conch gave a lurch. They charged back towards the opening of the tunnel.

It was comfy enough to fall asleep in the shell, and Cole would have if he weren't so worried about crashing into a wall or getting caught by a mermaid who would do something far worse than throw them in a cage. He kept his shell ajar and peered around, bracing himself for any sudden danger.

In the adjacent conch, Gemma's rescuer seemed to be having the time of his life. Whooping and laughing, he, like his (quieter) partner, steered the conch like he had been doing it his entire life. For someone who had broken into mermaids' territory to set free a couple of prisoners, he was being rather cocky.

Gemma pushed open the shell an inch and was almost blown back by the force at which the water rushed past her. 'How did this crusty old thing manage to break through the cage?'

'What's that?' the boy yelled. Gemma repeated her question. 'Fairy dust, of course,' the boy called back.

They careened through the opening at the end of the passageway and straight up through a narrow blowhole that spewed them out into the sky.

And then they were in free fall. Cole felt his stomach plunge as they crashed back down onto solid ground. The clamshell bumped and skidded across the rocky surface before coming to a stop on a patch of grass.

'You really need to work on your landing,' Cole said to his driver, and received a glare in return.

* * *

At the sound of Cole's voice, Gemma hurried out of her shell to join him where he stood in front of his carriage. Next to him, a girl was untying the rope that bound the hinge of the clamshell to the conch.

'You really need to work on your landing,' Cole said. The girl only glared at him.

It was only when Gemma spotted the hemp bracelet around her wrists that she realized who the children were. 'Lost Boys!' she blurted.

'We have names, you know. And one of us is a girl,' the boy said from next to her. 'I'm Kittern. And that'—he gestured at his partner, the dark, silent girl—'is Meerka.' A tiny spray of light appeared before Gemma. 'And you know Nix, of course.'

'Nix!' Gemma cried, relief washing through her.

'How did you know where to find us?' Cole said.

'Nix told us,' Kittern said. 'Said you were going to cross the Silver Sea to get the key.'

Gemma was more surprised by the fact that the Lost Children came for them than by their ability to find them. As though she had read Gemma's mind, Kittern said, 'Nix said you two are our only hope. And your mother is that Katie girl Peter brought here years ago.'

'We need to find shelter,' Nix said. 'All that hubbub would have woken up the serpent, and I hear you have pursuers.'

'Who?' Gemma glanced around. 'Where are we? And what happened to Storm and the rest?'

Kittern, Meerka, and Nix shared a look.

'We don't know,' Nix said. 'The ship went down.'

Twenty

Gemma

Cole's voice, low and steady, rumbled in the background, filling the silence in the car. I half-listened to him, trying not to dwell on the fact that my mother was gone for good and I never got to say goodbye. I could try to pick out the clues that might explain her death, but my memory was still incomplete. The tales we made up so long ago felt comforting yet foreign.

That night, my dreams were ragged pieces of memories woven into a patchy story.

I dreamt about my parents, about Cole and his father. I dreamt of our old house and the garden bursting with flowers, my mother's fingers stained with soil. I dreamt of Hopewood, with its pristine lawn and padded, sterile rooms where everything was careful and measured. I dreamt of low, muffled voices and water, water everywhere, filling up in me until I burst through the surface and found myself staring at the darkened ceiling.

I dreamt long and hard, drowning in a sea of images. But I couldn't tell where the memories ended and the dream began. I couldn't tell between fact and fiction, real world and Neverland.

After Cole took me home last night, I had crashed into bed and lain there for a long time before sleep claimed me. By then, my insides felt like they had been scraped raw, from grief and anger and regret and other things I couldn't name. Jo and Boon hovered outside my room—I could hear them debating whether to come in and talk to me—but they eventually left me alone.

Thomas called shortly after, so I knew Jo and Boon must have told him about the state I was in. I let his call go unanswered. All I wanted was to escape to Neverland again, to go back to the time when I still believed I would one day find my mother there.

When I got to the Wild Ride the next day, Laura took one look at me and tutted. 'Now, is that the look of someone who just spent the night partying with the Gatsbys?'

I didn't even bother asking how she knew where I went. 'You do realize that the Gatsbys came with their own set of problems, right?' I glanced around. 'Is Thomas here? And, um, Cole?'

Laura narrowed her eyes, studying me. 'I see you two are already in that stage.'

'What stage?'

'The awkward *are we or aren't we* stage. If you want my opinion, I think you and New Boy are more compatible than you and Thomas.'

I rolled my eyes. 'Laura. Are they here or not?'

'Sheesh, Wendy Darling is cranky this morning. They're in the office. Cole got here not two minutes ago and was looking for you as well.'

'Thank you.' I made my way to the office.

Cole was just entering the room when I got there. Thomas, who was on the computer, glanced up when he entered. I lingered outside the room, just out of their sight, not sure what I would say in the aftermath of last night, but I pressed close to the open door.

'What happened last night?' Thomas said. 'Jo and Boon said Gemma was in a state, and she didn't pick up my calls.' My grip tightened around the doorknob.

'Oh, that's because she's not talking to you,' Cole said. 'Or me.'

'Why not?'

'Because I told her about the letters. And the text messages.'

'What?' Thomas exclaimed. He let out a sigh. 'Why would you—'

'She was going to find out sooner or later.'

'Didn't we agree that we'd let her remember it on her own?'

'She did remember. Well, sort of.'

'Explain, please.'

Cole recounted everything that happened last night, starting from the rumour I had heard and laying bare my hysterics and humiliation. I had half a mind to barge in there and make him stop, but it was easier to have Cole tell Thomas than telling him myself.

'You don't really believe they had a thing, do you?' Thomas said at last.

'Of course not, Thomas,' Cole snapped.

I chose that moment to make my entrance before Cole could rant against that possibility again. The boys fell silent when I pushed the door open.

My gaze settled on Cole. Somehow, his stare managed to reel me back to the ground, when before I had been pinwheeling in the sky. But I said, 'Go on. Don't stop on my account.'

Thomas got up and came over to me. 'Gem, I am so sorry. I didn't mean to lie to you, I—'

I shook my head. I had spent the better part of last night awake and alone with my anger, and the company was miserable. The truth was, a part of me was thankful for them—both of them. Because while they had lied to me, they had also kept my hope alive for this long. In the days after Jo and Boon found me, nothing could make me talk. My thoughts were all tangled up and I couldn't begin to make sense of anything. Those text messages and letters had given voice to all my confusion and fear, my worry and guilt and hope, and writing them had helped me get through each day.

So it didn't matter now if Thomas knew that the 'T' I mentioned in my letters (if he had read them) was him, or that Cole had read every single message I had sent to my mother. My friends had saved me, whether they knew it or not.

And maybe I had played a part in this ruse too, so willingly fooled into believing my mother could be pinned down to a random address and phone number.

'I'm starting to remember more,' I said. 'But I still need some help.'

'Whatever you need,' Thomas hurried to reply. 'No lies, I promise.'

'I need to visit Hopewood.' The name felt both familiar and foreign on my tongue.

Thomas and Cole exchanged a look. 'Are you sure?' Thomas said. 'I mean, you already know the truth about your mother.'

'I can't leave it at that, Thomas. I need to know what exactly happened to her and how she . . . passed.'

'The movers are coming today,' Thomas said.

'I won't take long.'

'Thomas, you stay. I'll go with her,' Cole said.

Thomas looked at me, expecting me to protest. But Cole was exactly the person I wanted to have along. He was the one who had been with me to Neverland all those years ago. Thomas, despite all his attempts to understand the place, was never quite able to.

He nodded. 'Keep me posted. And Gemma, I'm sor—'

I dragged Cole out of the office before Thomas could finish that sentence.

Memories of last night came surging back. I saw my hysterics play out over and over, felt the shame press against my chest and a fresh wave of grief wash over me.

We sat in silence in Cole's car, separate and together in the thick of our thoughts. I wasn't used to sitting in such a quiet car. Boon's old Toyota rattled when it was at rest on good days and clunked and coughed on bad ones.

I cleared my throat. 'I'm sorry about what I said last night.'

His eyes slid over to me.

'I didn't mean that your dad . . . you know.' I rubbed my neck. 'I just don't know what to think.'

The car was quiet in the aftermath of my apology. Too quiet. Quiet enough for me to hear my thoughts buzzing in my head. I itched to say something more.

'While we're in the spirit of remorse,' Cole said, 'let me also say that I'm sorry about the text messages. They were never meant for me, and I should have told you who I was from the start.'

'You should have,' I agreed. 'It was a despicable thing to do, leading me on like that. But you also kept my hope alive all this time. So, for that, I guess we're even.'

We came to a stoplight a moment later. 'Question,' Cole said. 'What are you going to do if you ever find your dad?'

'I don't know. Get some answers, I guess.'

'That's it? You meet the guy who abandoned you in an amusement park ten years ago, left you to die'—he ignored my eye roll—'and all you're going to do is ask questions? Aren't you even a little mad that he left you? I mean, who dumps an eight-year-old at an amusement park? You could've been kidnapped. You could've *died*.'

'Be a little more dramatic, Cole.'

'You could have,' he said in full earnestness.

'Well, I didn't. And that's what matters. Green.' I pointed at the stoplight. He put the car into gear again. 'Look, I've already lost all these years of knowing him. I don't want to waste another minute being mad at him.'

'I just find it hard to believe there are no grudges. So if you ever do find him, it's just going to be all rainbows and unicorns and you both live happily ever after?'

'It could happen,' I insisted.

He shook his head, staring at me like he couldn't believe a life form like me existed. Cole could be as cynical as he liked, but

I remembered the way he used to laugh, the way he had regarded Neverland with wide-eyed wonder, and how hopeful he had been about saving it.

'What if he doesn't want to be found? Ever considered that?' he went on.

'Why wouldn't he?'

'Uh, because he left you? If he has a conscience, he'd be eaten up with guilt for that. He's not going to want to see you.'

'I'm confused. Are we talking about you or me now?'

'You,' he said, shooting me a look, 'are a fool for hope.'

'It's been said.'

* * *

Hopewood Sanatorium looked exactly the way I left it ten years ago. Its walls and corridors remained stark and foreboding despite the fresh coat of sky-blue paint. The manicured lawn was just as I remembered, lined with trimmed hedges and dotted with bonsais.

I had been terrified of this place, of drowning in all the realities that existed within its confines. Each patient here carried a universe in them, so vast that they were lost in it. If you were lucky or skilled, you managed to reel them back for a while.

I hadn't even managed to reach out to my mother, much less bring her back.

She was nothing more than a statistic now, someone who had fallen through the cracks. *It happens*, people would say. *She wasn't of sound mind. Something like that was just waiting to happen*, like her life was a movie they had watched before and knew the ending to.

But my mother wasn't just a statistic. She was made of stories, wild tales that spilt out of her and consumed her like a fever dream. I saw them in her paintings, maybe even dreamt the same things as her. After all, we both shared the knowledge of Neverland; our adventures, while different, took place in the same treacherous landscape where we were always in danger of losing ourselves.

I felt her presence in the hallways, heard her stories from the walls that whispered their secrets to me, even caught a whiff of her scent in the air. Maybe everything here bore the mark of every patient, and some traces—like my mother's—were indelible.

Cole trailed through the hallways next to me, silent and subdued. When he spoke at last, his voice was low, as though he was afraid of shattering the fragile peace. 'Do you remember who her therapist was?'

York. Doctor York. My mother spoke of him enough, though mostly with scorn. My father, however, could quote him word for word. *Doctor York said dissociation from Neverland is the best way you can ever be free of it. You need to remember that we are real, Katie, not Peter Pan or Captain Hook. As soon as you see that, you're safe.*

Now that we were here, I wasn't sure what the next plan of action was. Doctor York might not even be here today, and we hadn't scheduled an appointment.

We managed to catch him by wrangling his whereabouts from the receptionist, then hunting him down in the cafeteria, where he was spending his lunch break.

Doctor York had the type of face that made you either very pacified or very furious. He even looked patient with his meal, handling his chicken steak with the focus and methodical precision of a brain surgeon.

Cole followed the direction of my gaze. 'That's him?'

I nodded but threw out a hand to stop him when he began to head towards Doctor York. 'We're interrupting.'

Cole stared at me. 'We didn't come all the way here to watch him eat lunch.'

He dragged me across the cafeteria, and somewhere along the way my footsteps grew urgent. It wasn't just the memory of my mother that propelled me, but also my rage at being kept in the dark for so long.

Doctor York glanced up from his food when we parked ourselves in front of him. His fork hovered in mid-air as he stared at us.

He didn't remember me. Of course he didn't. How easy it was to forget someone whose life you had altered without knowing it. Disappointment pricked at me, but Cole nudged me before I could back out prematurely.

'Hi, Doctor York,' I blurted. The words tumbled out, rolling over one another. 'You may not remember me, but my name is Gemma. I'm—'

'Joseph and Katherine's daughter.' He broke into a weary smile and set down his fork. 'It's a relief to meet you at last.'

When her father first mentioned the new work project, he made it sound like he was embarking on an adventure. One of his own, separate from Gemma and her mother.

Well, not quite his own. He was going with his business partner, Lionel Wu, who was also her father's old friend from school. They had big plans to bring their entertainment franchise to other parts of the world, her father said, and this was just the beginning so there was a lot of 'homework' to be done.

Gemma knew that this adventure meant she and her mother would have to leave everything behind, because her father had asked her how she would like to live in cities like London and Shanghai.

The first time Gemma met Lionel, she had immediately ducked behind her father after shaking Lionel's cool, large hand. He had a keen gaze that made Gemma more nervous than when she had to go to the front of the class for show-and-tell. He introduced himself as Uncle Lionel and told her he needed to talk to her father for an hour or so.

'Go play in the backyard, Gem,' her father said, which Gemma understood to mean they had secrets they didn't want her to know.

They talked in the living room, so Gemma sat outside on the porch swing listening, silent and worried that things were going to change.

Two days later, her mother returned from Hopewood. Her father brought her back on a Saturday afternoon, his hand at her elbow as she inched forward with the wariness of an animal released from captivity. Her parents were polite, murmuring thanks and apologies as they skirted around each other. They also tried to have dinner together again, ordering from Gemma's favourite pizza place and eating in front of the TV so they wouldn't run out of things to talk about.

They tottered along in a precarious calm until Uncle Lionel's visit three days later.

He came by in the middle of dinner. The doorbell rang midway through her father's compliment of her mother's attempt at chicken stew. When her father returned, he was joined by Uncle Lionel, who exchanged a curt nod with her mother.

'Hey, Gem,' her father said. 'Mummy and I have to talk to Uncle Lionel for a while. Finish up your dinner, then go to your room. Okay?'

But later, even in her room Gemma could hear the adults' raised voices coming from the study. She caught enough to piece together the situation and decided that she would go wherever her mother went, not just out of loyalty to her, but also because she needed to take care of her in her father's stead.

Later, Uncle Lionel stormed out of the study, sparing her not even a glance as he passed her in the hallway, and Gemma's mother locked herself in the art studio for the rest of the night, painting. Gemma saw the defeat on her father's face and debated whether to go over to him, but he shot her a tired smile that stopped her feet.

In the days following that visit, Gemma's mother began putting her ear to the walls and pacing the hallway in the dead of the night like a silent, wakeful ghost.

One night, Gemma roused to the rustle of footsteps outside her room. She threw off the covers and peered out from behind the door to find her mother creeping down the length of the hallway.

'Mummy,' she murmured, rubbing her eyes. 'What are you—'

'Shh!' her mother hissed, reaching over to cover Gemma's mouth with a hand. 'He will hear us!'

'Who?'

'Captain Hook!'

'Where is he?'

'In the walls. Everywhere. You can't see him, but he can always see you.'

'Well, what's he doing? Surely he needs to sleep.'

'He wants me to walk the plank, Gemma. He's pushing me to the end. He wants me to jump.'

'Don't worry, Mummy. I will rescue you.' She let out a yawn. 'In the morning.'

'He means to destroy the key. You mustn't ever let him have it. Neverland needs the key. Neverland needs you, Gemma.' Her eyes shone with moonlit tears. 'Don't ever give up on it.'

'I won't, Mummy,' Gemma said, fear starting to creep into her at the sight of her mother's wide, bloodshot eyes. 'I won't give up on Neverland.'

Twenty-One

Gemma

Doctor York called it regression. And what started out innocently enough as escapism—a brief foray into Neverland—turned into something much darker. Delusion. Fear of persecution, of being trapped, held captive. The desperate need for someone to save her.

My mother's fear had been as real as the stories she believed in. It had made its home in her mind and become her reality.

When I was done narrating the Neverland chronicles up to where I couldn't remember, Doctor York dragged a hand down his face and sighed.

'I was against your father's decision to take your mother home,' he said. 'She was not well enough, and I should've fought for her to stay.'

'What exactly happened?'

'The reports said it was an accident.'

'But you don't think so,' I said.

'When a patient suffering from delusions drowns herself, normal people would pin it on her mental condition and call it an accident. But something must have driven her to jump; something must have triggered that episode. That itself indicates it was not an accident.'

'What was it, then? What drove her to do that?'

'No one knows. After the accident, I replayed every session with her to search for clues, but there was only Captain Hook, on whom she blamed everything bad that happened in her life.' He shook his head, and I realized how worn he looked compared to my last memory of him. 'Your mother was the first patient I failed, and I owe all of you an apology.'

I could be mad at him. Here was someone ready to take the blame; he made it so easy. But there was no time for anger. I was this close to finding my father, the only person I had left now.

'I don't need an apology, Doctor York,' I said. 'I just need to know where my father is now.'

'I can't tell you that, Gemma.'

'Why not?'

'He's currently a patient of mine, and he's specifically told me not to let anyone know where to find him.'

So he *had* been around all this while, just out of my life, out of my reach. And that was the way he preferred it.

Doctor York's tone softened. 'Your father has never been the same ever since your mother died, Gemma. And while that doesn't excuse his abandoning you, he needs more time to sort out his life before he's ready to face you again.'

'Ten years is a lot of time.' The words slipped out, bitter on my tongue.

Doctor York did not reply.

'All this time . . . did he ask about me at all?'

'Your father could never forget you, if that's what you're asking. He just doesn't know how to face you after everything that happened.'

Doctor York had an appointment at two, so I let him wolf down his lunch in peace before he had to rush off.

'I know you have questions,' he said before leaving. 'And I promise to help find the answers. But your father will come to you when he is ready.' He got up. 'It's good to see you again, Gemma.'

I left Hopewood with more questions than before.

At least my father was still alive. Avoiding me, but alive nonetheless. The ache in my chest swelled, and with that came an alien, monstrous anger. Cole might be right, after all. Maybe all the sadness in me had, over the years, coagulated into something unrecognisable, a meanness lurking under the cloud of optimism I had used to keep myself afloat all this time.

Because that was what happened when hope died, leaching out day by day—rage became the only thing left that kept you going.

I was finally starting to understand where Cole was coming from.

Twenty-Two

Cole

There were a few types of social situations that I generally tried to avoid—the functions my father was so fond of throwing, and one-on-one meetings that involved sitting across someone to whom you had everything and nothing to say.

My mother sipped on her tea, her gaze darting away whenever it met mine. We had been here for a full ten minutes, and apart from the frenzied tapping my fingers were making on the table, we were both silent. Other diners made enough conversation to fill the space between us, but how much longer were we going to sit here like this? Granted, I could say something. But I wasn't sure what the situation was between us after that court case two years ago, so it was her move now.

After another sip of her tea, she cleared her throat. 'You said you know about Joseph Young. What do you know?'

I continued drumming, waiting for more. Nothing else came. My fingers stilled in their manic tapping. 'Guess we're skipping the pleasantries then. Why don't you start first?'

Something hardened in her face. 'Cole. Tell me what you know.'

A sigh escaped me as I reached for a fry. 'Did you have a thing with him?'

'What? No! Where did you hear that?'

'Just had to check.'

169

Her lips thinned. 'Is that what you think of me?'

Now I understood what Gemma meant when she expressed her doubts. 'I don't know, Mum. I don't know you well enough to have an opinion of you.'

She stiffened at my snark, then sighed as she leaned back in her chair. 'That's more like how I expected you to behave.'

For some reason, that felt like a counter-attack. I reached for another fry just so my fingers would get busy again. 'What does that mean?'

'Angry. Hateful. At me. That's how you should be.'

'Don't tell me how I should be.'

'You've always tried so hard for us to be together again when you should've been mad at me, not just for suing your father two years ago, but for leaving you both. I just didn't know what to do with your efforts. Your hope.'

She was right. It had been years since she left. My display of anger and resentment seemed a little overdue. But that wild hope I had seen in Gemma's eyes felt dangerously like the one I felt curdling inside me like milk left out too long. Did my efforts seem laughable to her? All this time I kept asking her out for lunch, tried keeping her up to date with my life, did she think I was wasting my time chasing something that was never going to materialize?

'So you decided to sue Dad and cause us a whole lot of inconvenience?'

'I sued him because his men were found trespassing on my property—'

'That he bought for you,' I couldn't help but add.

Despite the million other ways I had tried looking at it, Chelsea was right. My mother *had* used me to find out about the property my father had left under her name, then proceeded to engage him in a long-drawn-out legal tussle. I liked to think that I had nothing to do with it—that I had been a hapless accomplice to my mum—but Dad had never regarded me the same way since then, as though he had decided that I wasn't worthy of his trust since my loyalties didn't lie with him . . .

'We are not here to talk about this,' I said.

'Let's wait till your father gets here.'

I got up from my seat. 'You called Dad?'

Another sip. I hope she would reach the end of that cup just so she would look me in the eye for once. She set the cup down. It *was* empty now, but she continued nursing it.

Gemma was wrong. Everything didn't automatically work out once you had someone back in your life, even just for a moment. In fact, it upset the balance even more and knocked you off your feet just as you were starting to get used to the absence.

I'd thought getting an answer from my mother would be the key to fixing everything that was wrong with us, but all it did was stir up the anger and guilt—and, worst of all, the hope— sitting in me.

Dad arrived without preamble. 'Let's make this quick,' he said, signalling for a coffee.

That was how Lionel Wu rolled—filing away issues one by one, allowing no spillovers. Thanks to me, Mum was one messy entanglement he couldn't get rid of entirely.

Dad turned to me. 'Your mother says you've been asking about Joseph Young. Why the sudden interest?'

'Just tell me what you know.'

'You must be mistaken, Cole. You don't get to order me around, especially not after humiliating me in front of everyone yesterday with that girl.'

I snorted. 'Please. Like you didn't force me to attend it.'

'Actually, I didn't. I made you an offer, and you decided to take it up to help that girl.'

'How do you explain Wonder Town then? That wasn't part of the agreement.'

'It was either that or London, and you've already expressed your aversion to the second option'—he shot Mum a look—'for obvious reasons.'

Mum turned away from his stare.

'This isn't about Mum,' I snapped.

Dad flung me a look. 'It isn't? So you don't blame me for her leaving? Don't think I don't know you've been loitering around her apartment. Randy's been reporting to me—'

'You had someone keeping tabs on me? See, this is why I can't wait to leave. You treat everyone like a mess only you can salvage. And when you can't, you drive them away.'

'Do not comment on things you know nothing about,' he said. 'Nothing makes you sound more like a child.'

'What don't I know about? Didn't you drive me out of the house? Didn't you make Mum leave?'

'Cole.' Mum's voice cut me off mid-rant. 'It was my choice. I *chose* to leave.'

No. She didn't choose to leave us. She didn't willingly give us up for a new life. She didn't decide to leave me behind. She couldn't have. Blaming my father all this while had worked out well. I didn't want that to change.

'If you wanted to leave, you should've done a cleaner job of it,' Dad said. 'Cut us off entirely, not hang around like a loose thread in Cole's life. You made your choice—why not stick to it?'

'Stop it,' I snapped. Mum flinched. Several glances flitted our way. The waiter took a step back with Dad's coffee before setting it down and scurrying off. Fifteen minutes in and things were already turning ugly.

Dad turned to Mum like I had proved him right. 'My son hates me because of you.'

'Ever considered the possibility that I hate you because of *you*?' I said. 'Don't blame everyone else for what you can't handle. Mum and my friends aren't the problem—you are.'

'Cole,' Mum said, still in that deadly quiet voice. 'Enough.'

I leaned back in my seat and glared at Dad. 'So was Joseph Young a problem you had to fix too? Did you cut him out of your life because he didn't fit into your plan?'

Mum closed her eyes.

'As a matter of fact,' Dad said, 'I did.'

That confirmed the word on the street, then. But while it wasn't uncommon for business partners to fall out, where did Gemma fit into all this?

Dad took a sip of his coffee. 'Joseph and I were supposed to be partners. Wonder Entertainment was our project, until he decided to back out to take care of his wife, despite my repeated attempts to dissuade him.'

I reached into my pocket and pulled out a cell phone. Dad glanced at it as I set it down on the table. 'What about this?'

Dad stared at it like it might explode any second. 'Where did you . . . why do you have this?'

'It belonged to Gemma's mother. Why did you have her mother's cell phone?'

He held my gaze, coming to an understanding. Maybe I had guessed at his involvement all along and just needed him to confirm it.

'There's nothing in there that proves it was Katherine's phone.'

'No, I'm sure you deleted anything incriminating.'

He narrowed his eyes at me. 'What's that supposed to mean?'

'It means you're not supposed to have this phone, Dad. It means all those text messages Gemma has been sending out all these years were meant for someone else. It means you owe us an explanation.'

Ten years ago, a girl had lost her parents because of him. He hadn't just destroyed our family; he had destroyed someone else's too.

Mum and I exchanged a look as he nursed his coffee. When cornered by his past, would he keep hiding?

'It was an accident,' he began.

Twenty-Three

Gemma

Back at the Wild Ride, I found Thomas in the ticket booth with Laura. He came out to join me when he spotted me at the gates.

'How did it go?' he said. 'Did you find Doctor York?'

I nodded, feeling strangely drained and not in the mood to talk. All I wanted to do was crash into bed.

Thomas studied my face, then turned the topic to Cole. 'Have you seen him?'

My phone reported no missed calls or messages from him. 'He's having lunch with his mum,' I said.

'His mum? Didn't he fall out with her a couple of years ago?'

'What happened?'

'Some legal tussle over a house—sounded like his mum used him to gain ownership of it. I don't know the specifics, but he ended up crashing at my place for a couple of weeks before his dad came to get him.'

'Sounds complicated.'

'Things are always complicated when it comes to Cole and his mum.' He glanced over my shoulder. 'The movers are here.'

The entire process of selling the rides turned out to be shorter than I expected. Everything happened so fast I barely had time to reconsider. Soon after the buyers came for the assessment the other day, the rides were about to be cleared out.

By the end of today, the Wild Ride would be twice as empty and half as familiar.

I pulled out my phone. Still no news from Cole. Was he still trying hard to reach out to his mother, or had they chipped through the icy impasse? Would she tell him the whole truth, or would we be left with more loose threads?

Thomas gave me a nudge. 'Quit checking your phone every five seconds. Cole will be here soon.'

He was right. The Wild Ride was being hollowed out as we spoke. My own problems could wait. So I went to join Thomas, Laura, Cory and Beth in watching the movers dismantle each ride piece by piece and ferry them away.

It felt wrong that we were the only ones here to witness this.

'Where *are* Jo and Boon?' I asked. 'They should be here.'

'Didn't they go on a holiday? That's what the note said,' Thomas replied.

Yes, the handwritten note from Boon, in which he told me to take care of myself and not stress over the amusement park, that he and Jo were on a holiday and would be back soon. Wherever they had gone apparently had little or no cell phone reception, because I couldn't reach either of them. It was almost like they didn't want to explain themselves to anyone.

I had never thought of myself as clingy. But maybe the reason I felt so secure in the belief that Jo and Boon would always be within reach was only because they had always been here for me, making up for how my father had abandoned me.

But even though I pretended that everything was fine, I couldn't quell the panic rising in me. I couldn't pretend like it wasn't a scarily familiar sensation, one that brought back memories of the day I tried so hard to forget. Normal people didn't experience this kind of anxiety when their parents weren't around.

'Any idea when they'll be back?' I asked.

Thomas shrugged. 'When they feel like it? They've been working so hard for this amusement park. Don't they deserve a long break?'

'I suppose.'

It felt unceremonious, somehow, just watching each ride taken apart and loaded on to the back of a truck. Maybe it was better that Jo and Boon weren't here, after all. Maybe they had planned their holiday to avoid this moment.

Thomas took my hand, as though he knew exactly what I was thinking. I held on gratefully as the ground rumbled with each ride being demolished.

The movers came and left within the day, and by late evening the park grounds were decidedly emptier. All that remained in the Wild Ride were the bistro, the café, the slot machines and only a handful of rides. The park seemed more desolate now, and the signposts pointing to the roller coaster and Viking ship stood as obsolete references to something long gone.

My gut twisted with something I didn't want to acknowledge— that this time, I was being left behind by a place that I had come to know so well. The panic and fear at that thought felt more familiar than I would like.

'Everything feels like it's changing so quickly,' I said as Thomas and I made our way to the Peter Pan ride. It looked out of place now that it was the only ride standing in the middle of the grounds.

Thomas nodded. 'It is. But that's only because better things are coming along. The Wild Ride will come alive again. We'll make it happen.'

I stopped. 'What if we can't? What if this is really the end?'

I wasn't sure what I was referring to anymore. Ever since my dad left, this place was all I could hold on to. As long as the Wild

Ride was still around, as long as I stayed put, he would be able to find me. Now that I knew he had never meant to look for me after all, what was I holding on to?

Thomas peered at me. 'Gemma, what's wrong?'

'Nothing.' I made for the benches at the foot of the ride, and Thomas joined me there. 'I just haven't felt this unnerved in a long time. And with Jo and Boon gone without a word . . . Forget it. It's stupid.'

'It's not stupid.' He squeezed my hand. 'You've always tried so hard to assert your independence. It's like you want to prove you're not a burden to anyone.'

I had never admitted this to anyone before, not even Thomas, and no one had ever guessed. 'How did you know?'

'Cole figured it out, actually.'

'Cole?' I echoed.

'He said—and I quote—the distance you put between yourself and Jo and Boon is to compensate for your blind faith in your father.'

Was it so obvious that I tried not to be needy and desperate so that the people around me wouldn't decide that I was more trouble than I was worth?

'Even if everything changes, Gem, we won't,' Thomas said.

He couldn't know that for sure. No matter how hard we held on to everything, nothing remained the same forever. People changed, they moved on. I had waited years for my father, so certain he would find me eventually, but people were the least reliable of all.

Still, this was Thomas. If there was anyone who could make me believe in the constant, it was him. Thomas kept all his promises.

'If you ever find your father again . . . you're not going to leave Boon and Jo, are you?' he asked.

I frowned. 'Of course not. Why would you say that?'

'I mean, Jo and Boon may not be your biological parents, but this place is still your home.'

'I know. I'm not going to leave them.'

Finding my father wouldn't change anything between me and my foster parents. And the Wild Ride had been my home for as long as I could remember.

No, there had been another one. The one with the yellow walls and backyard full of flowers my mother grew. Geraniums and hibiscus. They flourished when my mother was on her medication, but suffered when she was lost to Neverland and feverishly creating art. She would come in from the garden and pick me up, and I would inhale the safe scent of geraniums on her. Safe, because that meant she was accessible, lucid. It was the sharp tang of turpentine that I had to be worried about, because it meant she was painting again. And Neverland, I came to learn, was a dangerous place to linger around.

RL had mentioned a house during our last encounter. Possibly *the* house.

I leapt to my feet.

'Gemma, where are you going?' Thomas called after me.

I was already making my way out of the Wild Ride. My feet had taken on a life of their own, driven by the memories that were coming back hard and fast.

'I'll be back,' I called over my shoulder. 'I just need to—' I spun around, only to bump right into someone's chest.

Cole gripped my shoulders, steadying me. The look on his face was as heavy as the air before a storm. 'We need to talk.'

'How did it go with your mum?' I asked. 'What did she tell you?'

In his eyes was a look I recognized. I saw it in the mirror on days when I just wanted to escape to Neverland. 'I'm sorry,' he said at last.

The words sent a chill down my back. The closer I got to finding out the truth, the more I felt as though I were hurtling towards something I wasn't ready for and might shatter against upon impact.

'Cole, what is it?'

'I know where your father is.'

They were now so close to finding the key. Gemma could finally focus on rescuing her mother from Captain Hook, even though she still hadn't lost hope that Peter Pan might come to help.

By the time they managed to put considerable distance between them and the spit of land they had been deposited on, dawn was breaking, smearing the horizon pink and gold. Gemma clung on to the clamshell (it turned out that the shells only had magical abilities underwater; above, they had as much use as driftwood), trying not to get distracted by the lovely sight.

Neverland still possessed beauty; it wasn't beyond repair. The thought buoyed Gemma all the way to Black Island.

Black Island, home of Old Limestone. They were here at last. Gemma had heard enough stories about the cursed island to constantly glance over her shoulder now for phantom guards and blood-sucking critters that might burst through the ebony sand and take a bite out of her.

Nix and the Lost Children joined Gemma and Cole on the beach. Cole shook the water off him and squinted in the distance. Gemma could tell he had just about had enough of this place, and she didn't blame him. She herself was ready for this quest to be over; all she wanted to do now was find the key and get to her mother.

But navigating around Black Island proved to be the biggest challenge so far. Vindictive mermaid soldiers she could deal with; but an island filled with the ghosts and bones of intrepid explorers who met their demise here unnerved her. Every snap and crackle made her flinch, and every rush of wind sent her heart leaping to her throat. Cole reached out to squeeze her hand. They could barely see anything beyond the fog rolling in, though Gemma was sure she spotted shadows drifting around them.

'Great,' Kittern said next to her. 'How are we going to find Old Limestone? I can't even see my own feet.'

Meerka spoke up for the first time since Gemma met her. 'We should take cover. I don't like standing out in the open like this.'

Gemma seconded her sentiments. She couldn't shake off the feeling of being watched. Nix flitted around them, the light from her wings feeble in the gloom.

'This way,' Gemma decided, making for a narrow path that led to the mouth of a cave.

'How do you know?' Cole said.

Gemma gestured at the cave. 'It's the only area not filled with bones.'

Nix flew ahead of them to light up the way. The cave grew danker as they ventured deeper, winding down slippery, narrow passages. As soon as her eyes had adjusted to the darkness, Gemma noticed the slick, gleaming cave walls, the potholes at her feet collecting pools of luminescent turquoise water, and the minerals that had crystallized in the rock crevices above them, creating a strange constellation that illuminated the rest of their way.

Old Limestone, according to her mother, was linked to a cave that many—if not all—died mid-passage, beguiled by its treacherous beauty. We have to make it to the other side, Gemma thought. She didn't travel all the way here just to die in a cave, no matter how pretty it was.

But when they reached a fork in the passage, it became clear that they didn't have a fighting chance. Jaws of crystalline stalactite and stalagmites fenced one route, while the other path led them down a stream towards a roaring waterfall.

'Great,' Cole said. 'Now what?'

'I say we turn back,' Kittern proposed. 'Find another way through.' Meerka nodded in agreement.

'That's going to take us more time,' Gemma said.

'Would you rather bash your head on those rocks?' Kittern retorted.

'How about I push you down that waterfall right now?' said Cole.

'Now, now, children,' came a silky voice that made everyone fall silent. 'Let's all play nice. You're all going to die anyway.'

They whirled around to find a figure emerging from the shadows behind them. His slow smile was as unmistakable as the gleaming curve of metal where his right hand ought to be.

Gemma wasn't sure which of them broke the silence. In the yawning cavern where they were trapped, his name resounded like doom.

'Hook.'

Twenty-Four

Gemma

As Cole packed me into his car and drove away from the Wild Ride, the Neverland chronicle played out in my mind in starts and stops. It seemed like we hadn't stopped running since the moment we landed in Neverland. Like I was, till this day, chasing something only to reach a dead end every time.

Not anymore.

Cole was waiting for me to snap back to reality. His gaze was fixed on the road, but I could tell his attention kept flicking over to me.

'What's the story?' I murmured.

He launched into his explanation. 'Our fathers were friends in university. After graduation, they set out to be business partners—Wonder City was their dream. But then your father married your mother, and she fell sick soon after. Postpartum psychosis. Your dad pulled out of the partnership to take care of her, but my dad kept persuading him to return to the venture.' We came to a stoplight. 'My dad resented your mother for holding him back, and I think the feeling was mutual.'

It was. I remembered how she always regarded him with a narrowed stare, and in the height of her psychosis would call him a villain, a clear-cut storybook character who thwarted the hero every step of the way in his quest.

'My dad had almost convinced your dad,' Cole went on, still with that cold, detached fury. 'They almost left together to attend a meeting with the board. Not for good, of course. But your mother was distraught.'

We turned into a slip road that took us down a lane lined with neat rows of well-tended houses. As we ventured deeper into the estate, the houses appeared more ramshackle, their walls stained with rain. Wild blooms grew where before there were trimmed hedges and freshly mowed front yards.

'And then?' I prompted.

'And then she took you and left.' A crease appeared between his brows.

'You don't think that was it.'

'I think he knows more about your mother's accident than he let on.'

By now, I knew where Cole was taking me. I had barely been able to remember my old house, much less find my way there. But now that we were weaving back to the past, everything around me grew familiar again, as though the memories were right where I left them, guiding me home.

'He said it was here . . .' Cole muttered, slowing down as he contemplated the houses.

'It's further down, after the frangipani tree.'

Cole glanced at me. 'You remember?'

'I'm starting to,' I said, watching a couple of kids cycle past us.

We came to a stop after the tree. Cole parked under the shade along the kerb, then killed the engine.

'He's still living here,' he said. 'Moved back a few years after the accident, though he cut off contact with almost everyone.'

My father had been right here all this while. I could have found him if I had remembered anything about that day. Just like he could have found me if he had bothered to return to the last place he had left me.

I got out of the car and ventured towards the house. The gate was unlocked, as though the owner had nothing to lose by leaving it open.

Nothing had changed, yet everything had. The house was preserved as carefully as the pages of a worn book, but it was a much lesser version of itself. The yellow walls and red letterbox out front needed a new coat of paint, and the overgrown yard needed tending. Weeds had taken the place of the geraniums and hibiscus, and the fence was speckled with rust.

'Hello?' My heart thrummed inside me as I pushed the gate open. 'Anybody home?' No answer. I took a step in.

Behind me, Cole said, 'Gemma, maybe we should . . .' He glanced over his shoulder and froze.

Then I saw him. He stood at the end of the lane, watching us. His outfit made him look at odds with his living environment, as if he had wandered into this half-forgotten wilderness from a board meeting. I remembered how his shirts used to smell of cologne and a tinge of Mum's turpentine.

Even from a distance, I recognized his eyes right away. His face, now lined and worn, reminded me of tree rings, but his eyes remained the same. They were the eyes that smiled whenever he took me out for pancakes or watched my mother read me a story.

I wondered if *I* was anything like he remembered. Did he even recognize me?

My breaths rattled shallow and hard, but my body had fallen so still that it felt like the world was spinning around me.

He didn't come any closer, just stood there waiting for my move.

My voice quivered when I spoke. 'Cole. Tell me I'm not dreaming.'

'You're not dreaming.'

'Pinch me.'

'What? I'm not going to pinch you.'

'Just do it,' I hissed.

He did.

'Ow.' I rubbed my arm half-heartedly. 'What should I do?'

'Say something before he leaves.'

'Dad!' I blurted.

The word sounded foreign coming from me. I had tried uttering it a few times before—even contemplated calling Boon that—but it felt funny on my tongue, and I stopped after a few attempts.

Now, even when directed at the person it was meant for, it sounded strange to my ears.

In the silence that followed, the air seemed to stretch and fold around us. My heart was a wild, buzzing thing like a forest in Neverland. A bird cried from among the trees, eager for us to move things along.

'Why isn't he saying anything?' I hissed to Cole.

Cole raised his hands and declared, 'We're not burglars.'

My father continued staring at me. Any minute now, I might crack under the weight of his gaze.

'Gem—Gemma?' he said. My name sounded just as foreign coming from him.

I had imagined a million ways this moment would play out, but nothing could prepare me for what he actually did.

He turned tail and ran.

Cole nudged me. 'What are you still standing here for?'

But my legs remained where they were.

'That was my dad, Cole.' That fact blocked out every other thought in my mind. 'My dad,' I said again.

It felt unceremonious, the way he just appeared at the end of the lane. He should have entered with some kind of soundtrack, or the universe should have sent a sign this morning to prepare me for this moment. I shouldn't have been caught off guard like that. I had an entire speech prepared. I was ready. I *would* have been ready if he hadn't just shown up like that.

Cole let out an exasperated sigh and gave chase, but I stayed rooted to the ground.

All this time, he had been here. All this time, we could have found each other. Instead, we had let those years pass us by, each hiding in the last place we felt safe in.

No. *I* had tried. I had made the effort. I had spent years searching for him only to find him now, fleeing at the first sign of discomfort. *He* had chosen to remain out of reach.

Why had I been the only one holding on all this time, believing that we could still be a family again, when my father had given up on us—on me—a long time ago?

Ten years hadn't been enough to change his mind, and ten minutes here definitely wasn't going to. But I would be the biggest idiot if I let this moment go by just like that.

Laura and Cole and everyone else could call me a fool, but it wasn't hope that spurred me on now. Rage was good; it made me feel stronger than I really was, and kicked me into action.

I raced down the lane.

Twenty-Five

Cole

Going after Joseph Young gave me something to focus on other than the look on Gemma's face, even though it was all I could think of as I gave chase.

The sight of him scurrying away made me angrier. What kind of coward did that?

'*Hey*,' I called. When he didn't stop—didn't even turn around—I sped up and overtook him, then planted myself in front of him and held him by the shoulders.

He flung my arms off. 'What do you want?'

'I want you to stop thinking about just yourself for one second and go talk to your daughter. She's still waiting for you. She's been waiting for years.'

'She was not supposed to find me here. She was supposed to have forgotten what happened over time.'

'She was eight,' I snapped. 'Pretty hard for her to forget her parents, even if she managed to block out some unpleasant memories. So you were just going to hide out here forever, hoping that she'll never remember you?'

'It's for the best.' He sounded like he had just about convinced himself.

'For whom, exactly?'

'For both of us.'

'Wrong. This arrangement only works in your favour, because then you won't have to face her. You won't have to account for dumping her at an amusement park when she was a kid.'

'You seem very concerned about my daughter.'

'Her business is my business.'

A beat passed as recognition slipped into his gaze. 'You're Lionel's son.' I gave him neither affirmation nor denial. 'Look, I'm not—this isn't going to be some big teary reunion. I lost her the day I left her behind, and I don't expect to have her back.'

'Funny how it all seems to be about you.'

'How is she?'

'I didn't think you gave a shit.'

His jaw tightened. 'I don't. As far as I'm concerned, my daughter's dead.'

He turned to leave, only to find Gemma standing not two metres away from us, her stony gaze fixed on her father.

'I had dreamt of every possible scenario where I might see you again,' she said. 'I believed that the moment would make the entire wait worth it. It was the only thing I wouldn't give up on.'

Joseph's gaze fell to the ground. 'Things don't always turn out the way we want them to, Gemma,' he said quietly. 'The sooner you understand that, the less disappointed you'll be.'

Before Gemma could reply, Joseph edged past me down the lane. I was about to go after him again, but Gemma reached out for my arm.

'Let him go,' she said quietly.

'You've been hunting him down for ages and now you're just going to let him go?'

'Didn't you hear what he said? There's no point anymore.'

'That's because he's an idiot who doesn't know how to deal with his feelings.' There was that look on her face again. It made me want to spring into action just so I didn't have to see it. 'No, I'm getting him back.'

'I said let him go.'

I relented. We stood there in silence, watching as Joseph got into his car and fled.

'So, what now?' I said once we were alone again.

'Now, nothing.' She turned and walked away stiffly.

I fell into step with her. 'He'll come around.' Even I didn't believe myself.

'Whatever.'

'Hey, you're the one who's supposed to be all unicorns and candy floss. I'm cynical enough for both of us,' I said.

Her silence was flinty.

'You don't have to hold back if you can't,' I went on. 'I promise not to say anything about this. You have every right to be upset. The guy's a—'

Her sneakers squeaked as she came to a halt. She whirled around to glare at me. 'I'm not going to cry. I'm going to get my father back. I didn't wait all this time for him just to watch him walk away from me.' She drew in a long shaky breath, her eyes daring me to contradict her.

I said nothing and reached for her instead, pulling her to me.

She didn't react immediately, nor did she resist, even when I wrapped my arms around her.

'I told you,' I said. 'You don't have to hold it in if you can't.'

She gave in slowly, warily. I held her tightly. Then, as she sobbed in my arms, I held her even tighter. Later, we would pretend none of this had ever happened. But for now, she let me gather all her pieces and hold her together.

At last, she pulled away and dragged a hand across her face. 'This was not how I planned for it to go.'

'Well, you know what they say about the best-laid plans.' I squeezed her hand. 'He shouldn't have left you behind. Not then, not now.'

'He's not a bad person,' she insisted. 'He was just really sad because of my mum. Sometimes, grief can drive you to do things you don't mean.' She turned and headed back down the path to the house before I could refute that.

'Uh, I think we're going that way?' I called, jabbing a thumb over my shoulder.

'He'll be back,' she replied without turning around.

I stayed where I was. 'Are you serious?'

Her footsteps didn't falter. 'He can't hide from me forever.'

There was no talking her out of this. I stepped back through the gates and headed into the house after her.

It wasn't a shabby space, although the leather sofa was cracked and the TV console was coated with a light film of dust. Like the front yard, the house toed the line between quaint and ramshackle, as though the owner was trying his best to preserve the house in its original state.

Gemma wandered through the living room, surveying each item—the stack of bills on the coffee table, the downturned photograph of the family on the mantle that she waved at me with no little amount of smugness, as though it were proof of the person her father was.

The fridge was bare, save for a few cans of beer and a jar of jam. Gemma slipped through the screen door into the backyard, treading with the reverence of someone visiting a museum. I tried picturing her spending her days out here, trailing mud from the garden after traipsing through Neverland.

She stared up at the sky, as though Peter Pan might come swooping down any second. Her eyes had filled up with tears. She was beginning to remember.

A text message made her jump. She glanced at her phone, then turned it off and slipped it back into her pocket as she headed up the stairs. I followed her, pausing only to check a text message that had come in from Thomas.

Where are you guys?

G's old house. Met her father, I replied.

We came to a room with pale yellow walls and gauzy curtains that did little to keep the afternoon sunlight out. Dust motes floated around her as she stepped in.

'She would paint here,' she murmured, partly to herself. 'Once, she was so lost in her work that she didn't notice I had climbed out of my playpen. She never let me out of her sight after that. She said if either of us got lost, we would always find each other in Neverland.' She sent me a sad smile. 'She didn't say where exactly in Neverland, and I think that was the whole problem.'

'Neverland isn't real,' I said, as gently as I could. 'You lost her because she was sick.'

She ignored me, going over to the easel by the window. A thick green cloth sat atop it, and a plume of dust exploded in our faces when she pulled off the cloth. Gemma coughed.

When the dust settled, we saw what Joseph Young had been trying to protect all this while: a stack of paintings preserved with varnish, their colours leaping off the page as though they had just been painted yesterday. It was Neverland portrayed in the most painstaking detail, from the cocktail birds to the jade-green lagoons, the fairies' iridescent gossamer wings to the Lost Boys' paint-streaked faces.

To Gemma's mother, Neverland wasn't just a storied place; it was an entire world that she had immortalized with her art.

Gemma laid out each painting on the ground and sank to the ground before them. She stared at them intently, as though listening to the story they were telling her.

Based on her mother's descriptions of Captain Hook, Gemma expected to see a scarred, ragged man with hatred in his eyes and vengeance in his hand. But all she saw was a tall, slim man in a long, dark coat. His face was set in an eerie, unreadable calm that reminded her of Cole's father.

'I must say, you children got much further than I ever thought you would.' He shook his head. 'Storm was a fool for aiding you in your quest and thinking he can save this place.'

'We just might succeed. Storm believed in us,' Gemma said.

'You will never find the key.'

'Watch us,' Cole snarled.

Hook sent Cole a pitying look. 'There is no key, silly boy. There never was. It's just something Peter Pan made up to fool the Council and Neverlanders to make them believe they're safe.'

'Peter wouldn't,' Kittern snapped.

'On the contrary, he would and he did. He's a liar, always has been and always will be. Didn't he promise to always be here for Neverland? Yet, strangely, he's nowhere to be found when Neverland needs him most.'

None of them could find a retort for that.

'Then what's in the cave that's got you chasing us all over?' Cole demanded.

Hook's smile curved up his face. 'You.'

Nix flitted over to Hook's side and perched on his left shoulder, away from the gleaming hook on his right hand.

'Thank you, Nix,' Hook said. 'You were a tremendous help.'

Gemma gasped. 'Nix! How could you?'

Shame flickered past the fairy's face before she pushed it aside. 'Peter Pan abandoned us. He had lied to us all this time about the key, he failed to protect us. The Otherworlders come here and destroy the place before shaking off the fairy dust and returning to their world. Neverland is dying and it's all because of them.'

'So you decided to join Hook?'

'Captain Hook, mind you,' Hook said, waving his right arm at her. Gemma did not flinch.

'We've got a better chance fighting those Otherworlders than keeping them out with an imaginary key,' Nix said.

'Otherworlders,' Gemma repeated. 'You mean us?'

'No, not you . . .'

'Now, now,' Hook said. 'Don't let sentimentality cloud your judgement, Nix—'

A distant rumble cut him off. It shook the walls of the cave and made the turquoise-coloured pools tremble at their feet. The sound of rushing water grew louder. A hiss echoed through the winding passages behind them as the ceiling let out a loud crack.

Rocks and stones rained down on them, forcing them to duck for cover. A large shadow loomed over them, revealing a giant monstrous body that glided through the tunnel at astonishing speed.

'The serpent!' Kittern gasped. Meerka clamped a hand against his mouth. Gemma reached around for Cole's hand, and they pressed as close to the slick, craggy walls as they could.

'You really shouldn't have slaughtered that mermaid, Hook,' Nix said, lifting herself off the pirate's shoulder. 'Now her blood is on your hands. The Serpent is coming for you.' To the children, she cried, 'Run!'

They ran, crashing clumsily across pools of water in the rocky ground. The monster was enormous, but it was also blind, relying only on its sense of hearing to navigate through the passages. Its horrific shriek pierced the air, making the ground and ceiling rumble.

When the sea serpent let out another unearthly cry that shook the walls of the cave, Gemma almost keeled over, but Cole pulled her through the narrowest passage, dodging the monster's spear-like fangs just as they grazed her ankle. The serpent might not be after them, but it had been affronted and was ready to unleash its fury on any of them. Nobody killed its mermaid warriors without suffering its wrath.

Meanwhile, Kittern and Meerka were cornered in a nook of the cave with Captain Hook. They watched with bated breath as the serpent's great body slithered past, its girth filling up practically the entire passage.

Suddenly, Kittern let out a piercing whistle and the beast came to a stop.

Hook clamped a hand over Kittern's mouth, but it was too late. 'You're going to get us all killed!' he hissed.

'No, Hook,' Kittern said. 'Only you have the mermaids' blood on your hands. I'm just going to get you killed.'

Hook drew his arm, ready to sever the boy's head with his right hook. 'You Lost Children have always been a pesky, interfering bunch,' he snarled. 'I'd be doing Neverland a service by killing you.'

Meerka crashed into him, fending off his weapon. The serpent doubled back for them, lunging for the bloodstained overcoat Hook was scrambling to slip off.

'No!' Gemma cried.

She was about to burst out of her hiding spot when Cole yanked her back. 'Let the monster finish the job!'

'I need Hook to tell me where my mother is!' She plucked out the knife Cole had stashed in his belt and dove into the fray, too quick for Cole to stop her. Before she could hesitate, she plunged the knife into the serpent's side.

Its scream was horrific, ripping the air and making them dizzy. Gemma withdrew the knife, then ducked back into the shadows with Cole as the cave walls hailed down on them. The monster thrashed and wailed, snapping uselessly at the air.

When she spotted Hook scrambling to escape, Gemma abandoned all caution and gave chase, ducking out of the serpent's range and almost getting crushed under its slick body.

Nix flitted into view. 'This way!' she called. Gemma followed the fairy.

Behind her, Cole was yelling for her to come back, but there this was the only chance she had. She could not let Hook escape.

Leaving the chaos behind, she burrowed into one of the tunnels after Hook, relying on Nix's fairy light to find her way.

When at last they arrived at a bottleneck and Hook whipped around with his weapon at the ready, Gemma pounced on him. 'Where is he?' she screamed.

Hook only laughed. His teeth were bloody from the earlier scuffle and his eyes held a manic gleam. Gemma had to quell the frightening urge to beat him senseless with one of the rocks lying around. Nix flitted before her face, as though sensing what she was contemplating. Gemma batted her away impatiently.

'I've had her sentenced,' Hook said. 'She's probably walking the plank as we speak. You will never see your mother again.'

A chill slipped down to Gemma's fingertips, making her loosen her grip on Hook's shirt. 'We need to get to Hook's ship,' she said.

The statement wasn't meant for Nix. Gemma had expected Cole to respond, but there was only silence aside from Hook's manic laughter. She glanced around and found no one coming through the gloom for her.

'Cole?' she called.

But she was all alone in the tunnel now—with the true monster who haunted her dreams.

Twenty-Six

Gemma

It was a long time before Cole picked me up from the floor, where I sat among my mother's paintings, lost in my memories. The chill that slipped down my spine was real, as was the fear in my racing heart. I could still hear the sea serpent's scream, the voices echoing in the cave.

It was hard to tell how much time had passed since we broke into the house. But even as the light outside faded, there was still no sign of my father.

Cole tugged on my elbow gently. 'Gemma, let's go. We can come back tomorrow.'

'He'll be back by tonight,' I said with more certainty than I felt.

'You're going to wait here the whole night?'

I perched on the window ledge and stared out the window, watching the sparsely lit lane for any sign of him. Cole sighed and sat at the foot of the reading nook before me.

'You can leave,' I said. 'I'll be fine on my own here.'

But he remained where he was and pulled out a magazine from the bookshelf behind him. For a while, there was only the sound of him flipping through the pages. I could tell he wasn't really reading, but I wasn't in the mood to talk either.

The stack of paintings sat on the easel next to me, glossy, perfect, and frozen in time. It disguised all the ugliness underneath like our memories often did.

For the longest time, thoughts of Neverland and my mother and Peter Pan had comforted me; I had believed that as long as I held on to them, I would still exist. But the paintings had filled in the gaps, and I now saw everything else that had been masked by the golden glow of Neverland. How sick my mother had really been, how it broke my father's heart, how her illness ate away at us until we became sad, dry husks adrift on a sea of longing.

I remembered Cole's father, who glared at me and my mother as though we had stolen something from him, as though we were the poison in my father's life—and maybe we were.

I remembered the treacherous Neverland adventure Cole and I had embarked on together.

I remembered the Council, Captain Storm and his ragtag crew, Captain Hook, the mermaids, the sea serpent, the Lost Children, and Nix.

But the story got cut off where I was trapped with Nix and Hook in the cave, in Old Limestone's belly. It seemed vital that I remembered what happened next, but all I got for my efforts was another pounding headache.

Cole glanced up at me as he absently turned another page. He had to be hungry by now, but he only said, 'If it hurts so much to remember, then maybe you should take it slow.'

'I don't care if Neverland wasn't real—'

'Isn't,' he corrected.

'The fact is, I left her behind. I was starting to grow out of that place. I was starting to hate it. It grew uglier and uglier by the day, and I was losing faith in Peter Pan.'

He set down the magazine and straightened. 'You know why we had to leave, didn't you?'

I shook my head.

'Because there was no more room left in Neverland for all the Lost Children in the world, the ones who still believed and the ones who refused to grow up. We had no choice but to leave, so it wasn't your fault you had to leave her behind.'

He didn't get it. Whether or not I *had* to was beside the point; the fact is, I left. Even though I grew to realize Neverland wasn't real, I was the only one who understood that place, and I had left her there alone in the end.

'I'm sorry,' I said.

He frowned. 'For what?'

'I left you behind in Neverland too.'

'Gemma.' His voice was unbearably soft, like he was careful not to shatter the obsidian night that contained us. 'It was just a story.'

'I don't think I've said this before, but . . . I'm glad I found you again.'

He broke into a smile like the one he gave me years ago, when I said I'd take him to Neverland. 'You and I both.'

He leaned closer, close enough for me to catch a whiff of the woody musk lingering on him. My heart raced in anticipation of what he was about to do, and I found myself inching closer in return. He pushed himself up to meet me.

When our lips found each other, I was surprised at how natural it felt, as though our story had come full circle and we had finally arrived where we were meant to. The spinning in my head wasn't the starry-eyed adoration I had for Thomas, but something that wound deeper and shook me from within in the most exhilarating way. Cole wasn't an escape; he wasn't a dream. He was solid ground, and it was a relief to find my footing again.

Sometime during the night, we fell asleep. It was only when Cole shook me awake that I realized it was completely dark outside. Cole handed me his cell phone, his face grim. 'Thomas,' he mouthed.

'Thomas?' I said into the phone.

Thomas let out a sigh that sounded like relief. 'Gemma, where exactly are you?'

'My old house. Cole brought me here. Thomas, I found my—'

'Come back quick.' Something wasn't right. His voice was tight with panic, and Thomas *never* panicked.

'Thomas,' I said, struggling to keep my voice steady. 'What is it?'

'It's Jo.' My stomach twisted. 'She's sick.'

She was eight. A milestone, her mother claimed. 'My baby girl is growing up so fast.'

'Will I be too old for Neverland?' Gemma asked.

'You will never be too old for Neverland unless you stop believing in it.'

She took Gemma to the Wild Ride amusement park that day, just the two of them. The amusement park had just acquired a new ride that was inspired by the scene where Peter Pan and the Darling children flew to Neverland.

Gemma's father had spent the night at the office. Ever since that last visit from Uncle Lionel, he had been lost in his own head, going around with a pinched look on his face and barely paying any attention to Gemma. Her parents were still being painfully polite to each other, giving each other enough space to fit two Gemmas in between.

The night before the trip to the Wild Ride, Gemma hovered outside her father's office. He was not alone—she heard his voice and Uncle Lionel's through the door and pressed close to listen.

'I'm still considering, okay?' her father said.

'The flight is—'

'Yes, Lionel, I'm aware that the flight's tomorrow. But you're asking me to leave my family behind for three months without warning. What's going to happen to them if I'm gone?'

He was leaving. It had come to this at last. Gemma had seen her father sad and absent for months, putting up a credible performance in front of her and her mother, and she had wondered when he would eventually tire of all this.

Should she tell her mother? A part of her didn't quite believe that he would go through with it, or that he would really leave them.

So, even when she and her mother left for the Wild Ride the next day without her father, Gemma kept mum on what she had overheard.

They left early in the morning after breakfast.

'But what about Daddy?' Gemma ventured as they boarded the bus.

'He said he'll join us later,' her mother replied. 'So it's just us girls for the morning.'

But as the day wore on and even after they had gone on all the rides—thrice on the Peter Pan one—there was still no sign of her father.

While her mother had been giddy with the prospect of freedom after weeks of 'soft confinement', she grew more and more anxious the longer she stayed out.

'We should have—no, he promised he'll be here,' she murmured to herself. 'We should wait for Joe . . .'

Gemma recognized the signs—her mother's eyes had grown wider, intent but unfocused, and her sentences came in starts and stops, as though her thoughts were jostling one another for centre stage.

Stupid! Gemma mentally chided herself. Why didn't she make sure her mother had taken her medicine before coming out today? She had been so desperate to convince herself that everything was okay—that her father wasn't leaving and her mother was getting better—that she hadn't allowed herself to consider the terrible alternative.

The amusement park suddenly felt like a scary place, filled with strangers she couldn't turn to for help. It was just her and her mother, and the disease in her mother's mind that threatened to swallow them both.

Gemma laid a hand on her mother's arm. 'Mummy, maybe we should sit down somewhere.'

'He said he'll be here,' her mother murmured. She reached in her purse for her cell phone but started scrambling when she realized it wasn't there. 'I put it in here last night, I swear . . .' Her hands shook harder with every passing second, and she barely noticed when Gemma dragged her to one of the shaded benches by the bumper car ring and sat her down.

Gemma watched the people passing by and wondered if they noticed anything amiss, if her mother's sickness cast a tell-tale pallor over them. At eight, she now knew the kinds of things people whispered behind her back, the fear and disgust and pity the kids and teachers at school regarded her with.

'Someone stole my phone,' her mother said. Her face was pinched with distress. How had her mood escalated so quickly in mere minutes? Gemma's heart started drumming. She had to stop this now. 'It has to be Lionel. He came by last night . . .'

'Mummy,' she pleaded. 'Let's go on the Peter Pan ride—'

The roller coaster ride nearby cut her off with a sudden roar and screams from the ride-goers. Her mother flinched and bit her lip, her eyes darting around as her hands continued groping for her phone. A sheen of sweat had formed on her forehead.

'Mummy,' Gemma said, in a voice quiet enough that she hoped her mother might miss. 'Daddy's not coming. I heard him last night.'

Her mother froze. 'I knew it. I knew it! Hook's got him. He's going to come for us next.'

'No, Mummy,' Gemma said, not bothering to disguise her misery anymore. 'There's no Hook. It's just Uncle Lionel.'

But her mother wasn't listening to her. She leapt to her feet, knocking Gemma's cup of sweet corn to the ground. Gemma barely had time to react before her mother ran out from under the orange umbrella and back into the blinding sunlight.

Gemma gave chase.

'Mummy! Come back, please!' she screamed, wending through the crowd after her. Her heartbeat reached a deafening crescendo, a relentless drumming that drowned out the noise of the amusement park. All she needed to hear was the one voice that mattered. 'What's the story? What's the story, Mummy?'

She didn't realize when she had started to cry, but her tears soon made her lose sight of her mother's receding back.

'Mummy, please! Tell me the story,' Gemma cried, ignoring the stares from everyone. As long as she was telling her the story, Gemma had time.

Her mother came to a stop at last. 'He's killed Peter.' Her voice broke on his name. 'He's killed Peter, and now he's making me walk the plank.' Her eyes shone bright and wild like a cornered animal's. 'Peter's dead, and I don't know how to get back.'

* * *

There was nowhere else to run. In the tight airless corner of the cave, even breathing became a laborious task.

But Gemma ran. She ran like the wind, faster than she ever had. She ran for her life, her life and her mother's. Time was running out. She felt it most keenly now, when the distance between her and Hook's ship seemed impossible to cover.

Beyond the passage, there was no one else around but the sea serpent, now squirming in its growing pool of blood. Cole and the Lost Children must have maimed it further before fleeing.

Gemma waded through the crimson tide, careful to keep a wide berth from the beast. But just as Hook emerged from the mouth of the passage, the serpent snapped its jaws, intent on taking its last shot at the brazen pirate. It finished off Hook in one bite, but almost immediately began thrashing again. A gash appeared halfway down its neck from within, revealing a sliver of the gleaming hook, now slick with blood.

Gemma continued running, not sparing a glance backwards. All she wanted was to leave this savage place behind, find her mother and flee Neverland for good.

* * *

This game of make-believe had stopped being fun. Gemma saw now what a terrifying place Neverland was. It lured you in and ate you up until there was nothing left of you in the real world. It took the hardiest, staunchest believer to truly survive Neverland, and it was a lonely place to be.

Even now as she ran after her mother, Gemma didn't quite understand the story. All she gathered was that her mother was walking the plank. Any minute now, she would throw herself into the choppy depths of the sea and be lost to her forever. Hook might be dead, but her mother's fear and hatred for him was inextinguishable.

'Mummy, stop please!' Gemma cried. People around made way for them, turning to stare at the little girl with the tear-streaked face chasing after her equally distraught mother.

They came to the pier at the edge of the seaside amusement park. Gemma's heart filled with dread as her mother continued in that direction.

Surely she wouldn't? The afternoon heat had driven most people in search of shelter, so the pier was mostly empty even though the cafés lining the boardwalk were packed.

Gemma's mother ran, unobstructed, towards the end of the dock. Before Gemma could scream for her to stop, she leapt off the edge, her slight frame tumbling into the water.

The beating in Gemma's ears reached a deafening pitch. People shouted from the pier, shouted around her, but Gemma ignored them all, squeezing through the railings and diving in after her mother.

The water was much deeper than she expected. Its brackish taste made her gag right away. She flailed, struggling to stay afloat, but she was powerless against the waves. Her mother was nowhere in sight.

'Mummy!' Her screams were soon cut off as another wave washed over her. The water was dragging her out to sea. She gulped down a mouthful of water and went under again.

The story wasn't over yet. It couldn't be over. In fairy tales, she would succeed in defeating the villain with her trusty sidekick and save her mother. They would return, triumphant, to the glorious kingdom they helped restore.

But the story of Peter Pan was never a fairy tale—in fact, Gemma had found the ending kind of sad when she first heard it. And even in her own Neverland chronicle, the ending wasn't quite what she had hoped for.

More onlookers gathered around the edge of the pier, yelling and pointing. Gemma's world was starting to fade into a blur of cold water, her mother's voice, and her own frantic, shallow breaths. Sunlight narrowed to a pinprick. When the sea claimed her eventually, she could barely muster the energy to fight.

But then a figure appeared. A boy-shaped shadow, floating in the sky. Against the sun, his features were indiscernible. Peter, *she mouthed. Air bubbles trailed to the surface, which now seemed so far away.*

How cruel that he should appear only now when her story was ending. She had failed, in both her missions to save Neverland and her mother. And Peter had been of no help at all.

But even as she prepared to give in, even as a man cupped her chin and hauled her out of the water and further away from her mother, even as he laid her on the baking boardwalk and people crowded around her and her rescuer roared at them to please *give them some space*, even when someone pumped her chest and made her cough up water, Gemma clung on to her last hope of saving her mother.

What's the story, Mummy? Tell me the story, please. She might even have said that aloud.

'I think she might be in shock, Boon,' said a woman—not her mother.

Where was her mother? Had she found her way back? Gemma tried to sit up, and the man— Boon?—propped her up.

'What's your name?' he asked. His voice was low, gentle, and he had lines around his eyes that made it seem like he was smiling at her even though his face was pinched with concern.

'Gemma,' she rasped.

'How old are you?'

'Eight. Today's my birthday.' And she started to cry.

Today was supposed to be a milestone. Her mother had said so.

* * *

Her father came to collect her at the hospital. Gemma could tell he had been crying, and the sight of his pinched face and red-rimmed eyes made her break into fresh sobs as she reached out for him.

They held on to each other, trying hard to fill the space between them. Her father didn't tell her that it was okay or that everything would be fine, and Gemma knew everything had changed. Everything had changed, and she was to blame.

They let her go home the next day. Her father barely said a word to her, even as he went about the funeral preparation. It seemed like he was slowly being eaten away from the inside, and Gemma was powerless against the creature that had made its home inside him. Uncle Lionel called once, but her father turned off his cell phone after seeing the name on the screen.

Gemma tried, on more than one occasion, to talk to her father, but stopped after he responded with a blank stare that terrified her with its abject emptiness. He must hate her for what she had done. Hadn't he always warned them that Neverland was not a safe place? And hadn't they always defied his warnings to stay away?

I'm sorry, Daddy. I'm sorry. If only he could hear her again, that was what she would say. But a terrible silence had settled upon the yellow house, and even the flowers in the yard had begun to wilt, folding up their browned petals for good.

Overnight, they had both lost their voices and there were no more stories left to tell.

Twenty-Seven

Gemma

What's the story? What's the story now? I recognized the panic in my gut, the fear of losing someone I couldn't afford to lose.

In the mad dash to the hospital, everything came rushing back fast and furious. The clamour of my memories filled my ears, drowning out everything else. Behind the wheel, Cole kept glancing at me, but I turned to look out the window, barely registering the sight of the world racing past.

It was my fault. Everything had happened because of me. My mother's accident. My father's departure. This was what I had been unable to remember, even though I didn't deserve to forget.

At the hospital, Thomas was sitting on the plastic benches with Cory, Beth, Anika, and Harris from the Wild Ride Bistro. Our footsteps echoed in the hallway, signalling our arrival.

Thomas leapt up from the seat when he saw us. 'Where were you? I called you so many times!'

'How is she?' I said, panting. 'What happened to her?'

'We thought it was just low blood sugar. But it turns out she has a tumour that produced too much insulin.'

My body turned cold. A tumour. That meant this had gone on for a while now, ever since Jo started losing weight and looking sickly.

'Where's Boon?' I asked.

'I told him to get some air outside. We've been waiting for a while.' The accusation sat in his eyes. If only I had picked up my phone earlier. If only I had come when I was called. I was too late yet again.

It was four in the morning, according to the clock on the wall by the vending machines. How long had she been in there? How long had she been sick? How long had they kept this from me?

'She didn't want you to worry,' Thomas said, reading my thoughts.

'But *you* knew?'

'I noticed.'

'How long?'

'Two months.'

'Two months and you didn't tell me?'

'No one expected things to turn out like this.'

'You should've told me anyway!' I was shouting, but I didn't care. Cole squeezed my hand. Beth looked close to bursting into tears, and Cory tightened his arm around her.

Thomas's eyes flashed. 'I'm sorry, but you seemed to be too busy chasing your deadbeat father to care about anything else. Not the amusement park, or Jo and Boon. I had to hold the fort here, keep Jo and Boon updated, and basically manage the whole project while keeping Jo's secret for her.'

I felt a lump growing in my throat and willed myself not to cry. 'That's not fair.'

'No, what's not fair is your obsession with your father. I get that you want to find out the truth and reconnect with him. But there are people in your life who actually care about you, people you seem to have taken for granted just because you think they're always there. Instead of chasing after those who keep turning their backs on you, why don't you pay some attention to those who have never left your side?'

Through the tears in my eyes, Thomas seemed like a completely different person, altered by anger and disappointment. In me. He was disappointed in me. It seemed like all I ever did was let people down.

'I found my dad, Thomas,' I said. It sounded like an excuse, a plea for exoneration.

'I heard.' Cole had clearly filled him in on the meeting with my father. 'You were planning to wait the whole night for him?' I didn't recognize this newfound hostility in Thomas. The edge in his voice scraped like gravel against skin.

'He was bound to come back—'

'Just as he was bound to come looking for you at the Wild Ride one day?'

It was just as well that the Wild Ride was closing. We should never have taken on this revamp project. I should have let go after holding on for so long for nothing.

'We'll have to close the Wild Ride tomorrow,' I said.

Thomas looked at me strangely. 'The contractors are coming tomorrow. We have to be there.'

'Just forget the whole thing! It doesn't matter anymore.'

'You promised Jo and Boon you'll save the amusement park, Gem,' Thomas said. 'Now you're just going to give up?'

'Jo and Boon meant to shut the Wild Ride anyway.'

'Only because Jo's sick! They never wanted to close the place. Don't take your disappointment at the way things ended with your father out on the Wild Ride. It deserves better than this. Jo and Boon deserve better than this.'

Cole stepped forward and laid a hand on Thomas's shoulder. 'Thomas. Calm down.'

Cole had to be hungry and tired after spending the whole day with me, wrapped up in my business. I wanted to ask if he was okay, but every time I looked at him, more questions rose in my head. Not just why he had my mother's cell phone or why he was the one receiving all my messages all these years, but also how Lionel had persuaded my father to leave on the day of the accident. Most importantly, how much of it did Cole know? How much of it had he chosen not to tell me, just like he had kept the truth about my mother?

Boon appeared in the hallway, pulling me back to the present. His eyes were ringed like coffee stains, and I could tell from the look on his face that he had overheard our conversation.

I rushed to him, feeling the comforting weight of his hand as he pulled me close and stroked my hair. 'I'm sorry. I'm so sorry.' I might have said those useless words aloud.

But he only shushed me. 'It's no one's fault, Gem. Things are just the way they are.'

Boon's kindness felt like a knife. I didn't deserve this. He and Jo were too good to have me in their lives. They didn't have to take me in or make me their responsibility. Negligence was my thing—it had led to my mother's demise and now it was leading to Jo's. There was always so much more I could have done but didn't. There was a wrongness living inside me, one that made me selfish and blind.

Thomas was right. Who would have thought that he would be the one to dole out the truth? Not Cole, who was busy protecting me from disappointment even as he helped me remember, but Thomas, whose words did irreversible damage. Damage I deserved.

I lost myself in Boon's arms, sobbing. Soon, the voices around me—Cole's low murmur, Boon's gentle shushing—melted away into the sweet cries of Neverland. The songbirds' lilting melody and the Lost Children's laughter chased me further and deeper in. I could see the water glistening off the mermaids' jewelled scales again; it was impossible to look away. Wherever I went, the lure of Neverland was undeniable. It was a place that promised happy endings, a place removed from blame or guilt or grief.

Everyone deserved to go to Neverland. It was as real as the scab on their wounds, the cuts and scrapes and bruises on their skin, and the sound of their own laughter. It was as real as the corner they curled up in, the warm whisper in their ear. It was as real as we wanted it to be, and it was the only place that would always have us.

I didn't realize that I had pulled free until I felt my feet pounding in tandem with my heartbeat, racing—fervently, inexorably—towards that fabled paradise. Voices swam around me, muffled and distorted like I was underwater.

Just get there. Just get there and everything will be okay. The noise will stop. The pain will stop. It was the only thought I clung to as I fled.

Twenty-Eight

Cole

There were gates to Neverland.

Despite how easy it was for Otherworlders to discover the place, it wasn't as easy to break in. There were walls to scale and hurdles that were near impossible to cross. And the road to Gemma's Neverland was riddled with them. She was the one who had given me access, after all, so she could just as easily play gatekeeper and shut me out like she was doing now.

But it wasn't just me she was pushing away. It was Boon, Thomas, and everyone else who fed her guilt and that voice in her head, the one blaming her for everything that had happened. The last thing she needed was to retreat into Neverland again just so she didn't have to face the real world.

I shoved Thomas in the chest. 'You really think that was necessary? Don't you think she feels guilty enough? This isn't just about Jo. She blames herself for what happened to her mum too. She doesn't need you giving her grief about this right now.'

'It's not fair for Jo and Boon either.'

Boon laid a hand on his shoulder. 'What's fair or not is not important. Jo's illness isn't fair. Gemma being abandoned by her father isn't fair. Her mother's accident wasn't fair either. Nor is it fair that you're left to hold the fort while Gemma gets reacquainted with her father.'

'I just thought it needed to be said,' Thomas muttered, staring at the hallway where Gemma had fled.

'Time and place, man,' I said. Thomas started to give chase, but I held him back. 'I'll go. You stay with Boon.'

Boon gripped my shoulder. The weight of his hand was as heavy as his gaze. 'Please. Find her.'

I knew he didn't just mean pinning down her whereabouts. But I wasn't sure I was able to reach her in Neverland anymore. It felt like all these years of waiting for her had built up to this moment, and now that I was this close to finding her, I was denied access to the place she believed so wholeheartedly in.

But I raced down the hallway all the same, pulling out my cell phone as I wove out of the hospital into the vast, empty night. He had to have known this would happen eventually when he gave me his number.

He picked up after three rings, his voice bleary with sleep. 'Hello?'

'Doctor York? This is Cole. I need your help.'

It was hard to tell when you had entered Neverland. Some days, you plummeted from the sky. Some days, you emerged from a lagoon. Sometimes you crossed over from waking to dreaming. And sometimes you simply found yourself in it with no warning or inkling of how you ended up there.

Gemma couldn't tell when she had crossed over to Neverland. Once she had left the fluorescent lights and noises and the smell of bleach behind, she found herself in a world far removed from the chaotic one she had been in.

But the sight that greeted her made her realize that she had run from one nightmare straight into another.

Neverland now stood as a whitewashed version of itself. The kingdom was, for once, silent. All their efforts to save it had been futile. There were some maladies that even the stoutest heart couldn't hope to heal, and some battles that even the bravest people could not win.

The cocktail birds had gone into hiding. Grey-green algae coated the once crystal-blue lagoons. Neverland was now a bleak world that had lost its colour and voice.

She saw it now. Neverland was never meant to fit everyone. It took in the stragglers, the ones left behind, and those who needed a place to hide. Eventually, too many tears and fears made a world sick.

Gemma stood alone in the barren clearing that once bloomed with life. Trees reached out for her with their shrivelled arms. A cold wind moaned as it gusted past her, and a deluge of rain left her soaked to the bone.

'Kittern! Meerka! Storm!' she cried.

But the wind threw her cries back at her. The silence was vast and empty, save for the rustle of rain. There was nothing left for her here anymore. Neverland had dissolved, the way dreams often did when stark morning light chased away sleep.

Sands shifted beneath her feet. Gemma couldn't tell when the ground gave way and rendered her airborne. But soon she was falling, dead weight plunging through the air.

It felt all too easy to let gravity take her. It felt right, somehow, that she should fall away with Neverland. She waited for the final rush, the view of the world folding close over her, the taste of oblivion—

She crashed to a stop, caught in a grip that pulled her back to consciousness. Her eyelids flew open.

'I've got you, Gemma,' said a male voice close to her ear, too muffled for her to discern. His body shielded her against the flaying winds.

No! she wanted to scream. Leave me be. But her voice died in her throat, and she let herself be picked up. Her feet found solid ground again as Neverland ebbed away with the glare of street lights.

Maybe that was all Neverland ever was—a dream, now destroyed by the growing realization that it was all inside her head, and that she had never gone anywhere except deeper and deeper into herself.

'I've got you,' the voice said again. And this time, she knew who had found her.

Twenty-Nine

Gemma

Street lights hovered above me, sharpening into focus along with the two figures next to me. Cole's silhouette broke the stream of streetlight, providing some respite from the glare.

Beneath us, cars sped past in a blur of taillights and headlights. The roar of tyres against slick tarred roads echoed through the night. It was still dark, and traffic was sparse. The smell of rain lingered in the air. Everything shimmered like a fever dream.

Cole's arms were wrapped around me, even though we were now safely away from the overhead bridge railing. My body throbbed with the rush of almost falling, my head spun from vertigo.

Neverland. Each time it tried to steal me away, I was powerless against it. How many times had I lost myself to that place and almost never made it out? How many times had I cut myself off from the real world, strayed too far out of its realm?

My breath slowed from shallow rasps to long, shaky sighs. Cole loosened his grip around me but didn't let go. Doctor York stood before me in sweatpants and a T-shirt speckled with rain. It was still drizzling. I flinched at every drop of cold rain that landed on my skin. Cole shielded me against the wind, but he couldn't chase away the lingering traces of Neverland.

'Next time, I suggest you bring a sweater along for a night-time stroll,' Doctor York said, as though running out into the rain in the middle of the night and almost leaping off an overhead bridge was an everyday affair.

'I don't know what's real anymore, doctor.' Rainwater slipped into my mouth. 'One minute I was in Neverland, and the next I'm here.'

He looked me in the eye. 'Our reality is psychologically constructed based on motivations, experiences, what we believe to be true and want to believe in, and many other things. Neverland is real to you because of all the things you have been through and all the things you desire.'

'I believed in that story. I built upon it. I led the Neverlanders to their deaths, and I let my mother die.'

I didn't know what to believe anymore. What if everything I remembered about my mother—about Neverland—was nothing but distorted memories? Who could be sure that our reality was real, and not just a version of the truth polished by time?

The question clawed its way out of me. 'Am I c-crazy? I've been trying so hard to fight it, but now I'm scared I'll turn out like her. What if I let Neverland consume me like she had? What if I get lost there forever too?'

Cole was the one who replied. He gripped my shoulders and fixed his gaze on me. 'Gemma, listen to me. I've been to Neverland. I know it too—probably not as well as you do, but I know it all the same. I know there's a way out of it, just as there is always a way to fall back in.' He grasped my hand and squeezed it. 'Don't go to Neverland without me.'

I didn't fall back in. I *couldn't*, not with him holding on to me so tightly. So I let him pull me out into the cold, wet night, shaking off the vestiges of the dream I had trapped myself in for so long.

It was a Saturday when her father finally spoke to her. Weeks after the accident, there was only the constant ring of silence at home. It followed Gemma everywhere she went, even to the darkest, tightest corners.

Outside, birds kept her company during the day and crickets took over at night, but the silence was unrelenting. She kept seeing her mother everywhere—in her studio, in her room, in the library—a spectre willed into existence by the sheer power of her hope.

Gemma knew her father missed her mother too. He had taken to flipping through old photo albums and lingering on each photo as though they were a book to be read, a song to listen to over and over again. Gemma had just about grown used to his ignoring her—she deserved the silent treatment, after what she had done—until one day he knocked on her door.

She shot up, ready to be on her best behaviour. 'Come in?'

He pushed the door open and hovered in the doorway. 'Gemma, how would you like to go to the Wild Ride?'

How would she! Was that a trick question? Gemma didn't dare to reply immediately. Because why would he bring her to the same amusement park where the accident happened?

'I miss her,' he said. And that was all Gemma needed to hear.

They went to the Wild Ride the next day. Gemma's father packed her bag with an apple and a carton of milk, the way her mother used to before sending her off to school. In the car, they didn't sing along to the songs on the radio like they used to. This clearly wasn't one of their regular trips. Her father kept his gaze fixed on the road the whole way. His determination made Gemma uneasy. What renewed purpose was driving him to do this?

After the accident, the owners of the Wild Ride had fenced up the boardwalk, barring people from going down to the pier. Everything seemed to hum along to its original rhythm, as though nothing tragic had ever happened. Gemma's father didn't let her read or listen to any of the reports about the accident, but she could tell that nothing was ever the same again.

They entered the amusement park unlike other families. Theirs was a sombre return to a nightmare, their wounds still fresh. Gemma still didn't understand why her father wanted to come back here, but she didn't let go of his hand even as they passed by the boardwalk and she desperately wanted to run as far away as possible.

Her father bought her a cup of sweet corn although she wasn't really in the mood for it, and they walked in their bubble of silence—always that silence—to the Peter Pan ride. Her father seemed out of it, barely taking in the noise and laughter around them. It was everything Gemma had grown used to over the past weeks, but something felt different today, as though he was readying himself for something.

She looked up at the carriages spinning in the sky, squinted against the sunlight glinting off the face of the clock tower. She and her mother had taken this ride thrice that day. She looked away, trying to quell the unbearable ache in her heart. There was nothing quite as excruciating as missing someone who was no longer here, and everything in the Wild Ride reminded her of her mother.

'Wait here,' her father said, breaking into her thoughts. 'I'll be back in a bit.'

'When you get back, can we go up the Peter Pan ride?' she asked meekly. All she wanted was to pretend, if only for a moment, that they were all together again.

'Mm,' was all he said before giving her a tight hug and disappearing into the crowd.

Gemma stood at the foot of the ride with her cup of sweet corn and wished more than ever that her mother was there with her. Amusement parks were strange—they teemed with lights and sounds and voices and laughter, but could still make you feel incredibly alone, frozen in your own shoes.

As she waited, Gemma kept up a stream of bargains with the universe, trying with each deal she made to beat down the panic and fear rising in her chest. He'll be back when this ride is over. He'll be back when I finish my corn. He'll be back once the sun sets.

But countless rides started and ended. Her cup of corn had long been devoured. The sky gradually turned into a bruised shade of purple. And still there was no sign of her father.

The crowd grew thinner as the day wore on. Gemma, who had caved in to her lethargy and eventually sat waiting on a nearby bench, emerged from under the umbrella, still holding on to her empty cup of corn. She watched the other children around her, collected in their parents' arms or begging their parents for one last ride. She looked at their tired but blissful faces and tried not to resent them.

She understood at last. This trip to the amusement park wasn't redemption; it wasn't borne out of longing and grief and hope for a new life for the two of them. It was punishment. Her punishment. For her neglect, for believing in Neverland, for being of no help at all when it came to her mother.

She hadn't allowed herself to cry all day, even though she grew tired and hungry and the seed of uncertainty took root in her heart. But as she came to this realization, Gemma could no longer hold back her tears.

He couldn't leave her here. He wouldn't. In all the years of knowing her father, she had never known him to be cruel.

But her father had changed into someone she barely recognized anymore. This stranger that had taken up residence in her father's body was brusque, moody, and absent. Leaving her all alone at an amusement park seemed like the sort of thing he would do.

Gemma didn't know how long she cried. She felt like all the pain and sadness in the world had coagulated inside her. She cried for her mother who had been eaten alive by Neverland, and for her father who had always been an outsider. She cried for Cole and the Lost Children who were stranded in that far-flung kingdom, for Captain Storm and his crew who had died to help her, for all the people real and make-belief, for the friends she had made, and the bedtime story that had grown into something much bigger than she had ever imagined. She cried until she was wrung dry, and all that remained of her was a husk that the wind could sweep away. Another Lost Child for Neverland.

The couple had found her sitting at the foot of the Peter Pan ride, tear-soaked and curled up on a bench, half asleep. The ghost of their voices drifted through her sleep-muddled mind.

'It's her, Boon. It's that little girl who almost drowned. Gemma.' A woman's voice, the same as the one she had heard after being rescued from the sea.

The couple had found a note tucked in the side pocket of Gemma's bag, only six lines long.

To: Boon and Josephine

I cannot thank you enough for saving my little girl. I am now leaving her in your trust as I believe that you will succeed where I have failed. I alone am inadequate in providing her the happiness she deserves. She needs a complete family not taken to flighty delusions or crippling self-doubt. If possible, create a new life for her so she will forget the one she had. Please keep her far, far away from Neverland.

Yours in gratitude,
Joseph Young

'Who does that? Who does that?' Jo said, her voice shaking. She thought it was unfair that while some people like her couldn't have children no matter how hard they tried, others threw theirs away like yesterday's dinner.

'We can't keep her, Jo,' Boon said gently.

'We can adopt her.'

'He probably did this in the heat of the moment.'

'Then we'll keep her until he comes to his senses.'

So they kept her. They kept her without knowing when—or even if— Gemma's father would ever return. They kept her even when she had no recollection of what happened over the past month. They kept her even when she grew older and began asking questions about her parents and taking it upon herself to uncover the truth.

But Neverland wasn't a place they could keep her out of, not when they didn't even understand it themselves. Gemma was a Lost Child given a second home, but Neverland lived inside her, wild and beautiful and deadly like always.

Thirty

Gemma

The night wore on, and it seemed like dawn would never arrive. But first light eventually broke through the relentless night, washing away the last dregs of my memory.

Doctor York gave me and Cole a ride back to the hospital, tired and silent and soaked to the bone. Cole kept me close to him the entire way, but as much as I wanted to draw close to him, something elbowed its way between us.

Neither Cole nor I listened to Boon when he told us to go home, although Thomas complied upon his insistence. Thomas gave my hand a squeeze before leaving, offering a silent apology for his earlier outburst. I squeezed back and shook my head.

'I'll stay,' Cole said, even though he looked more tired than I had ever seen him.

'It's fine. Just go home.' It came out harsher than I intended, and the look in Cole's eyes was unbearable. I hadn't even begun to thank him, and I was already resenting him.

He nodded. 'Keep me posted,' he said before leaving.

The wait continued, now a lot lonelier than before even though the world was rousing. Boon and I leaned against each other on the bench. Weariness settled into my bones, and my eyelids fluttered shut even though my mind was still racing.

'Do you remember when I had a really high fever when I was ten,' I murmured, 'and you and Jo rushed me to the hospital?'

He nodded. 'You kept saying you were okay even though you were hot as a barbeque grill. Halfway there, you started talking about Neverland. It was almost as though you were *there*.'

'Jo always asked me, "What's the story about Neverland?" And she didn't mean the original story. She meant what was going on in my head. But I never dared to tell her, because I was afraid she would get lured in too, the way my mother and I had. And then I would lose her there like I had lost my mother.'

'We didn't mean to hide the truth from you, Gem. We just didn't want to upset you.'

Anger felt like an overdue, petty response now that we were faced with the possibility of losing Jo. Boon and Jo had given me everything they possibly could, and sometimes even more than I expected. Whatever they did, they did with the best intentions—likewise for Thomas.

Cole's words echoed in my head. 'I needed to remember on my own. It's the only way I can come to terms with it.'

'Still, I'm sorry. I've wanted to say that ever since that day.'

'For what?'

'For not being able to save her.' His voice cracked on the last word.

I shook my head. 'It was no one's fault, yours least of all.'

It was close to noon when we finally received news about Jo's condition. She needed to undergo surgery to remove the tumour, but her condition was stable for now.

'She's okay,' I breathed. 'She's okay. She's okay.'

Boon's eyes shone with relief. He took my hand, and I held on to it with both hands like I used to when I was little, as we made our way back to Jo's side.

Thirty-One

Cole

She was beginning to remember everything. I saw it in her eyes. The way she faltered as she reached for my hand or flashed me a small smile, the way she banished me in the hallway. Her guilt, her doubt, I saw them all stacked between us like brick walls.

I had only managed to grab an hour of sleep in the car before Gemma's text woke me up.

She's okay.

This was the first time she had texted *me* at this number, not her mother.

And then: *We need to talk.*

When I got to the Wild Ride in the evening, Thomas was already at the ticketing area, directing the contractors. A one-man show, like he said. It had barely been a month, and aside from Thomas, all of us were losing steam. This project was founded on wild hope and blind faith, after all, and anything that came out of either of those was bound to fall apart eventually.

At half past eight, Gemma stumbled into the ticketing booth, bleary-eyed. She hesitated when I handed her the cup of peppermint tea that I bought for her.

'It's just tea, not lies and bad memories,' I said.

Her eyes flashed upon the reminder. She accepted the tea but launched straight into her interrogation. 'How did you get my mother's cell phone?'

'I found it in my dad's drawer when I was ten. Two years later, I started receiving text messages from a girl named Gemma and I've kept that number ever since.' If the number had expired, if Gemma's mother hadn't been using a prepaid phone card, things would have turned out differently. Gemma's messages wouldn't have been sent through and she might have given up sooner.

'Then how did your dad get my mother's cell phone?' she asked.

I could tell she already had her own theory and was just waiting for me to confirm it. Anything I said now would shake her trust in me. The truth was the best I could offer.

'He took it from her,' I said.

'You mean he stole it.'

She was right. He had stolen Katherine's phone because he didn't want her to distract Joseph and change his mind about joining him in Shanghai. Because he knew that it was impossible to turn off Joseph's phone, so taking Katherine's phone was a way to ensure that she had no way to reach him—that by the time he and Joseph flew off, Joseph would have no way of knowing that Katherine was looking for him.

Yet, as filthy as I thought my father's actions were, I didn't want Gemma to think the same of him. Or brand me as the same villain as him.

'What he did was wrong,' I said. 'But—'

'*Wrong* is an understatement. If he hadn't stolen her phone, she wouldn't have had an episode, and she wouldn't have . . .'

'It wasn't entirely on him, though. Your mother was sick to begin with—'

'Which is why she didn't need the antagonism from your father! And then what, he tried to cover it up and pretend he never did something like that? He thought he could just move on like he hadn't just destroyed someone else's family?'

'It wasn't just your family he destroyed. My mother . . . this is the reason she left.'

Gemma held my gaze, considering whether to fight me over this. At length, she raked a shaky hand through her hair. 'This was a mistake,' she muttered, setting down the cup of tea on the table.

I wasn't sure I wanted to know what she was referring to. But I could feel her slipping away from me already, and that scared me more. I reached for her hand as she turned to leave. 'Gemma, wait.'

'I can't, Cole. I just—can't. This goes beyond you and me.'

'I'm not him.' I hated the plea in my voice.

She shook her head, then headed out of the booth. At the door, the arrival of Thomas and Chelsea made her stop short. They looked like the most unlikely pair, but Thomas nodded at Chelsea and told me, 'Chelsea's looking for you.'

'Hello, stranger,' Chelsea said to me.

Gemma pushed past them and left before any of us could call for her. I watched her race out through the park gates, wishing she would change her mind and turn back. But she didn't.

Chelsea laid a hand on my arm. 'I heard what happened to Gemma's . . .'

'Her name is Jo,' I said.

Gemma had to be going back to that house. She would go back to waiting for her father, waiting for him to spare her a scrap of attention or concern, despite what he had said to her. Nobody spent ten years waiting for someone without developing a stubborn streak.

Chelsea was still talking. 'You see,' she said, 'Wonder Town can help them.'

My gaze snapped back to her. 'Is this what this visit is about?'

'Your dad—'

'I don't want to hear anything about him.' I was done believing his stories and promises. That he could do something as low as steal someone's phone, indirectly cause someone's death, and then pretend like nothing had happened sickened me. I didn't blame Mum for leaving him.

'Chelsea has news,' Thomas said. 'It's about the director of J&K Enterprises.'

I was just about done with this conversation too. Gemma had just pushed everyone away, and it was anybody's guess whom she would turn to now. Someone who chose to dump her at an amusement park and then keep her out of his life. I had no time to lose right now.

'What has the director of J&K Enterprises got to do with *anything*?' It took everything in me to keep my irritation in check.

'It's Joseph Young. Gemma's father. He wants to buy over the Wild Ride too.'

Thirty-Two

Gemma

In a way, I knew this was how things would turn out. Even after all these years, I would still be waiting, wishing, wanting. Pride was something you threw out the window after holding on this long for someone and going through every means to find him.

If my father knew about the things I had done to look for him, would he find me pathetic? I knew Cole did. I saw the sympathy in his eyes whenever he looked at me.

But even now as my memories resurfaced and I finally understood the reason behind my mother's death, there were still gaps to be filled before everything made sense.

Whether he liked it or not, my father was going to give me all the answers. He owed me that much.

Doctor York was infuriatingly analytical about the whole thing when I called him the next day during my afternoon shift. I was beginning to see why my mother used to make fun of him behind his back. Her impressions of him would make me squeal with laughter.

'The reason you weren't able to remember anything about the accident is because you had shut out the guilt and grief,' he said. 'And now that the memories are coming back, you have so much to contend with, you can't think straight. How do you really feel, Gemma? What do you really want?'

Over the phone, the steady rhythm of his breath crackled as he waited. And for the first time since I remembered, I felt that wanting in me. Alive and pulsing like an organ.

'I want . . .'

I wanted none of this to have ever happened. I wanted to go back to Neverland. I was homesick for a place that didn't even exist but somehow filled me up and made me all the things I wanted to be—brave and strong and resourceful. I wanted a solid plan of action, a path that I could take with certainty.

I wanted my father without his sadness, my mother without her all-consuming fantasies and fears. I wanted to know Cole outside of Neverland, to find my Lost self in him, and have him find a piece of himself in me too. I wanted Jo and Boon to have their amusement park for as long as they wanted it. I wanted all the good people to get what they deserved.

But all I said was, 'Wanting doesn't necessarily mean having.'

That sentiment was contested the next moment, however, when my father appeared right before me like a vision I had conjured up. He glanced around at the empty food carts like he had no idea how he had ended up here. He seemed completely out of place in his pressed shirt and leather shoes, but I knew now that all that polish was only disguising the person he was inside.

Did he still remember how the Wild Ride used to look? What would he make of it now, with all its life sapped from it?

'Gemma?' Doctor York called in my ear.

'I'll call you back,' I said, hanging up just as my father spotted me. 'What are you doing here?' I hated the hope in my voice. Even up till now, that hope. I forced myself to stay where I was.

He turned and walked away. 'Scouting out the land.'

He was a stranger. I barely knew him anymore. There were other people worth my attention, my concern. I kept telling myself that, but I found myself tailing him all the same.

'What for? What does this place mean to you?' His footsteps slowed, but he didn't stop. 'Why are you back? You made it clear enough that you don't want me in your life.'

'This place isn't going to last. You need to reconsider your options.'

'What do you mean?'

He surveyed the faded paint on the signs, the lone carts all packed up and chained, the empty spaces where the rides used to be, coming to a stop at the foot of the Peter Pan ride. It made me mad, for some reason. I wanted to show him there was more to the Wild Ride than this, that my life had been perfectly fine without him, that Jo and Boon had given me much more than he ever had.

But there was nothing left here. I had nothing to show him.

'I'm here on behalf of J&K Enterprises,' he said, still in that stiff tone that made me keep my distance. 'To buy over the Wild Ride.'

'What?'

'Joseph & Katherine Enterprises would like to buy over this place. Please consider my proposal. I spoke to Jo and Boon previously, but they said they wanted to take your vote into account too.'

The knowledge that he had been in contact with Jo and Boon all this while but never once sought me out stung.

'Why?' I demanded. 'This place holds nothing but bad memories for you. Why would you—'

He turned to walk away, leaving his answer barely audible. 'Because it's the only way I know how to erase them.'

'You blame me, don't you, for what happened to Mum?' I called after him.

His feet stilled. I remembered how he used to piggyback me when I was little, though his shoulders seemed a lot narrower now. He turned around, instantly betrayed by the tell-tale glimmer in his eyes.

'I don't blame you, Gemma,' he said. 'You were never the one at fault. I blame Lionel. I blame the illness. I blame that stupid Peter Pan story. But most of all, I blame myself. But not you, never you.'

'Then why? Why did you leave me behind?' I swiped away the tears that were starting to well up in my eyes.

'Because you needed someone who was strong enough to pull you out of Neverland, out of that accident. And I'm just *not*.' His voice cracked at the last word.

'I don't need you to be strong. I just need you to be *here*.'

There was nowhere to run now that I had thrown those words out in the open.

His steps were uncertain, careful, as he came closer. 'Why did you keep waiting? I left you. I never once came back for you.'

'*All the world is made of faith, and trust, and pixie dust.*' That felt like reason enough. An involuntary smile slid halfway up his face before the sadness took over again.

'She would have this light in her eyes whenever she talked about that place,' he said. 'It reminded her of *her* mother, did you know?'

I shook my head. I knew nothing about my own parents, much less my grandparents.

'They died just before you were born,' he said. 'It hit your mother hard. She was never the same after that. I think dreaming about Neverland kept her alive, in a way . . . until it killed her.'

The wind sighed in the wake of his revelation, stirring the faded bunting strung between the empty booths behind us. Before us, the Peter Pan ride loomed, a behemoth of a memory that threatened to crush us at its feet. I had spent so many nights and days staring up at it, wishing I could ride it again with my parents, but now I wasn't sure I wanted to anymore.

'Come away with me,' he blurted, his voice urgent now. 'This is what your mother would have wanted—to see us reunited and happy again.'

I let out a snort. 'Just last week, you said that I'm dead to you. Now you're telling me what my mother would have wanted? She probably would have wanted you to be a father instead of leaving me somewhere and then promptly forgetting about me.'

'I've been keeping tabs on you over the years,' he said. 'How do you think RL had so much inside information?'

'You sent RL to spy on me? He tried to *rob* me.'

He shook his head. 'He wasn't supposed to be in touch with you directly. He acted on his own, and I've terminated his services.'

I gave no reply.

'Come on, Gemma,' he said. 'We'll start over. I'll buy over the Wild Ride. We'll turn it into something else. Not an amusement park—your choice. What would you like? As long as Lionel Wu doesn't get his hands on it, Wonder Entertainment cannot have this place. I'll do whatever it takes to make sure of that.'

'What's the point? Just so you can get your little revenge on Lionel?'

He flinched. 'If not for him, your mother wouldn't have—'

I shook my head. 'It wasn't all him, though. Mum was sick to begin with, and you could have chosen to stay.'

The gleam in his eyes died. 'What Lionel did was still wrong.'

'Is this what you've been doing all these years? Cole said J&K Enterprises has been thwarting Wonder Entertainment for almost every project. Is this how you've been trying to punish Lionel Wu?' He didn't reply. '*Dad.*'

'Come away with me,' he said again.

I had waited so long to hear this. Even when I was supposed to feel angry and betrayed, I still clung on to the shreds of my memory, what little I remembered of my father. Even up till now, after learning of his inglorious past and petty revenge scheme, a part of me wanted to leave with him, to believe that there was hope for us yet, even with my mother gone and no Peter Pan around to save us.

But maybe the magic was inside us all along. Maybe we would be able to do anything—save a kingdom, an ailing amusement park, ourselves—once we stopped looking to someone else to rescue us.

My father's breath shook as he waited for my response. It probably wasn't the one he wanted to hear, but it was the only one I could give for now. He owed me this much.

'I want you to help us save the Wild Ride,' I said.

Thirty-Three

Cole

When Chelsea broke the news about Gemma signing the Wild Ride over to J&K Enterprises the next day, I was more relieved than I should be.

'We've lost,' was the first thing she said when I answered her call. Of course, to her this was a competition, just like everything else. We all saw this coming as soon as Gemma found out her father had his sights set on the Wild Ride.

There was nothing I could do if she was so intent on getting her heart broken by him again. She had more claim over it than I ever would. Gemma was harder to pin down than one of those cocktail birds in Neverland, revealing a flash of their plumage before flitting off with a lilting birdcall. But for some reason, I kept lingering on for another glimpse.

'Cole,' Chelsea snapped. 'We failed. The project fell through before it even began. Aren't you the least bit upset?'

'It was never a guaranteed acquisition, Chels.'

The amusement park had always been more than just another thing for my father to acquire, another seashell to put in his pocket—it held all the memories that reminded him of his ignoble past, memories that he would rather destroy and pretend never existed. And now he no longer had the ability to do that.

Chelsea's response was a noisy sigh through the phone before she hung up. Sometimes I wondered why she was still friends with me if she found me so exasperating. She and Thomas might have more in common.

My father, however, was much less patient. A giant rift now lay between us after I had confronted him about Joseph Young, so wide it seemed impossible to ever bridge. We stood side by side now, facing an entire boardroom of stakeholders and partners, Chelsea and her father included.

I fidgeted in my shirt and resisted the urge to pop open a button. Every fibre in me was screaming to escape the expectant stares around the table. Unlike Chelsea, who was all prepped and ready to dive into her father's business, I had never willingly been a part of Wonder Entertainment, much less attended a stakeholder meeting.

My father's voice resonated through the room. 'As you might have heard, the owners of the Wild Ride have decided to sign over the amusement park to J&K Enterprises.' Murmurs of disapproval and outrage rippled through the board. A few exchanged stormy glances.

Chelsea's father spoke over the rest of them. 'You said you were confident about securing this deal, Lionel.'

'Complications arose that I could not have anticipated,' my father replied, throwing me a glance.

'What connection does Joseph Young have with the owners of the Wild Ride to have acquired it so easily?' someone else piped up.

'Wasn't your son supposed to work from within and pave the way for the acquisition?' said another.

Soon, they were all rushing to give their two cents' worth.

'I told you it was too huge a task for the boy. He barely knows how this company works.'

'When has he ever acted in the company's interest?'

'Your faith in your son has clouded your judgement this time, Lionel. You should have listened to us when we proposed the takeover.'

'It's probably much easier,' I roared over the tangle of voices, 'for you to throw in some funds and then complain when things don't turn out the way you expect them to.'

'Cole,' my father warned.

But I wasn't through yet. 'The Wild Ride isn't a place you can forcefully take over. Do you even know the people who run the place? They're not going to let you destroy it when—'

'Destroy?' someone from the far end of the table said. 'Dear boy, is that what you think your father is doing?'

My father's hand settled on my shoulder. 'I trust my son did a thorough job in studying the Wild Ride.' I was about to say more, but he tightened his grip. 'We will, however, review the flaws we might have overlooked with this project so that we can avoid making the same mistakes for other projects in the works.'

This was as close as my father came to admitting defeat. But the board wasn't done.

'Trusting your son with such a crucial task was your biggest mistake,' someone piped up.

My father was unflappable for as long as I knew him—not even Mum leaving cracked his mask—but this time he flinched under the onslaught of criticism. At that moment, I had never felt more like a disappointment to my father.

But my rage easily elbowed out the shame. How dared they question my father and his judgement. How often had he failed them? Never. And because of me, because of something I never agreed to doing, they were pinning all the blame on him?

I found myself storming out of the boardroom and into my father's office, slamming the door behind me.

Wonder Entertainment belonged to my father. It was his lifelong project, one that not only made him fall out with his friend, but also drove Mum away because he seemed to care about nothing else apart from that. I had every reason to hate it, and that was probably why I wanted Wonder Town to fail.

But as hard as I tried to convince myself that Wonder had nothing to do with me, a part of me knew that was a lie. I had grown up in Wonder City, watching my father labour over his company, and—up until my parents' marriage disintegrated— hoping I could fill his shoes. It was mine as much as it was my father's. My stake in it was quantified in memories, in the time I had been a part of it.

I stopped pacing when I heard footsteps clipping down the hallway. The door swung open and my father stepped through, barely acknowledging me as he made straight for his chair. He stared me down from behind his desk and waved for me to sit. I remained standing.

'I trust that you now understand the ramifications of losing that acquisition,' he said.

I forced a shrug. 'A few irate stakeholders and board members.'

He wanted to say a lot more, I could tell, but he only went for, 'Explain, please.'

'It just didn't work out,' I said.

His stare narrowed. 'We had a plan, Cole.'

'No, *you* had a plan. One that I was never a part of.'

'Your sentimentality is your biggest weakness, Cole. We're running a business. There is no room for that here.'

The model for Wonder Town lay next to me in all its intricate detail. The amphitheatre and the water rides and viewing tower and other attractions stood expectant amidst the maze of streets lined with miniature tents and open booths. My father could put in that much attention to detail when it came to his work, but not to the people around him.

'Is that all that matters to you?' I said at last. 'The business? Not Mum? Not us? Not the fact that you destroyed a family?'

'That is all in the past.'

'Maybe to you it is. But Gemma and her father are still damaged by what happened. What you caused.'

His stare narrowed, cold and steely. 'Are you so determined to brand me as a villain? I might have given Joseph a push in the right direction, but what happened after was no doing of mine. Katherine was sick to begin with.'

'Is this how you justify what you did?'

'You're better off without that girl in your life.'

'That's just your opinion. You took me away from her, tried to replace her with Chelsea.'

'I didn't want her to fill your head with childish fantasies. You had better things to aspire to than play make-believe games with a girl who's not in her right mind. I won't have you ending up like Joseph.'

He had never liked Gemma. Even when we were kids, he had regarded her wild imagination, fantastic stories, and glassy-eyed wonder with undisguised disdain. And if that meeting at the party aboard *Wondrous* was any indication, his view of her hadn't changed one bit.

Realization hit me hard. 'You're just afraid.'

'Excuse me?'

'Everything has to be within your control. Anything outside of that is immediately bad or wrong. You don't understand Neverland, so you tried to drag me away from it. You couldn't do anything about Mum leaving, so you try to keep her out of our lives and pretend we're fine without her.'

He stared at me, his expression unfathomable. 'You are exactly right.'

My retort, ready to launch, sputtered to a halt in my throat. 'What?'

'You're right,' he said again, unclasping his hands and reclining in his seat. 'I *am* afraid. I'm afraid I'll lose more than I already have.

I'm afraid I'll hate myself if I think about Joseph and Katherine. I'm afraid you'll turn out like Joseph and I'll lose you the way I lost my best friend. I'm afraid you'll never stop hating me for your mother's departure. I'm afraid you'll spend your life chasing things that are just not meant to be.' He leaned back in his seat. 'But if I spent all my time being afraid, I'd never get anything done. At least with Wonder Entertainment, things are, like you said, within my control.'

This was throwing me off more than any project ambush ever did. He was Lionel Wu; he was not supposed to reveal his weaknesses. Fear was not supposed to be part of his emotional spectrum.

All this time, I had tried to cajole, antagonize, and wring out a reaction from him, but now that he was finally offering a confession, I realized I wasn't ready for it at all. There was less pleasure and triumph in having him cornered into this than I'd expected.

By now, my anger had burned away what was left inside me. By now, it was clear that my mum was never coming back to us. And I was tired of resenting my dad, tired of hanging on the frayed hope that we would all be together again, especially now that I knew the truth.

Maybe, without Neverland, we were all just doing whatever we could to survive and reassuring ourselves with lies—*it's not my fault, she will return, everything will be okay*—was just our way of living with ourselves. It made things more bearable.

I looked at my father now and wondered how I had missed it before. Every rule he enforced on me and every project he pushed through was his way of beating down his fear— of failure and loss and all the things beyond his control. For him—and maybe the rest of us, too—everything was a leap of faith. Even after his confession, his fear had not subsided. If anything, he looked even more unsure of himself, more than I had ever seen him.

'Not owning up to what you did isn't being in control,' I said. 'It just means you haven't even faced it.'

A wry smile curled up his face. 'I never thought you of all people would be telling me about facing things.'

I could be wrong, but that sounded like a concession.

'So what happens now?' I asked.

He had probably asked himself this question many times before. 'We keep on.'

And that didn't sound like such a bad idea.

Thirty-Four

Gemma

J&K Enterprises wasted no time in taking over the Wild Ride. By the end of the week, preparations were set for renovations and new rides. Everything from walkways to the signposts, shops and cafes to booths and viewing galleries, was given a complete overhaul. The Wild Ride, my father promised, would be a newer, better version of itself.

In between overseeing the renovations with my father, Boon and I took turns to stay by Jo's side as we prepared for her surgery. Eventually she and Boon told me to stay at the amusement park, if only to spare me from the guilt and dread.

Now that Wonder Entertainment was out of the picture, so too was Cole out of mine. I kept expecting him to stroll into view and reach for my hand to tell me an anecdote about Neverland that I had forgotten. I kept wishing he would appear from one of those Neverland chronicles like a Lost Boy who had found his way home.

But there was only me and the amusement park that was gradually taking on a new life, edging out my old one with Cole.

One night, for the first time since the incident on the overhead bridge, I dreamt of Neverland. I dreamt of all the things I wished had been able to do, the grand plans I had for the dastardly mission I had planned to carry out. Neverland was magical in that it made anything possible, and in turn you believed that you could do just about anything. I found myself back in the middle of the forest again, standing amid a verdant sea embellished by the cocktail birds' jewel-hued plumage.

And I dreamt about Peter. The boy who never grew up. The boy who left us all to fend for ourselves. I would spy a glimpse of him—a shadow here, a flash of that impish smile there, a fresh peal of his laughter—details that were too abstract for me to paint a full picture of him.

Since then, it had been a string of sleepless nights, all tainted with lucid dreams. As I settled into what was becoming my usual spot on the balcony that night, Boon appeared by my side. It was a day after Jo's surgery, and the first night in a week where we had both come home to rest.

Boon looked like he had wrenched Jo back from the jaws of death himself, but he offered me a smile as he took a seat next to me. 'Guess I'm not the only one who can't sleep.' On his own, Boon seemed unlike himself, incomplete. We both were, without Jo.

'It feels different without her here,' I said. 'Wrong.'

'I miss her too.' He glanced at me. 'Your father told us you might leave with him.' I hated how hard he was trying to keep his voice light to keep the pressure off me. 'If that's your decision, we will respect it.'

'Boon . . .'

'Really. You don't have to think that you owe us anything, because you don't. If being with your father is what makes you happy, then you should go with him.'

'Boon.'

Boon was usually economical with words. That he was on a roll like this meant he had kept these words inside him long enough.

'*Boon.*' I reached for his hand. 'You and Jo, you're my family. And I don't intend to go anywhere without you two.'

'But your father . . .'

'He had his chance the past ten years. And I'm not in the habit of leaving behind those who need me.'

As soon as I said it, I realized how presumptuous it was to say that they needed me when it had always been the other way around, ever since they found me all alone in their amusement park.

But Boon pulled me to him, ruffling my hair like he used to when I was younger. I inhaled his soapy scent, remembering what family really felt like. Not promises and lofty proclamations, not guilt and grand plans, but just being there when we needed them the most.

Thirty-Five

Cole

'Cole, please tell me you're on the way,' Chelsea barked through the speakerphone. 'Thomas said the ceremony starts at ten *sharp*.'

I glanced at my mother to see how she was taking this. Not everyone could stomach Chelsea's intensity. But Mum only quirked a brow at me and went back to navigating our way through the parking lot.

All the hype that J&K Enterprises had built up over the past year about the new and improved Wild Ride had paid off. People were flocking from Wonder City to this novelty now. As we inched closer to the entrance, my heart began pounding harder, as though my verdict lay in those rides.

'Your dad's already here,' Chelsea added.

That was the main reason for my nerves. A decade of avoiding Joseph Young, and now my father wanted to meet both him and Gemma for an overdue chat. But it had taken him this long to get here. This was a start, no matter how small that step might seem.

'Cole?' Chelsea said.

'We're in the parking lot. Meet you at the ticket counter,' I said before ending the call. In the silence that followed, my hesitation found its voice. 'Mum. You trust him, right?'

She steered into a parking space, glancing at the rear-view mirror. She didn't respond until she had killed the engine, leaving room for my doubt to grow. 'I wouldn't be here if I didn't.'

It wasn't until I saw the Peter Pan ride that I understood what I was anxious about—that none of this was going to change a thing between me and Gemma. Where would that leave us then?

'Some things take time, Cole,' Mum said, like she had heard my thoughts. 'We just need to believe they're worth the wait.'

We had all done our share of waiting. Sometimes, it seemed like that was all we did.

The last time I stepped into the Wild Ride with my mother, I had gone home with a bunch of half-answered questions and the realization that even the people you counted on the most could leave you.

Mum slipped her hand into mine like she was thinking the same thing. I didn't want to believe in promises again, but this was one I badly needed to believe in.

Thirty-Six

Gemma

'Maps, we need more maps!' Cory shrieked as he burst into the office.

I glanced up from the carnival pack I was rearranging. 'Have we run out already? We printed a bunch of them!'

'Maybe we wouldn't if people would stop grabbing a few at one go and then throwing them everywhere,' Beth said.

'We still have carnival packs left, right?' Cory asked.

I nodded. 'About fifty or so.'

'Fifteen minutes to ten, everyone,' Boon announced on the walkie talkie. 'Get ready.'

We leapt into action, Beth and Cory helping me shove the cookie packets, bottled water, wet tissues, amusement park map, Wild Ride keychain, paper fan, a pair of complimentary tickets to the Peter Pan ride (now officially named the Sky Carousel), and a ten-dollar dining voucher for the Wild Ride Bistro into the bright red tote bags.

We were about to leave the office and make our way towards the Sun Stadium, where the open circus was performing, when we found Lionel Wu standing at the door. Behind him were Chelsea and a couple I had seen at the Wonder Entertainment boat party, whom I assumed were Chelsea's parents. Chelsea's gaze met mine, then she led her parents away towards the attractions.

Lionel Wu stayed put, looking oddly out of place in his forest-green polo shirt and brown trousers. His back remained ramrod-straight as his gaze flitted around the room.

'My dad's not here.' I didn't know why I said that. My father was probably the last person he wanted to see, given that J&K Enterprises had practically snatched the Wild Ride from right under Wonder Entertainment's nose.

'Gem, we're running late,' Beth said quietly from behind me. Cory gave me a nudge.

'I wanted to catch you both before the ceremony started,' Lionel said, ignoring our audience. He surveyed the frozen chaos in the office and the carnival packs in our hands. 'But I suppose this is a bad time.'

'It is,' Beth answered on my behalf, shoving me out the door and past Lionel before I could say anything.

We left our carnival packs with Laura at the ticketing counter and sprinted towards the Sun Stadium. I clutched the stack of maps as I ran, my heart pounding wild with hope—if Lionel was here, did that mean Cole was too? What *was* Lionel doing here?

At the Sun Stadium, my father was already heading for the podium with Jo and Boon watching by the side. Thomas and the new ride master Rashid were directing stragglers to empty seats and handing out maps and bottled water.

I scanned the crowd, but it was near impossible to find Cole here—*if* he was even here. Cory and Beth split up to help Thomas and Rashid, while I headed to the first row of seats in front of the stage.

My father began after the applause died down.

'Almost ten years ago, I brought my daughter to this amusement park. We were going through a very trying time and coming here was supposed to be a reprieve. But I made a terrible decision that day that I regret to this day. This is J&K Enterprises' most significant project to date, because it made me understand the world that my wife and daughter lived in. In a way, this is a belated birthday present to my daughter, and an anniversary gift to my wife.'

His eyes found mine as he paused to compose himself.

'Josephine and Boon have placed a great deal of faith in J&K Enterprises and its vision,' he went on. 'So I hope everyone finds a piece of Neverland here in the newly revamped Wild Ride too. Thank you.'

Dad left the podium to let Boon take over, then joined me at the front row. After his speech, Boon announced the first act, the open circus. I turned back to survey the crowd again, but still there was no sign of Cole.

'He'll be here, I'm sure,' Dad said, like he knew exactly what I was thinking.

It was Lionel who appeared just as Dad and I were leaving the Sun Stadium. Alone in an amusement park that was not his, he didn't seem as intimidating as before. His approached us backstage, his footsteps measured and gaze wary.

I looked to my dad for an appropriate response to our new company. There were so many things that we could say, but none of us knew where to begin.

Out front, raucous applause and a jaunty trumpet tune welcomed the ringmaster onstage.

Lionel cleared his throat. 'You did a good job with this place.'

The ringmaster's booming voice lingered on words like *amazing* and *wondrous* and *spectacular* as he introduced the troupe. I wished I were out there with the rest of them, eagerly anticipating the first act. But my third act was playing out right now, a climax of its own thankfully out of the audience's sight.

Dad nodded once, seeming at a loss for words. I took his hand and he grasped it tight, like that might stop him from going for Lionel's throat. 'Thank you for coming,' he said before leading me away.

Lionel called after us. 'I was only trying to help you, Joseph.'

Dad whirled around, still gripping my hand, all attempts at civility gone now. 'Help me? That wasn't help, Lionel. That was you trying to control me. I became something you had to fix as soon as Katie got sick.'

It was the first time he had brought up Mum this way, and it hit me harder than a slap. Applause rose from the gallery, filling the silence we stood in.

Lionel nodded. 'I'm a control freak, as I've been told.' He glanced at me. 'Up until recently, I was ready to keep your daughter out of my son's life.'

'People are not things you can fix or manipulate to suit your plans, Lionel.'

'So I've realized.' I could be mistaken, but that sounded like an apology. 'I never meant for any of that to happen.'

Dad's jaw tightened.

'Congratulations on the revamp, Joseph,' Lionel said. 'I mean it.'

Dad stared at him, as though waiting for a 'but' to come along, but Lionel left it at that. Finally, Dad unclenched his jaw. 'Thank you,' he said.

Lionel turned to me. 'He said he'd be here today.'

I nodded dumbly.

Later, as I watched Lionel leave, I tried to ignore the pang in my chest, the one I felt whenever I thought about my adventures in Neverland with Cole, the one that drove me to almost text Cole on several occasions.

Dad nudged me. 'Funny, isn't it? Ten years without acknowledging each other, and now we can't find the right words to say.'

'No,' I said. 'I think you both said all the right words.'

Thirty-Seven

Cole

They disappeared backstage. After the ringmaster took the stage, I spotted Dad following Gemma and her father into the back exit of the stadium.

Last I heard from Thomas, Jo had recovered from her surgery and Joseph Young was actively trying to mend his relationship with Gemma. Joseph wanted her to live with him after the amusement park had hit the ground running, but Gemma would continue to work at the Wild Ride.

She had got the ending she had hoped for, but I couldn't help wondering if this was really the end. Was she truly happy now? Where did I fit into her story? Did I even have a space in her life anymore?

The circus launched into their first act, and I watched absently as a couple of trapeze dancers somersaulted their way across the stage.

Mum nudged me. 'You didn't come here for the circus show, I'm sure.'

'Do you regret leaving Dad?' I didn't include myself in the picture because that wasn't the point right now.

She turned her attention to the dancers on stage. 'We both needed time and space to grow. Away from each other, and back to each other.'

A year ago, I would have scoffed at the corniness. But now I held it close to me as I made my way towards the back exit.

By the time I got there, my father was already leaving, heading in the direction of the bistro. Gemma's father caught up with him shortly, leaving Gemma alone to make her way out.

She emerged soon after, watching the two men go and then taking off in the opposite direction. Over the walkie-talkie, Cory and Beth reported that the 'carnival pack situation' had been resolved, so she could 'rest easy and focus on more important things'. Gemma rolled her eyes, then strode down the tree-lined path. Dappled sunlight made her flicker in and out of the shadows. Was she imagining herself in Neverland again?

She looked different now. It might have only been a year since I last saw her, but something seemed unrecognisable in her. She didn't have that lost, wild look in her eyes this time. She seemed fully present, taking in every shift in the light and life around her. She had never looked more beautiful.

I walked in tandem with her, matching my footsteps with hers from across the crowded lane. The sounds of the circus receded, giving way to music and sounds from the other attractions—the carousel, the fun house, the pirate ship . . . . We strolled past these at the pace of memories. Gemma waved to a new staff handing out balloons by the food carts and stopped to inquire about their remaining stock.

Nearby at the help booth, Chelsea was helping Thomas sort out a stack of maps and pamphlets as he helped a family of four with directions. I raised my brows at her when our eyes met, but she only smiled. When Gemma flitted into sight again, Chelsea glanced between me and her, then gave me a head-nudge in Gemma's direction. I nodded and went on my way.

We walked for ages around the amusement park. The Wild Ride had become a larger version of itself, not in terms of physical size, but in the way it filled out the empty spaces, not unlike how Gemma had come into herself.

It was only until we reached the Peter Pan ride that she came to a stop. The ride was called the Sky Carousel now, but I had a feeling she still secretly dubbed it the Peter Pan ride. It was evident from the way she looked up at it that she hadn't gone up the ride yet, even though I knew she yearned to.

The ride loomed over us, silhouetted in sunlight. Its carriages spun in lazy circles against the cerulean sky, gleaming golden under the rays.

I stepped forward into her line of sight. Gemma shifted aside to make way for a family joining the queue. Her gaze landed on me after they had passed.

I made my way towards her. Seeing her before me again made me forget everything I had planned to say to her. She seemed to be struggling the same way, so I fought the lump in my throat and said, 'I thought you'd get rid of this old thing.'

'The Peter Pan will always stay.'

I couldn't stop the grin from spreading across my face. But her next words sobered me up.

'I've been dreaming of Neverland a lot these days. And my mum.'

'What does she say?' I asked.

'A lot of things, actually. She said—' Her words caught, and she took a deep breath to get them all out. 'Neverland will always be waiting for me. But right now, I need to live. She said I need to live the life she couldn't.'

'I assume she means right here and now, not in Neverland,' I said.

She offered a small smile. 'That's what I think too.'

I held out a hand. As the Sky Carousel made its final trip around the clock tower, she slipped her hand into mine. It was a promise, one that felt much truer that the ones we were used to.

The ride slowed to a stop before us. And there was no question at all that we would get on the next one.

Years had passed ever since the two Otherworld children tried to save Neverland.

The kingdom had never quite healed. The disease that plagued Neverland was too deep-rooted for Gemma and Cole and all the wild, hopeful Neverlanders to exterminate. What ailed it from within had no cure.

But still they had tried. Oh, how they had tried! They had battled vengeful pirates and a beast that dwelled in the depths of a tumultuous sea; they had lost friends and comrades and placed their hopes in all the wrong people— those who failed to show up, those who turned their backs on them, and those who betrayed them. They took on the burden of another world, casting aside the one they knew for one that promised them magic and adventure.

Cole and Gemma stood on the sun-bleached sands of the Halcyon Coast. They were different now, grown. And they now understood that they didn't have to just be characters of a story. They could be the authors; they could write the ending for Neverland.

There were villains who fought for the greater good and heroes who abandoned you. There were children who never grew up and children who were afraid to. It didn't matter if Peter Pan never showed up, because he had been living in them all along. He had driven them halfway across the kingdom, made them believe, made them hope.

There were places that they never really grew out of, places that remained inside them even if the world changed around them. They were lucky to have found a place like that.

On a cliff where they now stood side by side, Cole gave a shout when he spotted the ship. It was a dark spot looming in the distance, so small that he and Gemma had to squint. Beneath it, the waves of the Halcyon Sea crested and fell, iridescent under the sunlight.

The Thunderstorm *came into full view, its sails billowing in the breeze like a silent greeting.*

And there they were, every single one of them. Storm and his crew, Kittern and Meerka, and all the Council members, all aboard the ship like a dream.

'They're alive,' Gemma said, laughing through her tears.

They had done this, she realized. They had brought the Neverlanders—and this place—back to life simply by believing in them. They had kept the magic of Neverland alive with their fierce, stubborn hope.

'We give life to whatever we believe in,' Cole murmured, echoing her thoughts.

They had let Neverland languish and almost die because they were too afraid to believe that they had control over its story. But even though it now bore battle scars and the footprints of all the children who had once traipsed across it, Neverland had always been a kingdom of their making.

Gemma and Cole raced down the hill, towards the Neverlanders who were heading for land. Otherworlders or not, they had family here, family that was now sailing towards them. And they knew that no matter how much time had passed, Neverland would always be there to welcome them home.

Acknowledgements

I often call *No Room in Neverland* the book of my heart because it meant so much to me when I wrote it back in 2015. It was escapism, loss of childhood innocence, a dark *Peter Pan* retelling, a girl's stubborn optimism and a boy's cynicism all in one, and I think they all reflected a part of me.

When I was querying, I learned that this book didn't have much commercial appeal because it was too sad, too strange, and too difficult to categorize. I had almost resigned myself to the fact that it might never ever see the light of day, when Penguin SEA expressed interest in it in late 2022.

Thank you to Nora for taking a chance on this book and the PRH SEA team for making it come to fruition. This book carries so many memories, along with a piece of that hopeful, persistent twenty-five-year-old Joyce, who was struggling to realize her dreams and find a way to share this story with the world. Thank you for giving *No Room in Neverland* a home, and for giving stories set in this part of the world a chance to be heard.

Thank you also to the usual suspects: scribe sisters Kayce Teo (Leslie W.), Catherine Dellosa, and Eva Wong Nava, whose candid text conversations keep me going daily; Muse sisters Meredith Crosbie and Nicole Evans, who read the early drafts of this book and have been constant companions all these years in spite of us being in three different time zones; and all the authors in our wonderful group chat and many more I've met along the way.

You all make this writing journey less lonely, and I'm so thankful to have met you all. I am constantly inspired by your creativity, kindness, dedication, grit, and resourcefulness.

Thank you to Mr. Martin Chan, as always, for igniting that spark way back in 2001. Without your encouragement, I would never have dared to believe I could ever become a writer, much less an author.

Thank you to the readers—too many to list, but you know who you are—who have supported, shouted about, read, reviewed, and recommended my books to other readers. Authors in this part of the world don't get that much exposure, so your help in providing some visibility goes a longer way than you may know. I am truly thankful for every one of you who reached out in whatever way, as it's the best kind of direct feedback to know that my stories aren't just floating out in the ether but actually connecting with people. To see readers resonate with our words and stories is one of the biggest motivators for us writers.

Lastly, thank you to my stubborn self who persisted with this book, despite all the soul-crushing, heartbreaking rejections and hurdles. We will always carry a piece of Neverland with us wherever we go. As Peter Pan said, 'All the world is made of faith, and trust, and pixie dust.'